Joyce Emmerson Muddock

The Star of Fortune

A Story of the Indian Mutiny

Joyce Emmerson Muddock

The Star of Fortune
A Story of the Indian Mutiny

ISBN/EAN: 9783337407995

Printed in Europe, USA, Canada, Australia, Japan

Cover: Foto ©Andreas Hilbeck / pixelio.de

More available books at **www.hansebooks.com**

THE STAR OF FORTUNE

A Story of the Indian Mutiny

BY

J. E. MUDDOCK

AUTHOR OF

"THE DEAD MAN'S SECRET," "STORIES WEIRD AND WONDERFUL," "MAID
MARIAN AND ROBIN HOOD," "STORMLIGHT," "FOR GOD AND THE
CZAR," "FROM THE BOSOM OF THE DEEP," ETC.

LONDON: CHAPMAN AND HALL, L^{D.}

1895.

NOTE.

It may add somewhat to the interest of this story if I state that during that tremendous struggle which nearly cost us our magnificent Indian Empire, I was stationed in India. I went through a very trying time, and though exceedingly young, met with many exciting adventures. Not a few of the scenes and incidents I record in the following narrative came under my own personal observation, and even at this distance of time they are still vivid in my memory.

J. E. MUDDOCK.

CONTENTS.

THE STAR OF FORTUNE.

CHAPTER I.

UNREASONING PREJUDICE.

"Sweet, sweet Dick, Dicky, come here, you rascal. Oh, you naughty boy, how dare you fly away like that when I want to catch you!"

These words were uttered in a clear, musical voice, by a young girl, who seemed radiant with health, and whom "the world's slow stain" had not yet touched. The scene was a well-furnished room in which there was ample evidence that it was the sanctum of a woman of refined and cultivated taste; and the room was part of a house situated in one of the best parts of the classic city of Edinburgh. The speaker addressed her command and admonition to a very beautiful canary which had been liberated for the nonce from a brass cage that stood with open door on the table. But "Dick," in the fulness of his enjoyment of the temporary liberty thus accorded, had flown from point to point which afforded him foothold, such as picture frames and ornaments, and had resisted his pretty mistress's attempts to catch him in order that she might caress him.

It was a charming tableau, this girl and the bird,

B

one that would have transferred well to canvas, and have made a gem under the deft hands of an artist of feeling and taste.

"You cruel, naughty Dicky, not to come to me," continued the young lady, with a pretty pout and an attempt at a frown that was altogether out of place on the fair, bright face. At this point the door opened and a gentleman entered, looking thoughtful, solemn, and even sad.

"Why, papa, whatever is the matter with you?" exclaimed the girl as she glanced at the intruder. "There is something wrong, for you have the tell-tale expression that so clearly denotes the state of your mind."

"Yes, Hester, there is something wrong. I am troubled," was the answer in a positively melancholy tone. "I want to talk seriously to you, but you had better put your bird into his cage again, for we cannot talk while he is flying about."

"I had better take him from the room altogether if what you have to say is so dreadfully serious, and especially if you are going to be cross with me, for Dick is very sensitive, and would be frightened out of his life if he heard his mistress scolded." The bird had alighted on the top of his cage, she managed to secure him, and, having pressed her lips to his bill and fondled him with many caresses, she placed him gently in his little prison-house, and put the cage on a table near the window which was gay with ferns and flowers. "Now, dad, I'm ready," she said with a smile as she dropped into a chair and folded her hands.

"I am afraid, girl, you are hardly in that serious frame of mind which would be more in keeping with the circumstances," said her father, with some severity. "Indeed, I am sorry to notice the seeming levity with which you are disposed to treat everything."

"But surely, father, you wouldn't have me going about the house with a soured, Puritanical expression of face, as if this world and the beautiful things it contains were hateful to me. It was never intended, I am certain, that we should view life through a distorted medium of crabbed discontent."

"You do not understand me," he replied, with increased severity of tone, as though he considered that her expression of feeling was altogether out of place. "My remark applies to the present moment only. I have no desire that you should look at life through dun-coloured spectacles. Your happiness is too precious to me, and it is my regard for your happiness that has induced me to act as I have done, and it is that act I now wish to discuss with you."

A little shadow of concern swept over his daughter's finely-cut face as some inkling of his meaning dawned upon her.

"What is the act, and what have you done?" she asked quickly.

"I have written to Lieutenant Hallett to tell him in a very emphatic manner that the intimacy between you and him must cease."

Hester's face grew red now, while a light of anger came into her eyes at this unexpected revelation; and there was an unusual warmth in her tone as she answered—

"Then, father, you must excuse me for saying that you have done that which you had no justification for doing."

"There you are wrong, girl. A father is justified in watching over the happiness and welfare of his child."

"But I am no longer a child," she exclaimed indignantly.

"Not in the literal sense, but for all purpose of argument in the present sense you are. At any rate, it cannot be expected that you should be able to form that dispassionate judgment of a matter in which the affections are concerned that I, your father, can, and there can be no doubt in my own mind that if this connection between you and Hallett is persisted in, it will be destructive of your own future welfare."

"Why ?" she demanded, with a force of expression that seemed to cause him some astonishment.

"Because he is in every way unfitted to make you happy."

"Why, again ?"

"Without going too much into detail, I may answer your question by saying that he is extravagant, reckless, unprincipled——"

"Unprincipled ?"

"Yes. I am sorry if the word offends you, but I use it advisedly."

"In what way is he unprincipled ?"

"In nearly every way in which that word can be applied. But more particularly in the lack of honourable regard for his actions, which any man who was proud of his reputation would certainly have."

"This is a very serious charge, father," said his daughter sadly, while her face assumed such a look of dejection that it presented a marked contrast to her appearance of a few minutes previously.

"I am fully alive to its scriousnes," he answered, "and I accept all the responsibility of my accusation, for it is an accusation. But, as I have said, it is your happiness I am consulting."

"A curious way of consulting my happiness, truly," she remarked sarcastically. "My happiness is bound up in Lieutenant Hallett, and yet you insult him and wound my feelings."

"To say that I insult him is not correct. I have been to the trouble to learn a good deal about his career, and I have no hesitation in saying that that career has been shameful and dishonourable. Therefore, to tell such a man the truth is not to insult him. As regards your feelings, it may be doubted if you are capable of rightly understanding even your own feelings, for girls of your age are generally led away by mere sentiment. There is such a thing as calf love, and that should not be mistaken for the genuine article."

"Well," replied his daughter dryly, "that may be your opinion, and I will not quarrel with you about it, but you will admit, as a just and upright man, that every one is liable to err—even you, my clever, precise, and usually accurate father."

"Yes, of course, I admit that; but in this case there is no error. I have convinced myself that Hallett is not a man who would do honour or credit to my family, and I must repeat again and again that if you were to marry him you would rue the

step as long as you lived. At any rate, the fact
remains that I do not approve of him, and will not
countenance your continuing a connection that is so
distasteful to me, and so well calculated to cause you
shame and misery. In speaking thus, I can have
no other interests at heart but yours. If I were
indifferent to you, I should allow you to take your
own course and do as you like. But as your loving
and affectionate father, I cannot sit still with
folded arms and see your future destroyed. And
you as my daughter must acknowledge my right
to control you, unless you wish to set yourself in
opposition to my desires and requests, in which
case you would have to take your fate in your own
hands."

"It is far from my intention," she answered, in a
cool and collected way which suggested that, though
young in years, she had the power when occasion
required of acting and thinking as a matured
woman of experience, " to set myself up in
opposition to your just parental authority, but I
would point out that your charges against Hallett
are too vague, too ambiguous for serious consideration——"

"This is absolutely insulting," her father exclaimed, with unusual anger, for he felt that his
judgment was being called into question and his
rights as a father flouted.

"Pray hear me out. No good can result if this
matter is discussed with warmth and temper. What
I was going to say is this. I have never observed
anything in Hallett's conduct or speech but what
was perfectly consistent with the character of a true

gentleman and an upright and honest man. I gather from what you say that you have felt it necessary in my interest and out of a jealous regard for the good name of our family to inquire into the private character and past history of Lieutenant Hallett, and presumably you have been told certain things which induce you to believe that he is not a desirable person to know. Well, that may be the case, father, but in common fairness I must ask that you will request him to come here, and in his presence that you will formulate a distinct charge against him, so that he may have full opportunity of answering it."

Mr. Dellaby looked at his daughter in astonishment. He knew that she had a far-seeing and reasoning mind, no less than a determined will, but he had always persuaded himself that in that household he was the supreme ruler, that his word and will were law, and that when he had once delivered judgment no one had any right to gainsay it. It was an unfortunate weakness that, and one which was in every way calculated to bring about the very discord he was so anxious to avoid. Herein, of course, he displayed the spirit of a martinet, a spirit which had been developed and fostered during long service in India, and to brook contradiction or questioning on the part of his daughter, whom he was unable to look upon in any other light than as a child incapable of forming a safe conclusion upon anything, was what he could not do. Of course, this was very unreasonable and unfair, but he did not think, and probably nothing in the world could have persuaded him that it was so. Under these

circumstances he must be credited with conscientious-
ness, for it cannot be supposed that such a man was
actuated by mere malice or petty spite. He believed
himself right, and men who believed that, however
wrong they may be, are entitled to a certain amount
of respectful consideration.

It was pretty clear from his manner that he had
not anticipated such opposition from his daughter,
and the frame of mind he was then in did not allow
him to view the subject dispassionately or with a
cool and unbiassed judgment, and this was the
answer he made to her suggestion—

"I consider it outrageous that you should call my
statements into question. The sources from whence
I have drawn my information about this young man,
who seems to have charmed away your usual good
sense and reasoning power, are above suspicion,
therefore I should regard it as an act of imbecility
were I to fall in with your view. Hallett shall never
cross the threshold of my door again, and unless you
wish to shut yourself out of my heart for ever and
ever, you will regard my injunctions. I will not
tolerate any disobedience on your part. Dare
to go against my will, and I'll bar the door
against you as sure as the heavens are above us.
There is no appeal from Cæsar. Bear that in
mind."

He had worked himself up to a pitch of unusual
excitement, and appeared to have lost all control of
himself, and having given this forcible expression to
his views, he waited not for any answer or further
comment from his daughter, but hastily left the
room, feeling, no doubt, that he could not trust him-

self to prolong the argument then, for his anger had got the better of his discretion.

Poor Hester was terribly distressed. There were tears in her eyes, but she dashed them away as being out of place on such an occasion. She had always been a loving daughter, and a dutiful daughter, but not even her love or sense of duty could blind her now to the manifest injustice of her father's behaviour. She was greatly put out, her feelings were wounded, and they found expression in a remark she addressed to her bird, which at that moment burst forth into a full gush of song, and, turning to the cage where the little songster trilled so beautifully, she murmured—

"Ah, Dick, happy Dicky; how I envy you! This world might be such a paradise if men were only more considerate, more reasonable. But, 'Man's inhumanity to man makes countless thousands mourn.'"

It was not often that she was cast down and dejected, for her disposition was a very happy and contended one; but now it was a question of forfeiting a lover's love or a father's affection. From the unexpected turn matters had taken, it seemed that she must certainly forfeit one or the other; it is little wonder that she found it difficult to decide which she should do, and after much earnest consideration and deep reflection, she decided to go to her mother and seek consolation and sympathy from her.

CHAPTER II.

IT was generally admitted by those whose privilege it was to be well acquainted with her, that Hester Dellaby could justifiably claim to be numbered amongst the belles of which Edinburgh had cause to be proud. She had many natural advantages, such as good health, a good physique, and a bright, cheerful, engaging manner. There are some women who embody in the very highest degree the attributes of fascination, and who draw around them by some irresistible power of attraction other people, in much the same way as certain flowers attract butterflies and bees. Such a woman was Hester. Her years at this time were but a score, so that she had all the advantages which youth offers, and allied to them was a sweetness of disposition, and a cheerful, even temper, which made her very popular with both sexes. She had been well nurtured, tenderly brought up, and educated with a view to her shining some day as an accomplished member of society, for her parents were ambitions, and a little given to boasting of the "good stock" they came from. Possibly the boast was justified, but anyway they ranked then amongst those who were pleased to think themselves members of "rank and fashion" in the so-called Northern Athens.

Hester's father had long and honourably served the Old East India Company in the Civil Service. He was a native of Edinburgh, though of English parents, and, marrying young, had gone out to India in the Company's employ. Three sons were born to him there, but two died in early childhood. The third grew up, and at the date of the commencement of this history he held a commission in the army, and was then stationed with his regiment in Malta. In addition to these sons, Mr. Dellaby had two daughters; his eldest, Margaret, was born at sea while her mother was on her way home; and the second, Hester, drew her first breath in Edinburgh. Mr. Dellaby had at that time been compelled to leave India, as his health had broken down. Margaret subsequently became the wife of Lieutenant-Colonel George Henry Pritchard, and had gone out to India with her husband, so that Hester was her father's and mother's solace in their old age. A just and upright man, he was nevertheless a severe one where he considered there was any dereliction of duty, or a lack of obedience to lawful command, or what seemed to him lawful command. His wife had long been content to be guided by him, and she would have no more thought of calling. his decisions into question than she would have thought of flying. She was a gentle, submissive woman, and believed that her husband could not err.

There was one point upon which Mr. Dellaby was disposed to be very arbitrary indeed, and that was with reference to his daughter forming a connection with any one of the sterner sex. At first she had laughed at his petty tyranny, and was amused by his treating her as if she were still a child. But this laughter and amusement underwent an entire change soon after she made the acquaintance of John Montague Hallett. They met at one of those little social gatherings, in which young people of both sexes are brought into contact with each other and dream dreams of an earthly paradise. It is an impossible paradise, of course, but youth takes no count of that, for to the young nothing seems impossible, and they firmly believe that the mirage is reality and that shadow is substance. You greybeards and wiseacres may argue as much as you like, with a view to convincing them that they are wrong. but be assured you will fail.

In the case of these young people it was almost love at first sight. An hour or two of each other's society, and then they both felt they had found their counterpart. A little later in the evening the hostess at whose house the gathering had taken place said to Hester—

" Well, dear, what do you think of young Hallett ? "

At the question a little tell-tale flush dyed the girl's cheeks, and she answered demurely—

" He seems very nice."

" He's *charming*, dear," the hostess exclaimed. "He's my very ideal of what a young man should be — so different to the stuck-up, stiff-collared, pomatumed-haired fops of the present day, who would scream if they found themselves alone in a room with a mouse. I shouldn't be at all surprised if young Hallett makes a noise in the world some day. All his people have been prominent in one way or other, and he's got go and grit in him."

This praise, which, by the way was only a spontaneous testimony to Jack's worth, and not uttered with any underlying motives such as often actuate ladies when they din the praises of young men into the ears of simpering maidens, had its effect on the listener, although she made no further comment one way or the other. But she had seen with her own eyes, and heard with her own ears, and she was quite capable of forming a perfectly independent judgment, though it may at once be said that her judgment was in accord in the main with that of her friend.

So it came to pass that the acquaintance thus begun ripened. Hallett gave every sign that he had come within the sphere of Hester's attraction, and was being drawn towards her as one orb that has got out of its orbit is drawn towards another. Opportunities were made for meetings, and after a time Jack was invited to Mr. Dellaby's house. Hester had a little gathering of friends, and he was included amongst the invitees. The attention he paid her that evening attracted the attention of her parents, and her father subsequently questioned her about him. She concealed nothing, made no attempt to prevaricate. She told the pretty little story from its initial stage up to the very point at which it had then gone. It was painfully obvious it did not please her father. He listened with frowning brow and stern countenance, and reproached his daughter with having been indiscreet, whereupon she exclaimed—

"But you don't suppose that I am going to lead the life of a recluse, and never open my lips to a man unless it be yourself?"

"No," he said sharply, "I don't suppose anything of the kind. But I maintain that you have no right to form an acquaintance with a young man without first taking steps to ascertain that he is honourable and of good report. And in order to do that your father is certainly the proper person to appeal to. In this instance I shall, beyond doubt, go to the root of the matter ; for I have too much regard for you, and too much respect for my own good name, to remain silent and indifferent where your happiness is concerned. For aught I know or you know, this fellow may be an unprincipled adventurer."

Hester winced a little, for she did not like to hear it suggested that the man she admired above all others might possibly be what is usually termed "an adventurer," meaning in plain words a scoundrel who sticks at nothing to further his own ends. And yet she displayed no feeling, but quietly remarked—

"You forget, father, that an officer and a gentleman are inseparable terms."

"In theory, yes. But in practice it is not so, for many an army and navy officer is an unmitigated blackguard. However, I make no reflections on Hallett, because I know nothing about him at present. We will renew the subject later on, however."

Mr. Dellaby was a persistent man, and having

resolved to do a thing, it took a good deal to turn him from it. So the first thing he did was to wait on young Hallett at his quarters in the Castle, and demand from him what his intentions were; having been assured that they were honourable, and based on a hope that the young fellow might be found acceptable in the young lady's sight, and the sight of those who had her welfare at heart, he next requested to be referred to Hallett's family, a request that was very promptly complied with.

So far as all this went Mr. Dellaby could find no flaw. The Halletts, as he proved, were people of high standing, and something more than merely respectable. But in the story of Jack's college career there was a black page. While at Oxford he had given way to extravagance and recklessness that had plunged him into serious difficulties, and his mother was unable to discharge his liabilities, but a scandal was avoided by an uncle coming forward and doing so. This was not all, however, for the young man had had an intrigue with a girl, the daughter of a farmer, and had, so it was averred, promised her marriage. Into the merits or demerits of this matter it is not in the least necessary to enter here. It may be mentioned in passing that it was the means of prematurely, to some extent, closing the young man's college career, and his friends had to pay over to the girl's friends a very liberal sum of money to hush the affair up.

Armed with these facts Mr. Dellaby returned home, not altogether sorry, perhaps, that he had found a weak spot in Jack's armour, for the fact could not be disguised that he had felt annoyed, and very much annoyed indeed, that Hester had dared to form such an acquaintanc without first taking him into her confidence and asking his advice. In dealing with the Oxford incident he was not in the least disposed to make any allowance for the proverbial weakness of human nature, nor did he care to consider how highly probable it was that if the incidents in the youth of any eminent man one might like to single out were inquired into, no man would come out unsullied. Youth, it has been said, is the time of folly, and wisdom comes with whitening hair. But Mr. Dellaby was strongly prejudiced, and, quite disposed to view the affair through a magnifying-glass, he clearly proved this when he again discussed the subject with his daughter after he had exhausted his inquiries, for he said to her—

"I don't want to be unkind or unduly severe," showing thereby that he was not speaking strictly in accordance with that high regard for unswerving accuracy which he claimed to have. But men often err from lack of judgment, and it is charitable to suppose that Mr. Dellaby did so in this instance.

"There can be no question in my mind," he went on, "that Hallett is a blackguard." When he saw how Hester was stung by this all too severe condemnation he qualified it by saying—"Well, what I mean is, he is a man of little principle, one who is not likely to have much respect for any woman's feelings. Under these circumstances I shall resolutely decline to recognize him, and I hereby give you strict injunctions to at once sever the connection. Let there be no mistake as to my meaning. You must treat him as if he were an absolute stranger. Do you understand ? "

Poor Hester tacitly admitted that sho understood only too well. And while not prepared just then to set herself in direct opposition to her father's wishes, she certainly did not intend to accept his dictum as irrevocable.

To what an extraordinary concatenation of thrilling events this difference of opinion between herself and her father was to lead will be disclosed as the narrative proceeds ; but Mr. Dellaby himself had no foreshadowing of what was to come. He considered his word law, his commands final, and in order to give, as he thought, the final blow to the whole affair, he penned the following severe letter to young Hallett—

" Sir,—As my daughter's happiness is more precious to me than aught else in this world, I am naturally anxious that she should do nothing calculated in any way to jeopardize that happiness. I must therefore request—nay, demand in the most emphatic manner, that from this moment you cease your attentions to her, for I do not regard you as being in any way likely to promote her well-being. In fact, it would be nothing short of a calamity if she were to become your wife, and I, her father, as well as all those who love her, would regard it as a dire infliction if by your insidious arts and wiles she were induced to disobey my wishes. As the receipt of this letter will give you clearly to understand how very objectionable you are in my sight, you surely will not have the audacity to persevere in forcing

your unwelcome attentions on my child. I have been
very outspoken because I consider that any ambiguity
would have been a fatal mistake.

"WILLIAM HENRY DELLABY."

Mr. Dellaby read this letter over two or three
times, and he evidently considered that its strong
language was fully justified, for he did not alter a
single word, nor soften down an expression. But
sealing it up, he dispatched the missive to Hallett at
his quarters in the Castle, and having done that he
sought an interview with his daughter, as recorded
in the opening pages of this story.

CHAPTER III.

"Jack" Hallett was still a very young man, not more than four or five and twenty. He was a lieutenant stationed with his regiment, then quartered in Edinburgh Castle. He represented a long line of ancestors, who had honourably and loyally served their country either in the navy or the army. His father had been an admiral and had greatly distinguished himself during the Crimean War for conspicuous bravery and devotion, but during the bombardment of Sebastopol was mortally wounded at the post of duty by a bursting shell. John was his youngest son, and having elected to enter the army in preference to the navy, he had been well educated, and launched upon his career with the prayers and good wishes of his loving sisters and widowed mother.

The lad had the misfortune—the word is used advisedly—to be singularly handsome. He really seemed to embody all the physical attributes which go to make up a perfect man, while face and feature were full of the pride of goodly stock and high heritage. It was a patrician face, with clear, frank, blue eyes and a delicate chiselled nose; a mobile face, that in certain moods told of the true soldierly

c 2

nature, a nature, stern, determined, defiant, unyielding, and full of courage and fire. He who would
have set Jack Hallett down as merely a pretty boy
would have made a woeful mistake. He had the
vivacity of the boy, the laughter of the boy, the
joyousness of the boy. But let the occasion arise for
the manhood to display itself, and then—what a
change! This can best be exemplified by the following
little incident in his career. He was barely twenty,
when one day as he was strolling along the high-
road near his home, he was suddenly startled by a
roar of voices, and looking back beheld a sight that
might have turned an older head than his. A
magnificent pair of horses attached to a brougham
had taken fright, and were thundering on towards
him utterly uncontrolled, for the coachman, as was
subsequently proved, had been seized with apoplexy,
and pitching forward on the backs of the animals had
startled them into madness; and on they flew to the
certain destruction of themselves, the carriage, and
its occupants; for, a couple of hundred yards or so
ahead, the road bent at an acute angle, and at that
angle was a deep stone quarry into which the frenzied
horses must necessarily dash. Hallett took in the
situation at a glance, and never a muscle quivered,
never a nerve quailed. It seemed as if he was
doomed to certain death if he dared to oppose
himself to those maddened steeds, and the swaying
and jolting vehicle that flew along the road and shook
the solid earth. But no fear of death was there; no
thought of self disturbed him. He placed himself at
the side of the road, he breathed hard, his lips were
tightly set. As the panting beasts neared him he

sprang at their heads, caught the bridles, was carried along for some distance, until he managed to regain his feet, and by sheer strength stopped the runaways on the very brink of the quarry. But for this act of heroism—for it was heroism—the elderly gentleman and his daughter would have been dashed to pieces. As the people who had been following in hot pursuit came up they lustily cheered the young man, but he only remained long enough to assure himself that the young lady and her father were safe, then in the excitement and confusion he slipped away, and it was not until some time afterwards that the old gentleman knew to whom he owed the lives of himself and child. Then he had the stupidity to send young Hallett a money present of a hundred pounds, which was returned with scorn and indignation and a wrathful message that he was not a hireling, to want payment for doing that which any man worthy the name would have done.

The foregoing details will bring into prominence a good deal of Jack's disposition and character. Proud he was with the pride of independence; and brave he was with the courage and instinct of a true soldier; and reckless he was with all the recklessness of youth. Gloominess formed no part of his composition. He revelled in life, and he had no sympathy with those who groan and sigh and moan because things are not quite in accordance with their own views. He believed that the world had been made beautiful that man might enjoy it, and, imbued with the tincture of Bohemianism, he had hitherto followed on the lines of "Hail, fellow, well met," and "A fig for to-morrow." By his comrades and

messmates he was regarded as a " jolly good sort,"
and his attractive manners, his *bonhomie*, his cheerful
spirits, and his handsome person and beaming face
made him an especial favourite with the fair sex.

On the first blush it almost seemed as if no more
fitting couple could have been mated than Jack and
Hester.   She, on her part, possessed sufficient
seriousness to counteract what might have been
termed the levity of his nature.   Perhaps "levity"
is hardly the correct word to use, for after all it was
nothing more terrible than the levity of lusty,
joyous, good-looking youth.   And whether boy or
maid, such a youth can hardly be expected to wear
the countenance of a philosopher, nor the gloomy
brow of an ascetic, who seems to think it is his
mission to go through the world groaning and
smiting his breast for the sins of his fellows.   From
what has now been said of these young people it is
not difficult to understand how the acquaintance
between them once begun ripened.   Opportunities
were made for meetings.   Hester had found out that
at or near a certain hour of the day she had
business to transact in Princes Street—the fashion-
able promenade ; some tradesmen to call upon, or
some trifle to buy which only could be bought in
that famous and most beautiful thoroughfare, with
its picturesque gardens and grim fortress on the one
hand, and its row of stately buildings on the other.
And by a remarkable coincidence the young lieutenant had come to consider it necessary to be
passing along the street at the same hour, and the
inevitable result was a meeting between the two.
Then there were mutual expressions of admirably

feigned surprise, a hearty handshaking, rippling laughter, and pleasant chat, until the parting came again. And Hester would wander to her home with a growing feeling that the handsome, dashing young soldier was exercising an irresistible influence over her, and she yearned for the next meeting.

Up to this point the girl had kept her feelings secret. Herein perhaps she was prudent, for at the most there had been nothing more serious between her and Jack than a mild and innocent flirtation; and it would have argued singularly bad taste on her part had she tacitly or otherwise led any one to suppose that the young officer had an eye to matrimonial potentialities in displaying a preference for her company. So she held her peace, she preserved her secrets, she dreamed her dreams, and when the busybodies and the tattlers and the prying little minds exclaimed—"Oh, I saw you yesterday again in Princes Street with that handsome young fellow, who seems so vain about his beautiful, even, white teeth that he is always showing them," she would answer quietly and ironically—

"Did you?"

And when the point-blank question was put—"I say, Hester, is there anything serious between you and that fellow?" her answer was no less quiet and dignified, and would run somewhat as follows—

"Surely I have a right to speak to a gentleman to whom I have been introduced under the roof of a friend's house without its being thought that I am about to rush into matrimony."

When Hester heard from her father what he had to tell about young Hallett, her feelings were not quite what the narrator expected they would be. To her there was nothing very dreadful in it. For a youngster in his salad days to protest by all the stars in heaven that he was madly in love with the first silly girl who chose to listen to him was no new phase of the human story. It had been repeated almost every day since time began.

Hester had the good sense to understand that a young man could not be gauged and controlled by the same fixed standard by which a girl's conduct is judged. A greater freedom and a greater licence are allowed to the man, and it has ever been so since man walked the earth, and right it is that it should be so. Of course, the shrieking sisterhood, who talk so glibly of "woman's rights," will protest against this doctrine, but, happily, they are in a very insignificant minority, and the generality of the fair sex, who prefer to remain women, will make no murmur. At any rate, Hester Dellaby, rightly or wrongly, regarded her lover's faults as venial ones. The blackness her father saw she could not see. The impression Jack had made upon her heart was far too deep to be removed easily. To her he had always been the most chivalric, courteous, considerate gentleman, and she could not possibly view him through any medium that was calculated to distort him to her view, and deprive him of that glamour which now surrounded him as she looked at him from her standpoint. Notwithstanding all this, she could not help but feel some concern that her father should display so strong a prejudice, and show no hesitation in referring to her lover as "an adventurer" and "a blackguard." Those were strong terms indeed to use, and as serious as they were strong, and unless a man is prepared to justify them to the hilt he should not breathe them, lest he bring himself into grave trouble, or wrongly blast the good name and reputation of him against whom he speaks. Hester knew her father too well to suppose that he would easily yield in his prejudice, for as long as he believed himself right nothing would change him. Under these circumstances the poor girl considered that the best course—even if it were not a duty—was to take counsel of her mother, and so to her mother she went.

CHAPTER IV.

A VIOLENT SCENE.

But in determining to lay the matter before her mother, Hester was not altogether hopeful that she would get that lady's full sympathy.

To use a common, but at the same time an expressive phrase, for it conveys a great deal of meaning, Mrs. Dellaby had no mind of her own. That is to say, she preferred to be swayed by others, rather than make any attempt to sway. She was a quiet, unostentatious little woman, who was content to live a humdrum life and follow blindly the lead of her husband. She had unbounded faith in him. He was truly her "lord and master," and so highly did she estimate his cleverness and ability, that she would have deemed it something only a little worse than treason on her part to have called his decisions into question.

Although Hester was fully aware that her parents lived in perfect unity, it did not seem to her possible that in this case her mother would refuse altogether to exercise some independent judgment. For, after all, it was purely a woman's question. At any rate the sentimental part of it was; for when a young woman falls in love with a young man sentiment runs high. It is no use asking her to be practical, no use asking her to sit down and coolly and deliberately go into certain calculations as if she were trying to solve a Euclid problem. Love takes the reason prisoner, and fetters it so that it has no power, and it is the merest fatuity to ask a girl to see through the same spectacles as her grandmother, or to understand the sermons of her elders when they dolefully tell her they have dreamed their dreams, and awakened to find that this world's idols are very common clay indeed. Youth is a sweet dream, and God grant it may be ever so.

Mrs. Dellaby listened patiently enough to what her distressed daughter had to tell, and then she admonished her to fall in with her father's views. This admonition was conveyed in a mild sort of didactic sermon, in which the duty of children to parents was lightly touched upon, and there were some vague hints thrown out as to the possible punishment that might hereafter result as a penalty for failing to strictly observe that duty.

The girl could hardly be blamed for her want of appreciation of the sentiment which her mother expressed. She had asked for bread and been given a stone; and the very source from whence she had hoped to draw consolation proving barren of sympathy, she found herself forced to act upon her own responsibility.

Under these circumstances she resolved, come what might, and let the consequences be what they would, to write to Hallett and then be guided by what he might do and say. Although she had not seen him nor heard from him since her father had sent that very violent letter—a copy of which he had subsequently read to her—which was destined to be productive of so much suffering, she did not believe for a single moment that he had abandoned her. Indeed, she pictured him bowed down with grief and crushed with despair. Nor was she altogether far wrong. Whatever his weaknesses were, and whatever his faults had been, he regarded her with a regard such as he had never had for any other woman; and if any one existed who could influence him to do great things and perform deeds which would add glory to his name, that person was Hester Dellaby.

The receipt of the very trenchant letter from Mr. Dellaby irritated Jack Hallett considerably, for it wounded his pride and insulted his dignity. He could not conceive what he had done to justify such a course as that which Mr. Dellaby had adopted, and his first thought was to send the letter back with an indignant reply; but his better sense prevailed, and he decided to await the tide of events, as he did not think it possible that Hester would allow herself to be influenced by her father's prejudices.

When he received her letter, therefore, which was very short, and suggested as the more practical course that an appointment to meet should be made, as they could discuss the situation so much better *viva voce* than by correspondence, his spirits rose, and he hastened to respond, saying that he could meet her that very evening, and he named a rendezvous where many a tryst had been kept before, and many a love-tale told.

When the first warm greetings had passed she asked—

"Have you ever done anything, Jack, to justify the course my father has taken ?"

"No, emphatically no," he exclaimed. "Foolish I have been, and——"

"Stay," she said, interrupting him. "It is enough for me to have your emphatic assurance that the letter he has sent you is unmerited. I want no confession of all your peccadillos, your escapades, your shortcomings. I am not so foolish as to expect to find a saint in the incarnate garb of a man. To me you have no faults now that I can see. But remember, sir, I look with love's eyes, and love is ever blind. Further, I would impress upon you that you have inspired me with a great passion that cannot be cooled down nor quenched by the mere bidding of a despotic father. That may be strong language for a daughter to use, but I must put my feelings into words since I cannot dissemble nor play the hypocrite. And forget not, Jack, that your honour is at stake——"

"And that honour has never yet been stained," he cried, with an expression of sincerity that could hardly have been assumed.

"I am glad to hear you make that declaration," she replied.

"And let me assure you, Hester," he added, "it never shall be stained. I am a soldier, and come of a race of soldiers who have ever placed honour above mere wordly gain. Your love for me is a very precious thing, and I should be worse than a scoundrel if I trifled with it."

"You would, indeed," she murmured, with a sigh.

" But you do not think me capable of doing so, do you ? "

" No, dearest, no, I do not," she exclaimed, with great fervency, as she tightened the pressure of her gloved hands about his arm, for they were walking arm-in-arm, and sauntering slowly and listlessly, as is the wont of lovers, towards the path that winds upwards to the summit of Arthur's Seat.

" And you will trust me, Hester ? "

" Aye, with my life ; with the essence of my life, my woman's heart."

" And may God forget me if ever I betray the trust. That trust shall keep me straight. It shall be my beacon star, and whatever my fate may be, wherever I may wander, I will not be unmindful of what I owe to you first, and through you to myself."

It was a pretty little speech, and full of lovers' vows as lovers have made them since love began ; and such vows have again and again and still again been broken. But he spoke sincerely enough then, and she, being a woman, reposed her confidence in him. How could she do otherwise ? Youth is trustful ; and love sees not.

It was the pleasant time of twilight as Hester Dellaby and Jack Hallett, with linked arms, and heads inclined towards each other, walked on the upward path that leads to the brow of the grey old hill which has witnessed so much that is stirring and strange in the world's story. But they had no eyes for anything but themselves ; no ears for aught but their own voices. Therefore were they all unconscious of the approach of a man who came after them with rapid strides, and whose every movement seemed suggestive of seething anger. And presently, when he overtook them, he made it instantly manifest that fierce wrath burned within him, for, though he was breathless with his uphill tramp, he exclaimed, addressing Hallett—

"You dastardly scoundrel!"

The speaker was Mr. Dellaby, who, having discovered his daughter's absence within a few minutes of her leaving the house, suspected that she had gone out to keep a tryst. So off he set in pursuit, for he had found in her room on a table Hallett's brief note, which she had carelessly left lying there. The young couple were necessarily disconcerted by this unexpected apparition, but the girl so far retained her presence of mind as to reprove her father for the strong language he used. This only served to exasperate him still more, and he said with all the rancour of a desperately angered man—

"Do not dictate to me. It is true you are my child, but I blush for you. I am ashamed of you. As for you, sir"—facing the young officer—"I feel that language is not strong enough to give expression to my disgust for you and contempt for you. You are a coward—a blackguard."

"I must take exception, sir, to both those terms," answered Hallett proudly.

"You may take exception to what you like," retorted the irate father. "I repeat that you are a blackguard; for in spite of my letter, in spite of my warning, you have had the temerity, and been deceitful enough to write to this silly girl, and to tempt her from the path of truth and duty to her parents, in order that you may corrupt her with your honied words and your shameless lying flattery."

"I resent this base accusation," replied Jack, growing very red in the face by reason of the great effort he made to suppress his anger.

"Resent that if you are a man," hissed Mr. Dellaby, as, entirely carried away by his feelings, he raised a walking-stick he had in his hand, and struck the young man across the forehead.

"Father, father, shame on you," cried Hester in an agony of distress, as she flung herself between the two men. But in this trying moment Jack displayed the coolness and self-possession of a true soldier, and he said dispassionately to her—

"Do not concern yourself, Hester, I shall not retaliate, but another man does not live whom I would allow to deal me such a blow with impunity. This man, however, is your father, so I accept the insult, and am content to let time bring its own revenge; and time will revenge me, of that I am sure. Good-night, Hester, and do not forget me; your father will escort you safely home."

He turned and walked away, and there was a touch of absolute grandeur in his dignified manner, and the absence of wrath under such trying circumstances.

Then, with a bitter cry, Hester covered her face with her hands and wept audibly.

"You ought to be ashamed of those tears," said her father, none of his anger abated.

"Yes, you are right," she replied warmly, as she wiped them away with her handkerchief. "They are a sign of weakness, and I ought to be strong. I will weep no more; but let me tell you this, that your mad conduct to-night fills me with a sense of burning shame, and if you think that that is the way to beget my obedience or retain my affection you will find yourself woefully mistaken."

"You shall either render me the homage a father, who has the true interests of his daughter at heart, has a right to expect from her, or you can go your ways as an outcast and a wanton, and I will tear you out of my heart, and never mention your name except it is to curse you."

Poor Hester thrilled with a little shudder at his violent language, but she had the sound sense to make no response, as no good could come of a prolongation of the argument. So she walked home in silence, and he followed, and she felt like one feels who has suddenly and rudely been awakened from a rapturous dream to find that the world is full of moaning.

CHAPTER V.

IT is difficult to imagine a more unfortunate position for a young woman of high-toned principles and conscientious scruples to be placed in than that of suddenly finding herself compelled to stifle down the natural feelings of the heart on the one hand, or to set herself in direct opposition to the expressed wishes of her parents on the other. It certainly was a position calculated to affect Hester Dellaby very deeply. For many days she endured a mental struggle which depressed her to an unusual degree. She had always been a loving, a dutiful daughter, but not even her filial love nor her sense of duty could blind her to the manifest injustice of her father's behaviour. She herself blushed with a conscious sense of shame, for no woman likes to be humiliated in the sight of the man who holds her heart, and certainly she had been humiliated that night as she had never been before.

When they reached the house her father said, with none of his habitual peremptoriness abated—

"I have something more to say to you, and you had better come to me in the library in half-an-hour."

Now arose within his daughter the spirit of

strength and self-will which he himself had given her, and, with but an ill-suppressed defiance in her tone, she made answer—

"No, sir" (the *sir* somewhat galled him) ; "no, sir, I shall do nothing of the kind. You can hardly expect me to be so utterly subdued, so meekly submissive, as to keep calm while you ruthlessly and rudely probe and re-probe a fresh and bleeding wound. I resolutely decline to hold further converse to-night on the subject."

She gave him no time to reply, but, leaving him looking almost dazed with astonishment, went to her room.

Now, there was no wonder Mr. Dellaby was astonished, for this mutinous spirit, as he was pleased to consider it, took him quite by surprise. In the egotism of his own esteem, and the blind belief in his own infallibility as a ruler of his household, he considered that his lightest command ought to beget silent and immediate obedience, while his judgment should be beyond question.

This doctrine was due no doubt to his Indian experience. When he first went out to our enormous empire in the East, the servants of the great "John Company" were very apt to develop the overbearing and masterful tone which at one time was considered necessary to the complete subjection of the varied races the Company ruled. Due allowance and some excuse should be made for this, as the positions in which the Company's servants were often placed were well calculated to make them autocrats. They as frequently as not carried their lives in their hands, and for their own safety, and the safety of all con-

cerned, they had to exact implicit obedience from
large numbers of natives. A man often found
himself in some wild district far removed from help
or succour if they should be suddenly needed, and in
the welfare of his employers, if for no other reason,
he was compelled to be determined, resolute, and to
make an autocratic and even despotic display of
power, for in those days India was truly held by the
few against the many, and the slightest show of
weakness would have been fatal to the tremendous
interests that were bound up in the Company.

This may all seem like an apology for Mr. Dellaby's
conduct, and frankly it is to some extent advanced
as such, for, after all, it was his head that was
wrong, and not his heart. Wrong he was in
principle, no doubt, but he erred conscientiously—
that is, he did not believe he was erring at all,
therefore was he conscientious. He could not but
help feeling some concern at the self-will which had
suddenly displayed itself in his daughter. He knew,
and he was proud to think that it was so, that she
was by no means lacking in character or individuality; but he made the lamentable mistake of
regarding her as a child, and, though a child might
be obstinate and self-willed, it was imperative on the
part of its natural guardian to subdue the obstinacy
and curb the will. Although Mr. Dellaby never
dreamed of allowing himself to be swayed by his
wife, he liked to discuss matters with her, and take
counsel with her, though it was always as one who
asks a friend for advice, but who has fully made up
his mind beforehand not to accept that advice, however sound it may be.

It is a contradictory and inconsistent trait of character, but one that is pretty common; undoubtedly it was strongly marked in Mr. Dellaby. So he went to his wife, and she was alarmed by the obvious signs which told her that he had been greatly upset, and was exceedingly distressed. With great circumstantiality he narrated to her all that had occurred, and when it came to the incident of the beating—in other words, the assault upon young Hallett—she looked up suddenly from her work, for she was embroidering a stool cover, and said plaintively—

"You don't mean to say, William, that you struck him?"

There must also have been a touch of reproof in her tone, or at any rate he thought so, for he responded sharply—

"Yes, of course I did. I felt it necessary to teach the impudent young beggar a lesson, and I am only sorry that I was not more severe."

Mrs. Dellaby subsided within herself again, and was silent. *interrupting*

"Now, I don't care a pin's point," he continued, "what Hallett may think. He was leading the child into the paths of disobedience, and he had to be sent to the right-about. But I am concerned for Hester. When once a girl gets all sorts of absurd notions about love and that kind of thing into her head, she can no longer be reasoned with in the ordinary way. Therefore, like all unreasonable beings, she must be treated without any regard for her feelings."

"Not quite, dear," very mildly put in his submissive wife, with a sidelong and timid glance at him, as though she was afraid of the effect her words were calculated to produce.

"I say yes," he cried, with a gesture of impatience, as though he couldn't brook her interruptions. "I repeat, that her feelings under such circumstances as these cannot be taken into account. A father who is really desirous of studying his child's welfare must be cruel only to be kind. Hester is wilful, and after all she is but a child. Why, it is only a day or two ago, so to speak, that I was dangling her on my knee."

Once more did Mrs. Dellaby look up from her work, and, in the deferential and subdued manner so characteristic of her, she showed that she was not in entire accord with him, for she remarked—

"I think, William dear, that we ought not to regard her altogether as a child. Remember that many a young woman at twenty is not only a wife but a mother."

"And shameful it is that it should be so," was her husband's rejoinder. "The idea of a girl of twenty taking upon herself the responsibility of matron and mother. It is monstrous, upon my word it is, for half the misery in the world is due to youthful marriages. Boys and girls come together and marry before they are capable of realizing the responsibilities of life. And what is the result when the false glamour of courtship and honey-moon has worn off?—all the defects in each other's characters and persons become visible, while the sordid and unromantic side of life is revealed. Then commences the misery, and out of misery cometh sin."

Poor little Mrs. Dellaby sheepily and feebly muttered—

"I fear you are right."

When her husband preached, she listened and bowed to him as one might bow to an oracle.

"Right! of course I am right!" he answered with his assertive egotism made painfully manifest. "Well, now, do you expect me to be a party to Hester's moral suicide?"

"Certainly not."

"Very well, then, why talk as though you thought I was doing something entirely wrong?"

"Oh, William," pleaded the submissive little woman, "how can you say that! You know what faith I have in your judgment; nor can I believe for an instant that you would stand in the way of anything you honestly thought would promote our dear girl's welfare."

"God forbid that I should!" he exclaimed with the emphasis of sincerity. "I would willingly sacrifice myself rather than throw a cloud over her life; but I am convinced Hallett is not the man for her. I believe him to be utterly without principle."

"Are you sure, dear, that that is so?" queried his wife with a frightened look; for though she had just expressed faith in his judgment, she could not altogether subdue her womanly nature, nor kill the motherly sympathy she felt for her daughter.

"Sure! I am as sure as a man can be sure of anything. I have learnt enough of his history to feel perfectly justified in my assertion. I say he is unprincipled. I say he is a vagabond in the worst sense of the word; therefore Hester will never have my consent to her union with him. Besides, why should the girl want to marry a soldier? The best of them are bad—that's been my experience; and, apart from that, there is always the probability of her being early left a widow. My own idea is that neither soldiers nor sailors should be allowed to marry."

"I am afraid, William," remarked his wife, with an attempt at a laugh, as though she wished him to suppose she was perpetrating a small joke,—"I am afraid, William, you would find that the majority of young women would be against you on that point."

"The majority of young women are fools," he answered irascibly; whereupon she gathered that she had made a mistake, and that it would be better to keep silent, having regard to his mood. She knew too well that his self-assertiveness, his unbending will—pig-headedness some people might have called it—his unyielding prejudices, and his obduracy, when he believed himself in the right and other people in the wrong, made it very difficult to reason with him. At any rate, she was sufficiently conscious of her own weakness to refrain from making the attempt. But notwithstanding this, and notwithstanding her blind faith in him, she could not subdue certain misgivings that disturbed the rhythm of her own heart with regard to her daughter; for she knew that Hester had inherited a good deal of her father's strong will, and if in this juncture of affairs the girl should refuse to obey, it might be provocative of disastrous consequences.

With that obsequious deference therefore that she-
always displayed towards her husband, Mrs. Dellaby
ventured to suggest the advisability of dealing with
Hester in a diplomatic rather than a commanding
spirit, and it was soon made clear to her that this
stern and despotic man was not without an underlying fear of the potential evils of any too high-
handed course with his daughter. For, while it
was very easy to speak of her in theory as a child,
it might be found in practice that she was capable
of displaying the will of a determined woman.
Anyway, he more than hinted to his wife that
she should see what her motherly influence could
effect in the way of inducing the girl to renounce
Hallett; and thus it came about that shortly afterwards mother and daughter were together, and the
mother, by such argument as came within her power,
was endeavouring to convince Hester that disobedience
and opposition to the wishes of parents were heinous
sins on the part of a child.

Hester was quite willing to concede that point
when the wishes were just, but she maintained that
there were times when a parent's wishes could be
legitimately opposed on the grounds that they were
inconsistent with common-sense, or not based upon
a fair and impartial consideration of the merits of
the case. Further, she fearlessly asserted that in
this instance her cause was a just one, and that her
father had behaved with a violence which was little
short of brutal. She was indignant and wrathful,
as well she might be. Firstly, because her father
had shown so little regard for her feelings; and,
secondly, because his insult to Lieutenant Hallett

was rather what might have been expected from an ignorant and ill-bred person than from one who laid claim to be considered a gentleman.

"It cannot be supposed," she said to her mother, "that I am going to dissever myself from Hallett simply because my father has taken a violent and unreasoning prejudice against him."

"But Hallett's career is well calculated to beget prejudice," answered her mother.

"Nothing in his career that my father has told me of warrants prejudice on my part. Besides, I have Jack's solemn assurance that his honour is unstained."

Mrs. Dellaby would not have been a woman if she had failed to appreciate at its full value such an expression of feeling on the part of a girl for her lover as this. It showed that Hester was not to be coerced against her will, and the motherly heart was disturbed with an anxiety that she found it by no means easy to conceal. But she was conscious also that the situation could only be saved by her, as neither heated language nor a display of will would avail aught, for the one would only irritate, and will would beget will. So she rose, or rather tried to rise, equal to the occasion, and her efforts were crowned with a certain measure of success.

Hester was not lacking in a proper sense of respect for, nor in loyalty and devotion to, her parents, and, therefore, when her mother pointed out that a little concession on both sides in this instance could hardly fail to conduce to a much better understanding than rashness at a time when tempers were ruffled and relations strained, she lent an attentive ear.

Mrs. Dellaby could not by any stretch of the imagination be described as a woman of any individuality. The reader will have gathered this from such analysis as has already been made of the lady's character. And it has further been pointed out that she really, if ever, attempted to call her husband's motives or his conduct seriously into question. She had, however, that intuitive power of arriving at a conclusion without reasoning which is a much more feminine than masculine characteristic. For while the man reasons by a process of deduction, a woman goes straight to the point, owing to some instinct—for the want of a better name—which is peculiar to her. In this instance the lady saw that her daughter might be led, but could not be driven, and so all the motherly influence was brought to bear to induce the girl to wait for a little while before attempting to renew her acquaintance with Lieutenant Hallett. Mrs. Dellaby emphasized the argument that time is a great assuager of wrath as it is of grief, and, given a little time, the father's views might *possibly*—she used the word "possibly"—might possibly change, and the course of true love be allowed to flow smoothly. Hester was so far impressed that she consented to her mother's suggestion that she should go away for a time—go to some relatives who were temporarily sojourning at a country residence not far removed from Flodden's classic ground. The distance from Edinburgh was not great, but the good lady considered it sufficient to separate the lovers. She urged, however, as the influencing consideration, that Mr. Dellaby would have time to cool down and think differently. Moreover, as it was utterly impracticable just then that Lieutenant Hallett and Hester could marry, persistency in open courtship could not fail to keep the wound already made open, and be productive of misery and pain. Whereas a period of quiescence would probably bring about in the end what the young people desired.

"This," pursued the lady, who, of course, held a brief for her husband, "will be infinitely better than open rupture with your father. You know how determined he is in the face of opposition, and it really would be a terrible thing if you and he were to be at constant strife. I do hope, therefore, that you will fall in with my views; and if you will give me your solemn promise that you will not communicate with Hallett, nor attempt to see him, for three months, I will use such influence as I may possess with your father on your behalf. Now, I certainly think this is a very reasonable suggestion, and you may depend upon it that if you are destined to become Hallett's wife, nothing can keep you apart, but it is far better to exercise patience than oppose your father's wishes, and henceforth live your life with a dark shadow over it."

Mrs. Dellaby certainly argued sincerely, if she did not argue well; Hester was influenced, and she gave the required promise of three months' silence. Very reluctantly she gave it, it is true; but she preferred peace to war, and three months might be the means of changing her father's views. So in the course of a few days she departed for the south, and Mrs. Dellaby felt that she had scored a triumph.

CHAPTER VI.

In falling in with her mother's suggestion poor Hester had in a sense failed to consider Lieutenant Hallett as a factor in the calculation. It was indeed very much like reckoning without the host, and the most momentous results were destined to follow the oversight. If the girl had seen Hallett, or written to him to explain, all would have been well probably, but, true to her promise, she did neither the one nor the other, and the consequence was, Jack fretted and chafed under his disappointment. He was a proud, high-spirited boy, and the shameful insult he had been subjected to at the hands of the irate Dellaby had wounded his pride terribly. Nothing could have testified in a more emphatic way to his love and high regard for Hester, than his meekness under the unwarranted chastisement. But for love's sweet sake what will man not dare and do! Therefore Hallett bore with his wounded pride, because, remembering Hester's words on the night of the outrage—for outrage undoubtedly it was—he felt sure that she would write to him or see him.

So day after day he haunted the place where he had been wont to meet her, and anxiously he looked to each post as it came in, expecting it would bring him the missive that would be as balm to his hurt feelings. But he met her not, neither did the hoped-for letter come, and then, as was but natural, he began to think that her words and promises were nothing more than the froth of an ebullient emotion which had suddenly cooled. He would have been a spiritless youth indeed if he had not taken this to heart. Perhaps if he had loved her less he would have scorned her more, but his love was a very real thing, and no words that could be used would do full justice to the stinging nature of the disappointment, and the crushed pride under which he laboured. And when by chance he learned from a lady, a mutual acquaintance who knew Hester, that the girl had been sent away from home, and was then sojourning with relatives in the Border country, it seemed that he had been befooled, that so long as it was a summer sky she was content to walk with him, and to talk with him, but with the first blast of an adverse breeze she had shrunk away, allowing her promises to wither like flowers that are plucked. Think as he would, and argue as he would with himself, he could find no excuse for her silence.

"If she had really cared for me," he mentally exclaimed, "nothing in the world would have prevented her writing to me, if it had only been one word to bid me hope. But women are all alike. They speak words only, and a man who places his faith in them is a fool. Like butterflies, women revel in sunshine and flowers, but when the first wintry blast blows they are seen no more."

This was terribly severe, and no less severe than unjust. But full allowance must be made for him. He was young. Of the practical side of life he knew little, and he judged woman under the influence of a bitter disappointment and a great wrong. In the dark and stirring future, however, that lay before him, he was yet to learn that woman's devotion, her self-abnegation, her silent heroism, her tireless patience, her magnificent tenderness are shown best in the hour of trial, sorrow, affliction, suffering, and death. Hester Dellaby had been to him a star that had made his world the brighter for its shining, and in a moment of emotional sentiment, of boyish gush, he had once penned the following lines to her—

> "I want no star in heaven to guide me,
> I want no moon, no sun to shine,
> While I have you, sweetheart, beside me
> While I am sure that you are mine."

But with a cruel suddenness the star had disappeared from his narrowed firmament, and he was like one who groped in darkness—the flowers and the beauty of the earth were obscured.

"She has mistaken me for a carpet soldier," he murmured bitterly; "but some day she will know better."

It often seems in our human story as if it was specially ordained that certain men and women should be subjected to crosses and disappointments, in order that the higher and better qualities of their natures may be developed. Many a man who has displayed magnificent heroism and made his name ring, would have remained obscure and unknown had some reverse of fortune or some startling circumstance not called forth his energies and noble qualities; and many a woman, around whose memory are now twined the bays of loving regard, would have died unsung had she not been called upon in the hour of awful need to show how much of the angel there is in the female nature.

Jack Hallett took his disappointment to heart in a way that his most intimate friends would hardly have thought possible, for he had generally been regarded as a lad who was incapable of any great or lasting emotion, and rather disposed to be inconstant if not insincere. But those who thus judged him looked no further than the surface, and saw nothing of the germs of the splendid nature that lay in the depths and only wanted the proper conditions to call them into active life.

It was about this time that one or two regiments which were then stationed at Colchester were under orders to sail for Persia, and one day Jack presented himself to the Colonel of his own regiment—an old warrior who had seen much service, and who, from his having been very intimate with Jack's father, was much interested in the lad—and to him he thus addressed himself—

" I am very anxious, sir, to have an opportunity to make a name for myself, if that is at all possible——"

The old Colonel laughed gruffly, and said—

"That is a noble ambition, young gentleman, and I applaud you for it. But you must have patience. The opportunity comes sooner or later to every man."

" Yes, sir, but I want to hurry on my opportunity, and I want you to help me."

"How? Why? What does this mean?"

"The 20th are under orders for Persia."

"Yes. I know that."

"Well, sir, I want to exchange into that regiment; and with your influence and assistance I may be able to manage it. Inactivity here goes against my grain. I want to see service. I should like to smell powder."

The Colonel looked hard at him for some moments from beneath his shaggy eyebrows, and then, in the deepest tones he was capable of sinking his voice to, he said—

"What does this mean, boy?"

"It means, sir, that I wish to go away."

"But why?"

"For the reasons I have stated."

"But you have another and more potent reason," replied the Colonel, making a shrewd guess at the truth, no doubt aided by something or other in the young man's expression.

"I *have* another reason, Colonel."

"There is a woman in the question?"

"Since you ask me bluntly, I will answer you frankly. Yes."

"Ah, I thought so. Women are devils. They drive men to destruction. But now, look here, youngster. Don't you let the best woman in creation turn your head. I admire your desire to distinguish yourself. That is all right. But I am not going to allow you to throw yourself away because some heartless minx has jilted you. Lads of your age see a pretty face, and at once think they are desperately in love. But it's calf love, that's what it is—calf love, and nothing more. Now go back to

E

your duties, and don't let any silly sentiment disturb
your serenity. It's a mistake, take my word for it.
Half the women in the world ought to be drowned,
and the other half kept chained up, for woman is at
the bottom of all mischief."

Jack waited patiently until the old warrior—who,
no doubt, had been as much a warrior in love as in
war—had blown some of his steam off, and then he
answered with quiet dignity—

"You do not quite gauge the situation, Colonel, as
far as I am concerned. Nor is it necessary, I
presume, that I should enter into minute details. I
have no doubt there is a good deal of truth in what
you say, and I am quite old enough to understand
that a woman is at the bottom of most mischief, but
still we should get on badly without women——"

"Oh, yes," broke in the Colonel, "they're useful
sometimes, I admit. They nurse our babies, darn
our stockings, put buttons on our shirts, can use a
needle without sticking it into their fingers, which a
man always does. They look after us when we are
ill, and that sort of thing, but damn 'em, they spend
our money, and drive us to the devil."

"Possibly, sir; but to come back to the object of
my interview with you," pursued Jack, unmindful of
the interruption; "pray let me urge my request with
greater emphasis. I want to go abroad, and I hope
and trust you will not throw any obstacles in my way."

"If you are really serious in this matter," mumbled
the Colonel, knitting his ragged brows into a stern
expression of thoughtfulness——

"Oh, sir, I am serious enough, I pledge you my
honour."

" You really want to go out to Persia ? "

" I do."

" Let me see, now. When do the 20th leave ? "

" I think it is in about six weeks."

" Ah ! well, there's not much time to be lost. Well, now, I will see what I can do. It is very likely the affair can be managed. At any rate I'll put matters in trim, and you can rely upon my doing my best for you; not that I want to lose you, on the contrary. I've watched you closely, and I am convinced you have the makings of a good officer in you. You're a smart lad, and as the son of my esteemed friend I should like you to make your way, and unless I'm mistaken you will." Hallett bowed, and the colour came into his face, but he made no answer. " Now go to your duties, but look here, young fellow, don't you get entangling yourself with wenches. They'll play the very deuce with your career if you do. Women are all very well in their way, and wine is a good thing to drink toasts in ; but the man who allows either the one or the other to muddle his brain is an idiot."

" I have no doubt you are right, sir, and speak from experience," replied Jack, with a sly look and an ill-concealed smile playing about his lips, for it was notorious in the regiment that the Colonel was a perfect lady-killer, and had had entanglements by the score in his time, while as a lover of good liquor he was scarcely to be surpassed. His shaggy eyebrows came together again as he growled sternly—

" No innuendos, young fellow, no innuendos. Go to your duty."

Hallett waited no longer, but saluted and retired ;

2

and when the door had closed upon his retreating figure, the old soldier relaxed his stern expression and murmured to himself—

" That's a fine lad, a fine lad, and he'll make a clever and plucky officer, or else I'm woefully out in my reckoning. However, he shall not lack opportunity if I can help it; and since he wants to go to Persia he shall go. I suppose the fact is he's lost his heart for the time being to some pretty puss. Well, they will do it. Girls will be girls and boys boys. God bless them all, say I. If I had my time to come over again, hang me if I wouldn't make love to every pretty girl I could speak to. Love and war are a soldier's trade. But young Hallett has evidently been seriously bitten, and he must go away."

Jack waited as patiently as he could for the result of the interview with his Colonel, until so many days passed that he began to despair and fret again. At last, however, he was ordered to go to the Colonel's quarters, and the old soldier thus addressed him—

" Well, sir, are you still desirous of going away ? "

" I am, sir; my desire has not abated one jot."

" Then I have to inform you that the exchange can be managed, and you must start for the south to-morrow."

" I am deeply indebted to you, Colonel, and no less grateful," said Hallett, with very obvious emotion.

" I want no thanks. I only hope you will not regret the step. The regiment you are leaving is a distinguished one, and has carved its name deeply on the tablets of honour. It has a glorious history, and any soldier may well feel proud of belonging to such a regiment."

"I beg and pray of you, Colonel," cried Hallett, unable to conceal his feelings, "not to think that I am indifferent to the honour of having belonged to the regiment, whose annals are indeed glorious, and the memory of whose great and heroic deeds can never fade. Fain would I have remained with you; but the current of our lives does not always run as we desire it to do. I yearn to go abroad; that yearning will not be suppressed; and I trust that I may never do an act or deed that will in the slightest degree reflect upon my own honour or the honour of those with whom I may be associated; nor will I ever forget that an officer and a gentleman are synonymous terms."

The Colonel extended his hand to his lieutenant, and said with what for him was an unusual display of warmth—

"You speak bravely and well, and there is a sterling ring in your speech. Old as I am, I may yet live to see you famous, and if I do I shall be proud of this day. God prosper you wherever you go. You will dine with me to-night, and I will invite your brother-officers to meet you and drink your health."

Hallett could scarcely find words to express his thanks, and his head was all in a whirl as he left the Colonel's presence. Such spare hours as he had during the rest of the day he devoted to writing to his sisters and mother, acquainting them with the step he was taking, and promising them that he would get leave of absence for two or three days to visit them before sailing for Persia, And when he had finished this correspondence he penned a brief note to Hester, of which the following is a copy :—

"When we last met, and you so solemnly renewed your pledges to me, I would have strangled that man who dared to assert that you would soon forget your vows. But it is the old story. Woman is as fickle as an April day, and she writes her vows in water. However, I must take my chance in the lottery of life. I hoped to win you, but have lost ; and so I go forth into the unknown future, with the prompting of a great recklessness moving me. I want excitement. I want the din of battle ; the roar of tumultuous war. My wishes may be gratified, for there is strife going on in Persia, and I am bound for Persia. I only hope the war will not fizzle out before I get there. At any rate in a foreign land I shall find distraction ; and when you and I are far from each other my sorrow may become less keen. But forget you I never can. Your name is graven across my heart, and I vow a vow on my honour and by my soul that no other shall replace it. Farewell ! and farewell again ! When you read this—if ever you do read it—I shall have started for the East. I have exchanged into the 20th, under orders for Persia, and the regiment embarks in a fortnight. Your portrait which you once gave me I shall retain. I ought to send it back, and intended to do so, but I find it impossible. I cannot let it go from me. It will keep me straight. I intend to have it fitted into a small morocco case, and shall wear it next my heart. That's ridiculous, isn't it ? I know I am foolish; but then I have loved you; do love you still. For the last time—Farewell !"

This was a manly letter, and though there was sentiment in it, it was wholesome sentiment. It was the sentiment of youth, and there was naught in it to be ashamed of. He put the letter into an envelope and addressed it to Hester at the house where she was staying, near Flodden; but he did not intend to post it until the very day that he was starting for the East.

That evening he dined with the Colonel and the rest of the officers, and when the cloth had been removed and the after-dinner wine was circulating, the Colonel requested the company to join him in drinking a toast. Then in a graceful, even eloquent little speech, he bade the young lieutenant God-speed, referring to him in the very kindliest way, and he wound up by the following facetious remarks :—

" Gentlemen, our young comrade-in-arms is leaving us, not because he is dissatisfied with us, for I am sure he would give us a good character if we need one, but because he is thirsting to flesh his maiden sword in some benighted Persian. Not that I think the chance to do that will be given him, for I fancy the bobbery will all be over before he gets there. It seems to me only a flash in the pan. But the truth is, and, gentlemen, the truth cannot be disguised, for as murder will out, so will truth—this fledgling has been trying his hand at another game; he has been laying siege to the heart of some pretty girl, but has had to withdraw his forces and beat a retreat. Well, we have all gone through that experience, I suppose, and a very pleasant pastime it is. It is generally supposed <u>that when a soldier is not fighting he is making love.</u> I shall say nothing now to disturb that fossilized idea, though we cannot always be on the winning side in love no more than we can in war; but a true soldier does not allow himself to be disgracefully defeated either in war or love, and though I know nothing of our young friend's little campaign, I am prepared to stake my reputation he has conducted it manfully and in a soldierly way, and though he has been defeated, he retreats with unsullied honour and his good name unstained. Gentlemen, let us pledge him in a bumper, and wish him the best of luck wherever he goes."

The toast was drunk with enthusiasm, and Hallett sat like one in a dream. The cheers of his comrades seemed to daze him, and the words of his Colonel pierced his brain, until his head was in a whirl, for he had had no idea that reference would be made to the cause which had led to the step he was taking.

When the clinking of the glasses and the cheers had ended he rose pale and agitated, and only by a supreme effort could he control his voice.

"From the bottom of my heart I thank you," he said; "and whether my life be long or short, wherever I go, or whatever may be my lot, I shall endeavour to thoroughly deserve Colonel Farquharson's opinion of me, and I will humbly try to so order my conduct that no man shall be able to honestly say that I have done aught that I need be ashamed of. You may trust me to uphold the honour of our profession, and to strive to add to its glory. That is all I can say, gentlemen, for I am not accustomed to make speeches, and I pray you pardon my shortcomings in that respect."

He could say no more, but resumed his seat amidst the applause of his brother-officers. The sincerity of his words, the earnestness with which he spoke, could not be mistaken.

The next day he took his departure, being accompanied to the station by many of his comrades; and a fortnight later, having bade a tender farewell to those who were near and dear to him, he embarked with his regiment at Portsmouth. Just before he sailed he dropped the letter he had written to Hester into the post, and as the night-mail bore that letter north, the gallant troopship that was carrying him and his comrades to the East was ploughing her way down Channel towards the steel-blue ocean.

CHAPTER VII.

WHEN Mr. Dellaby heard of the result of his wife's negotiations with Hester, he was, it is needless to say, exceedingly gratified. For though he would have hesitated to confess it, he had begun to feel rather alarmed lest his daughter, with an assertion of self-will, should persist in keeping up a connection with young Hallett. He was not unmindful of the proverb about taking a horse to the water, and if Hester had shown a disposition to give a practical illustration of the somewhat musty, albeit useful proverb, things might have been awkward. As it was, all was well. At least so it seemed, and he did not care to reflect on the possibilities of his wandering wilfully blind into a fool's paradise. It was the immediate effect that he concerned himself about, and not what might result at the expiration of the stipulated period to which Hester had pledged herself to refrain from holding any communication with Jack. In three months much might happen, and three months in some cases was long enough for love to wither in a girl's heart. At any rate, so Dellaby thought, and, thinking so, his wonted serenity returned, for the time being, at least. Just about this time there came a bundle of letters from his daughter Margaret, who was with her husband, Lieutenant-Colonel Pritchard, at Meerut, in India. "Madge," as she was always lovingly called in the family, was affected with the *cacoëthes scribendi*, and was an exceedingly diligent correspondent. She scarcely allowed a mail to leave without its carrying communications from her to her family. For though she had a doting husband and two sweet children—a girl and a boy—her heart was not entirely weaned from the loved ones at home. On this occasion she wrote a letter each to her father and mother, and one to Hester. To her father she wrote amongst other things as follows :—

Her letter was dated Meerut, India, November, 1856.

"We are beginning to wake up here after the hot season, which has been unusually hot and unusually trying. For a little while I was not very well, and went off to the hills with Fred and Amy" (her two children), "and they and I are now first-rate. You have heard, no doubt, that there has been some trouble with the native troops at Barrackpore and Dum Dum. A mutinous spirit displayed itself, but was speedily suppressed. It arose, according to common belief, because the native soldiers thought that their cartridges had been greased with pork fat—a most ridiculous idea, of course, but then the native mind is very apt to conceive wrong impressions, as you yourself are no doubt aware. The truth of the matter is, however, and it is known to those behind the scenes, that the little murmurings of discontent are due to the preachings of certain mendicant priests, who, whether on their own account or as paid emissaries of some of our country's enemies is not quite clear, have been secretly advocating the driving of the British out of India. An old prophecy has been revived to the effect that in 1857 India will be under Mussulman rule. Of course, George" (her husband) "and all the officers here laugh at the bare idea, but I confess that sometimes myself I have misgivings, for it is impossible not to notice that of late the natives are not as submissive as they were. Even one's servants show a greater independence of spirit, and they are not at the trouble they once were to conceal the contempt which we all know they bear for us as their conquerors. I often wish that George and I and the children could return to dear old England, for though my fears may be very foolish and the result of a morbid nervousness, I never feel quite comfortable here, and it seems almost a sacrilege to me to call it home. However, we have many dear friends. All the officers are exceedingly nice, and everything is done to make life pass pleasantly. It is a terribly long time, however, to look forward to 1859, when George's regiment will have completed its Indian service and return home. He often urges me to visit you with the children, but greatly as I yearn to do that, I confess that I cannot make up my mind to leave him, for if there *is* danger ahead I will share it with him. The place of a devoted wife is at the side of her husband in the hour of trial. I had a letter from Harry" (her brother) "at Malta the other day. He says it is on the cards that his regiment may be ordered to Bombay. I hope that will be so, as I should then have a chance of seeing him. We do seem such a scattered family somehow. But I would fain believe that all things are ordered for the best."

*　　　*　　　*　　　*　　　*

In this very womanly letter Mrs. Pritchard showed that she had a prescience which was lacking to those who ought to have been better informed, but who, with a somewhat egotistical consciousness of their own strength and might, refused to believe in any widespread dissatisfaction, but even if it existed they were confident they could cope with it in a very masterful manner.

"Madge's" letter to her sister was sent under separate cover. It was destined—unconsciously so to the writer—to influence Hester's future movements in a way that was never anticipated. How this was the case will best be understood by the following extract.

*　　　*　　　*　　　*　　　*

"Often, dear, when my thoughts wander away far across the sea that separates us—and, oh, how many times they do that in the course of a week—I wonder what you are doing, and, oh, how I yearn to have a glimpse of your dear darling face. How true it is that absence makes the heart grow fonder! You are a woman, dear, with a woman's heart, and a woman's mind, and mayhap you have given that heart into somebody's keeping. If so, God grant he may be worthy of the great trust, for you, my beloved sister, have such a sweet disposition, such a generous, noble mind, that the man who wins you may well be proud. Will it be your fate to have a soldier husband? Likely enough it will, for all our people seem to have an inseparable link with the army; and though the risks are many, for a soldier's life must ever be a precarious one, a soldier, speaking generally, makes a good husband. Of course there are good and bad among them, but I confess that I am strongly of opinion you are more likely to draw a prize amongst army men than amongst civilians.

"You will forgive this chatter, dear, won't you? but it is a woman talking to a woman, a sister to a sister, and you know how anxious I am about you, how interested in your movements, your thoughts, your hopes. Although it may seem selfish of me to wish it, for our dear father and mother have no one but you at home now to comfort them in their old age, I do wish you would come out to us for a few months, if *pater* and *mater* could manage to part from you for so long a time. You would be so intensely interested in everything here, for new-comers cannot fail to be interested. Everything is so totally different to what it is in our dear old fog-sodden country. Pa would have no difficulty in getting somebody to look after you on the passage out, for we have so many friends constantly going to and fro. You might come as far as Alexandria with Captain Milton in the P. & O. *Poonah,* and you would have plenty of company across the desert and on to Calcutta, where I would meet you, and we would travel up the country together. My dear little tots, at the bare idea of you coming, go into ecstasies. Fred is now seven years old and Amy is five. They are such bonnie children and talk so prettily. Freddy has made all sorts of plans should it chance that 'Tanty,' as he calls you, comes. But really, Hetty, I think I am indulging in a wild dream, for I cannot imagine either mother or father consenting to your leaving them even for so short a time as a little year. So, heigho! I must fain restrain my impatience for a sight of your dear face until our time here expires and we turn our backs on India. But oh! it seems such a long time to look forward to, and yet time passes rapidly, doesn't it? Fancy, it is over six years since we sailed from Portsmouth. George often talks about you. You know when he first saw you you were a little girl in short frocks, but what a sweet pretty child you were. Many a time has he said that, had you been a little older, he would have married you in preference to me. Of course he says that to tease me. But if your last photograph you sent me doesn't flatter you, I declare I should be afraid of George falling in love with you. You don't believe this, do you? It's only my fun, and I wish you could put it to the test. George is such a darling, doting old boy, that not Venus herself, I am sure, could turn him from me, although I have been his wife for upwards of eight years. I declare I seem to be growing quite an old woman.

"By the way, we heard recently that the 12th Lancers are under orders for India. They are to relieve the 10th Hussars, who have been on foreign service for fourteen years. When I first met George he was a captain in the 12th. It is funny that his old regiment should come out while we are here. It is very likely they will put in part of their time in Meerut. Well now, dear, I must close my letter. Tell me everything when you write, there's a darling. My prayers are ever for you.

"Your loving sister,
"MADGE PRITCHARD."

CHAPTER VIII.

THE HAND OF FATE.

THE people with whom Hester was sojourning were relatives of Mr. Dellaby's. Their name was Judson, and they had a daughter called Florence who was Hester's half-cousin. The two girls were about the same age, so that Hester did not lack companionship. Florence was a charming girl, and was engaged to a young man who had recently passed a very successful examination, and received an appointment in the Civil Service. Of course she was elated, and seemed never to tire of talking about her " dear boy " Reginald, or Reg, as she fondly called him. Hester on her part observed a discreet silence. Most girls in her position would have poured out their woes, and have sought sympathy from a companion like Flo. But she did nothing of the kind. As a matter of fact, her love affair was not a thing she cared to discuss, for had she mentioned it at all she must have referred to that humiliating scene between herself, Hallett, and her father, and she could never recall that without a sense of burning shame. So she listened to her friend, and lent a sympathetic ear to all she had to say, and her own secret, her own sorrow, she kept locked fast in the recesses of her heart. The house where she was staying was beautifully situated. Woodland, dell, and stream combined to make up a perfect landscape, which was shut in by rugged and scarped hills. There was a repose and restfulness about the place that accorded well with her mood, and she was never tired of wandering about the lanes and woods, for she was a great lover of Nature, and Nature's many tuneful voices delighted and pleased her. But though all her surroundings were genial and to her tastes, they could not possibly wean her thoughts from Hallett. Over and over again was she tempted to write to him, but she resisted the temptation, for had she not given her pledge and promise to refrain from writing or making any attempt to see him for three months ? To Love's impatience how like an eternity does three months seem. It is but an infinitesimal space of time when measured by the span of swift-rolling years, which so soon, alas! sweep us through our lives, and into that "great beyond," where there is an unbroken silence and a sleep that knoweth no dreams. But to a young girl whose heart has gone out towards him who has become her idol, and who is separated from her, how long, weary, and leaden-footed do the lagging hours seem. Where Hester felt her enforced inaction so much, was in the thought that he might deem her false and fickle, and when that thought did surge through her brain, she felt as if she could not control herself; that she must rush away, do something, break the seal that had been put upon her, though it was at the cost of her solemnly pledged word; and yet, on the other hand, how could she efface from memory's tablets the words she had uttered to him on the memorable night when she had walked with him under the shadow of

F

Arthur's Seat—that night when her father had brought the blushes of a stinging wrong and shame to her cheeks.

"Will you trust me, Hester?" Jack had asked.

"Aye, with my life; with the essence of my life, my woman's heart," she had answered. Now, unless those were mere windy words, was the pledge—for it was a pledge—to pass for nothing? Were they to have no binding effect upon her conscience? for let it be remembered how great was her faith in Hallett. Had he not declared with an emphasis of assurance that carried conviction with it, that he and his race had ever placed honour above worldly gain? and, unless it was a mere lover's phrase, she must set it in the balance against her father's prejudice, for which he had shown no better warrant than some story he had been told about a boyish escapade.

So poor Hester struggled with her heart, her thoughts, her desires, and she felt like one in a wilderness crying for sympathy; but her cry had to be stifled, and she had to wear a smile when she was ready to weep, and weeping would have been far more in consonance with her feelings.

"Does he dream of me?" she asked herself. "Will he continue to respect me? Will he wear my image in his heart during the dreadful three months? Oh, for some sign," she moaned, "some sign to tell him I am true to him and he to me!"

A sign came at last, but it was not what she hoped, wished, and prayed for.

She was sitting in her bedroom one evening. A charming little room it was, and filled with many a nick-nack of feminine taste and fancy. An oriel and latticed window commanded an exquisite view. She had thrown the casement open and watched the gloaming fade until the hills became shadowy and indistinct, and then the moon arose and spread a sheen of silver over the scene. Pensive she was and full of dreaming. How could it be otherwise? She was but in life's morning, and it is in the morning of our lives that we dream dreams, for youth is a time of desire; manhood of realization; old age of regret. When our fire burns low, and the ashes are turning white upon the hearth, we cast our eyes back over the track we have travelled, and sigh for the broken idols that we have found to be only delusive clay. "Alas!" we think, "we might have done so differently had we but known."

It is well, indeed, that we do not know as we stand upon the threshold of our career, for if it were given to us to tear aside the curtain that screens the future from our eyes, we should often shrink back appalled, and with white lips curse the fate that had given us the breath of life. And so Hester sat in an all-absorbed way gazing out to where the moon's rays shimmered on and transfigured the stream until it resembled a channel of agitated molten silver. And the pine trees on the hills, blended into solid shadow, could be likened to the portals at the entrance of some dark abode of mystery. Indeed, on such a night, the reins of fancy being free, nothing is too extravagant for the imagination, for it is on such a night that the real becomes unreal, and shapes and forms that are but airy nothings— phantasms of the darkness—flit before our vision. Perhaps Hester was trying to evolve out of the

F 2

visions of the moonlit landscape, something that she could construe into a prophecy of her future, some sign that would give her comfort in her great distress. Anyway, she was so wrapped in thought that she heard not a tap at her door, and when the door opened and a white-clad figure glided in, and a voice exclaimed—" Why, Hetty, girl, are you moonstruck ? " she sprang up with a cry, and said—" Oh, Flo, how you startled me ! "

" Why, I thought you must be asleep, for I knocked twice, and could get no answer," replied Flo, merrily. " But whatever are you sitting in the dark for ? Why, if I were to sit in the dark like that I should see ghosts. Ugh! I hate ghosts. My teeth chatter at the thought of 'em. Here, let's have a light. Where are the matches and the lamp ? I've got them ; it's all right. There, that's better. Now then, if you're a good girl, and promise you won't go mooning any more, I'll give you a letter."

" Has the mail-bag come in ? " asked Hester, with a little fluttering of the heart.

" Yes, about ten minutes ago, and I've got a letter from my dear old boy, and there's one for you ; no from my dear old boy, of course not, but I shouldn't be surprised now if *yours* is a love-letter. It' addressed in a man's handwriting, at any rate. Now I'm going to sit and devour every word of mine, and suck in all the kisses he sends me, so don't speak to me for half-an-hour."

She dropped down on an ottoman to feast on he lover's words, and as poor Hester glanced at th superscription on the envelope that Flo had thrus into her hand her heart leapt up, as the saying is, and the hot blood rushed into her face, for she recognised Hallett's handwriting. It was the letter he had posted to her just before he sailed with his regiment for Persia. For some moments she hesitated what to do. Could she trust herself in Flo's presence to read what he had written? But Flo seemed so utterly gone; so entirely without eyes save for the burning lines that her sweetheart had penned, that her presence could be ignored; and so kneeling by the table on which stood the lamp, Hester opened her letter with very varied emotions agitating her. She unfolded the paper, and when she had finished the perusal of the communication, every word of which was like a stab to her, she uttered a moan, and, bowing her head on her arms, burst into tears. Then up jumped Flo, and clasping her friend in a tender and sympathetic embrace, said—

"What is it, Hetty dear? Confide in me. Have you had some bad news?"

It was some moments before Hester could collect herself sufficiently to answer. She held the letter tightly clasped in her hand, and sobbed.

"Hetty darling, what is it? Do tell me," urged her companion.

Then Hester gave her friend the letter, saying, "Read for yourself," and, rising, she paced the room while Florence ran her eyes hurriedly over Jack's missive.

"A lovers' quarrel," remarked Florence at last. "You did not tell me you had a lover, though I understand now why you did not. But, look here, Hetty, that man evidently loves you yet, and you love him, or why do you weep? I suppose the fact is you've had some silly tiff, and he has taken himself off, and you are breaking your heart. Well, hang me, if it was my case, if I wouldn't follow him all over the world. For he vows a vow by his honour and on his soul that no one shall replace you. A man's vows are not always to be believed in, but that fellow swears deeply, and if you love him—well, you know there cannot be love without faith and trust. I have faith in my lad. I know he wouldn't deceive me, and I hope yours won't."

By this time Hester had regained her self-possession, and, having now betrayed herself so far, she felt that it would not do to halt midway, and thus allow her friend to remain under a wrong impression. That would certainly be a mistake, and might be productive of harm. So she told her the whole story, concealing nothing, but laying bare every detail. Flo listened with an intelligent interest, and, though she was by disposition some-what frivolous and at times light-headed, she showed now, when occasion required it, that she could be sensible and womanly, and sitting with her chin resting on her hands, the tips of her fingers on her lips, the while her eyes were bent earnestly on the lamp globe as though she had some hope that she might draw therefrom inspiration to talk to her kinswoman in words of wisdom, for wisdom was wanted in such crisis as this. And when she had thus pondered for a time, she murmured without changing her position—

"It's a serious business, Hetty, old girl."

"Yes," moaned Hester, distressfully, "for he has

gone away under the impression that I have deceived him."

"Had you no idea he was going?" and Flo abandoned the lamp now that she might look at the sorrowful, tear-wet face of her friend.

"Not the slightest."

"Well, he has been hard hit, Hetty," cried Flo, rising up and entwining her arms about Hester's neck.

"It is terrible to think that he believes me false. Oh, what a fool I've been! My mother had no business to exact that promise from me, and I was an idiot to give it. Tell me, Flo, dear, what shall I do?"

This was a little too much for Flo. She felt to the full the responsibility thus suddenly thrust upon her in being called upon to act as adviser in such a complicated and delicate case. She released her hold of her friend, sat down upon the ottoman again, crossed her legs, clasped her hands about her knee, and stared fixedly at the casement, and not for many moments did she venture on a reply, but when she did it only served to show how bewildered she was.

"Upon my word, Hester, I don't know," was the answer.

"You said just now," remarked Hester, "that if it was your case you would follow your lover over the world."

"Oh, yes!" exclaimed Flo responsively, and looking somewhat startled, "but one is apt to say things on the spur of the moment one does not altogether mean in a case of this kind. You see you've got your father and mother to consider. You are their only child, you know, at home. Upon my word it's a ticklish business."

Hester, who had continued to pace the room during the colloquy that had passed, knelt now before her friend and placed her hands on her shoulders, looking her full in the face, while with an impressive earnestness she said—

"Flo, put yourself in my place, or, better still, make my case yours. Suppose a breach not of your making had occurred between you and Reg, and supposing Reg, under a misapprehension that you were false to him, had started for a far distant land; and supposing you loved him with all the love a woman is capable of bearing for a man, what would you do? Would you fold your hands and say, it is willed so? Would you with a submissive meekness simper, 'It cannot be helped; I must make the best of it'?"

Flo was not equal to answering these questions. She showed by the distressful look on her pretty face that it was too great a tax upon her mental powers, or rather, if the strict truth must be told, she was afraid to answer as otherwise she might have answered, for she did not wish Mr. and Mrs. Dellaby to reproach her with having influenced their daughter. Therefore she endeavoured to dissemble somewhat, and with some halting of speech she answered—

"Well, the fact is, Hetty, I—I—upon my word, I don't know how I should act. It is difficult to tell what one would do in an imaginary case."

"But mine is not an imaginary case."

"No, dear, but how can I advise you?"

"Of course, I might have known that you could not advise me," replied Hester, with an irony that passed unnoticed, however, and rising up, she walked up and down again, while Flo, after some reflection, remarked—

"I tell you what, Hester. I think you ought to write and tell your mother what has happened."

"Do you?" said Hester, feeling bitterly sarcastic, and speaking with something like a sneer.

"Yes. You see one's mother after all is one's best friend."

"Sometimes."

"Well, I know *this*, I shouldn't like to think that my mother wasn't my best friend. But look here, there's the supper gong. Brush your hair straight and let us go down.

"Flo, I want you to make me a promise," said Hester, as she caught her cousin's hand.

"What is it?"

"I want you to promise me very solemnly that you won't mention to a living soul that I have had a letter from Jack."

"Well, of course, if you wish me not to do so, I won't. But still I think you ought to tell your aunt and uncle. I am sure they will advise you well."

"No, not a word shall pass my lips on the subject, and unless your protestations of love for me are false, you will promise me to keep silent."

"Oh, of course I'll promise," answered Flo, "though I don't agree with secrecy on an occasion like this."

"Well, Flo," said Hester, "we'll agree to differ in

opinion, but I have your promise, and I'll hold you to it. Come, let us go down."

The two girls joined the rest of the family at supper, and though Hester tried to look cheerful and be amiable, she was conscious that the effort was, partially at least, if not totally, a failure. The time seemed to lag so, for she was all impatient to be alone with her thoughts.

" Are you not well, Hester, this evening ? " asked her aunt, with an anxious manifestation of concern.

" Oh, yes, aunt ; well, that is, I have a headache. I think I will go to bed soon."

"Do, dear," replied the lady. "And look here, Flo, don't you keep your cousin up as you have been in the habit of doing every night. Why last night I heard you chattering till after twelve. You send her out of your room, Hester, and lock the door. She is such a dreadful girl to talk. I believe she would sit up all night if she could get any one to talk to. She likes the sound of her own voice, and would hold conversation with her shadow if it would answer her back."

Of course there was general laughter at this, and Flo protested that her mother was libelling her. In a little while ten struck by the mantelpiece clock, and Mrs. Judson, noticing that her niece was looking very weary, urged her to retire. Hester was only too glad of the excuse to do so, and hurried to her room, having previously wished Flo good-night as a sign that she wished not to be disturbed.

When she was alone Hester drew out Jack's

letter, and re-read and re-read it again. Every word he had written caused her a pang, and pitilessly did she blame herself for not having sent him some consolatory sentence that would have conduced to a better understanding. It was very dreadful for her to think that he should have gone away believing her to be so weak, so frivolous, so changeable, that in spite of pledge and protest, she had with the first adverse wind let him drift from her; and was it not possible that the current that was bearing him away was separating them for ever? It was something to be assured by him— and she had unbroken faith in all that he said— that no one should supplant her in his heart; but, after all, there was but poor satisfaction in that, and it offered no compensation for the bitterness of the cruel separation, for they had, as it were, been wrenched asunder, and he had left believing her to be without any will of her own.

These and similar thoughts that troubled her kept sleep away for several hours, and it was only when she had firmly resolved to send a letter after her lover by the very next post that she sank for the time being into forgetfulness of her sorrow.

With the coming of the morrow a new prospect was suggested to her, for the midday mail placed her in possession of Madge's letter. She had spent all the morning in writing to Hallett, but after perusing her sister's letter she came to another resolution, and she tore up what she had written. A little later she informed her relatives that she intended to return home at the end of the week. They were rather surprised at the suddenness of the decision, though

Flo understood the cause, and that afternoon as she and her cousin took their usual stroll she said—

"Hester, your going home so unexpectedly has something to do with Hallett's letter."

"You said, dear, when you first read it," Hester answered, "that if it was your case you would follow your lover all over the world."

"So I did."

"Well, I have had a letter to-day from Madge, and she expresses a strong wish for me to go out to India and visit her."

"And you are going?" cried Flo, opening wide her blue eyes in astonishment at this bold decision.

"Yes."

"But supposing your people object?"

"Under the circumstances their objection will have no effect."

"Do you mean to say you would go in spite of them?"

"I mean to say their objection would be so unreasonable that I should feel justified in taking my fate in my own hands. But you must remember I am going to my married sister, and she will advise and counsel me. My father is blindly prejudiced, and my mother is entirely influenced by him. Therefore I look to my only sister for advice."

"Well, perhaps you are right," murmured Flo, "and yet it is a bold step."

Hester was not indifferent to the fact that the act she contemplated was certainly bold in its way, but she felt as if Madge's letter had arrived at that important juncture of affairs in order to point out to her the course she should pursue. At any rate,

Madge's invitation was so opportune that she could not afford to regard it with indifference, and she intended to treat it diplomatically. If there was anything in her conduct which, even by a straining of the law of ethics, could be construed into deceit, she was prepared to justify it. Her happiness, the whole well-being of her life, was at stake, and she was quite prepared to risk everything on her own opinion.

In accordance with the arrangements she had made, she returned to Edinburgh at the end of the week, having previously apprised her parents of her coming. Necessarily they were astonished, and Mr. Dellaby even had some misgivings, for, of course, he did not know that Hallett had left Edinburgh; but his mind felt somewhat relieved when Hester laid her reasons for coming back so soon before him.

As she expected would be the case at first, he showed himself rather averse to the contemplated visit to India, but as Hester urged her sister wished her very much to go, and she herself was yearning to go, then he began to change his views; and, moreover, it dawned upon him that it might be the means of most effectually separating Hester and Jack, for, as already stated, he had not the remotest idea of Jack's departure, and Hester resolved to keep that secret to herself, whatever the consequences might be. The result was, her father informed her that he would take a few days to consider the matter, and during the interim he consulted his wife, as was his wont. Contrary to his usual course, he allowed himself to be influenced by her to the extent that while he wavered somewhat at first, he made up his mind finally, for Mrs. Dellaby, though averse to parting with Hester for so long, deemed it a good thing that she should go, and she told her husband so, with the result that he declared she was right.

"It will do the girl good," he said, "and, of course, Madge will look after her well; in fact, we will write to Madge and tell her about this silly affair. At any rate, before the girl comes back I have not the slightest doubt she will have forgotten all about this young upstart, and perhaps under her sister's guidance she will have formed a new and desirable attachment, for I suppose we must make up our minds to hand her over to a husband some day."

His wife endorsed that, and so, being mutually agreed, he subsequently informed Hester that it was decided she should pay a visit to Madge, and she could make her preparations at once. In the meantime, he would write to certain of his friends, who would take means to ensure the lady being well looked after during the voyage out, and a letter was also dispatched to Madge, asking her to meet her sister on her arrival in Calcutta.

Hester was delighted, and, yielding to an irresistible impulse to write to Hallett, she penned and dispatched to him the following brief note :—

"Whither thou goest, there go I also. You have deemed me false. You shall prove me true. I am going to India to my sister, who is at Meerut. Perhaps, as time moves on, we shall meet. Don't think me weak. Don't despise me when I say you have carried my heart off, and since I cannot live without it, I must seek it."

CHAPTER IX.

A HAPPY REUNION.

On a dusty plain, at a distance of less than forty miles in a north-west direction from Delhi, stands the city of Meerut. At the time of the great mutiny it was a strong military centre. From an early period in the history of the " Company Bahadoor," as the East India Company was called by the natives, Meerut had been regarded as of considerable importance from a military point of view. It was considered to be one of the most convenient stations in the North-West Provinces, and was noted for its extensive cantonments, European and native.

In this place the scene of the story is now for the time being laid. It is early in the month of March 1857. The summer heats have not yet set in, and though at midday the sun is powerful, the mornings and the evenings are deliciously cool. A little later in the year the heat of these plains is almost intolerable to Europeans, and ladies and children especially suffer much. March, however, is pleasant enough, and it was particularly so in '57, for the winter had been exceptionally cool—that is, for India, of course.

In one of the best parts of the town, and not far from the English lines, stood a large bungalow surrounded with an extensive and well-kept garden or " compound," in which the spring flowers made a magnificent show.   As was usual in European houses of this class, the garden was walled in by a mud wall, which was almost hidden from view by jungly undergrowth, while cocoa palms, interspersed by mango trees, overshadowed it.   This place was the Indian home of Lieutenant-Colonel Pritchard and his family.   He had been stationed in Meerut for a considerable time, and as it seemed then he was destined to remain for some time longer; for though signs had appeared, like handwriting on the wall, they had been ignored.   It was known that a spirit of discontent was abroad; but the authorities had chosen to ignore it, and the Europeans never dreamed of the terrible storm that was brewing; and amongst those who most firmly believed the natives were staunch as a body, was Lieutenant-Colonel Pritchard. Whenever he had heard fears expressed of possible danger, he had laughed scornfully, saying that he was prepared to stake his all on the fidelity of the Sepoys, who, he averred, clearly recognized how closely their interests were bound up with those of the white rulers, who, whatever their faults had been in the past, were then beyond reproach.   It is singular that his opinion should have been so extensively indulged in by those who ought to have been able to see the way the clouds were drifting.

It is true there had been great and formidable military mutinies in the past, and more than once the power of the " John Company " had been threatened. Only as recently as 1856 there had been a rising at Vellore, in the Madras Presidency, where two Sepoy battalions attacked the European soldiers and slaughtered one hundred and thirteen of them. These murders had been fearfully avenged, for eight hundred of the Sepoys fell before the terrific onslaught of the 19th Dragoons under Colonel Gillespie, who was ordered to put down the "riot" as it was called. The dissatisfaction which led to this outbreak was looked upon, strangely enough, as quite local, and men who had the temerity to hint at a widespread discontent seething throughout the native army were laughed at. Again, during 1856, small cakes of bread called chupatties were carried from village to village, and delivered to the head man of each place. It was well known that this was some strange and secret kind of freemasonry, but not the slightest significance was attached to it by those who ought to have known better and have been better informed. And so the British continued to live in a false sense of security. Beneath their feet was a volcano, but they knew it not, though the crust was getting daily thinner and thinner.

Colonel Pritchard was seated on the verandah of his bungalow in company with his wife, his sister-in-law Hester—who had only arrived from Calcutta a few days before—and two or three other officers and their wives. One of these officers was a Captain Sandon, who had seen much service, and done excellent work in the Crimean campaign. He was a young man of stalwart proportions, and a dark, handsome face. Every inch a soldier, and being ambitious to distinguish himself, he had purchased a commission in a crack cavalry regiment, and had been in India about six months.

Hester appeared to be exceedingly well. The voyage

G

had evidently agreed with her, and she had not been long enough in the Indian climate to feel its effects. Madge was a fine-looking woman, and her husband was an equally fine-looking man. They seemed, indeed, to be a very well-matched couple. The little party were partaking of afternoon tea, and were very merry and happy. As may be supposed, Hester was an object of peculiar interest, for she was fresh from the dear old country where there were so many ties, so many loved ones ; and, of course, she had numberless questions to answer and much to tell. "Handsome Sandon," as he had come to be called, was particularly attentive to her ; and this, and the burning glances with which he regarded her now and again, did not escape the notice of Mrs. Pritchard, who, although she had been to Calcutta to meet her sister, had had so many other things to talk about, that she had found no time to touch upon any affairs of the heart. Nor had Hester so far breathed a syllable about her connection with Hallett. Nevertheless, he was ever present in her thoughts, and she burned with an eager desire to know where he was, if he had received her note, and if he thought of her as she thought of him.

Sandon had only that very day been introduced to Hester. Mrs. Pritchard had organised a little excursion to a ruined temple on the banks of the Goomtee, and he was included in the invitations. But he had certainly made the best use of his time, and had shown a decided preference for the young lady's company.

"What do you think of this country, Miss Dellaby,

so far as you have seen it?" he asked, as he sat next to her at the little tea-table on the verandah, and lost no opportunity of paying her attention.

"Oh, I am charmed with it so far. Everything is so new to me, so strange, so fascinating. My sister, who is a capital correspondent and an excellent describer, had given me a good idea what to expect, but still no description can come up to actual experience, and no description could give one an adequate idea of the movement, the colour, the brilliancy, the novel sights and sounds and scenes which are peculiar to India."

"True," answered Sandon a little thoughtfully. "And yet after all India is not the place one would care to end one's days in from choice. Are you going to remain long?"

"I don't know. Possibly a year."

"A year!" echoed Sandon. Then he sighed, and added—"It strikes me a year will see wonderful changes in India."

"There," cried Mrs. Pritchard, with a merry laugh, "I declare, Captain, you are at it again. Do you know, Hetty dear, Captain Sandon is a regular Job's comforter, and is always predicting dreadful things for us."

"Well, you see," put in Colonel Pritchard, "he hates, or believes he hates, the natives. When he has known them as long as I have, he will perhaps change his opinion."

"No, I don't think so," replied Sandon. "I am sufficiently acquainted with their history to mistrust them, and the many little outbreaks recently have served to show—at any rate I think so—that there is a smouldering fire which, if it once gets a fair start, will set the whole country in a blaze."

"My dear boy, you are prejudiced and a pessimist," laughed Colonel Pritchard.

"Perhaps I am prejudiced," answered Sandon slowly, as he stroked his moustache, "for at the affair at Vellore last year, my only brother, Lieutenant Sandon, a splendid lad, and the hope and pride of his widowed mother, was killed. I confess I should like to have the opportunity of avenging his murder."

"Pray don't let us talk about such things," cried Mrs. Pritchard, with a little shudder. "Better to be cheerful than gloomy. If trouble is coming, I dare say we shall be prepared to cope with it. We have a fine array of brave men——"

"And beautiful women to inspire them with valour," remarked Sandon, with a furtive glance at Hester.

"Sheodeen," called Mrs. Pritchard, addressing one of the native servants in attendance, "tell the ayah to bring the children here."

The man salaamed and departed, and Hester, in order to keep up the conversation, asked Captain Sandon if he had yet made the acquaintance of her sister's children.

"Yes, Miss Dellaby, I have," he answered.

"And don't you think them very pretty?"

"Yes; I do indeed. I think they are two of the prettiest and best-behaved children I have ever seen."

Mrs. Pritchard's face coloured with conscious pride, as she thus heard her darlings spoken of. And in a few moments the merry ringing laughter of the children was heard as they came rushing on to the verandah, followed by their native nurse, who made a salaam to the company, and then stood in the respectful attitude common to her class. Both the children ran to Hester, and, climbing on to her knee, struggled with each other for the privilege of having their arms round her neck and kissing her.

"Now, dearies, don't be rude or rough," said their mother, as a warning that they were to be less impetuous, and to restrain their ardour.

"Mamma," exclaimed Fred, speaking apparently for himself and his sister, "we are not rough, and we are not rude. We can do as we like with our auntie. Can't we, auntie?"

"Yes, sweeties, of course you can," and she hugged them both.

"Oh, yes," remarked Mrs. Pritchard pleasantly, "your aunt is sure to spoil you. I suppose my nose will be put quite out of joint now that your aunt is here."

"Oh, ma, what a funny thing to say," screamed little Amy, with a childish laugh. "I am sure me and Freddy are not going to touch your nose, are we, auntie?"

Of course there was general laughter at this, in which the children joined, seeming to regard it as a huge joke that their mother should talk of having her nose put out of joint, and attached a literal meaning to what was a mere idiom. They were without doubt sweet, pretty children; both of them being of the purest Saxon type; fair, transparent skin, regular features, pronounced blue eyes, light golden hair, which, in the boy's case, clustered in long ringlets about his neck and shoulders. They were great favourites, and much petted, as it was but natural they should be; and yet they had not been spoilt, for their father was strongly averse to making them into "milksops" as he termed it.

As might be supposed, Hester was very proud of her little nephew and niece, and nothing seemed to delight them more than to be with her, while the fond and happy mother, now that she had got her sister, felt as if her cup of joy was nearly full. All that was wanted to complete it was the presence of her parents.

Presently the little company rose to depart, for the short Indian twilight had ended, and the night had come. Overhead was a canopy of brilliant stars, and on the languorous air rose the voices of the many insects that the night brings forth in India, while muffled by distance came the sounds of the mournful tom-toms, as the natives sang their wailing songs after their evening meal. Just as the ladies and gentlemen were about to go, a mounted orderly, fully accoutred, rode into the compound, and drew rein at the door of the bungalow. He had evidently ridden hard, for his horse was panting, and he himself was perspiring and covered with dust. Knowing that the man's business was with him, Colonel Pritchard went to him, and received some dispatches from his hand, and the trooper, having performed his duty, saluted, and turning his horse rode off again, while the Colonel retired to his room to read the official documents he had received.

In a little while Mrs. Pritchard and her sister

were alone on the verandah. The ladies and gentlemen had departed, and the children had gone off
with their ayah to be prepared for bed. Before he
went away Captain Sandon had shaken Hester's
hand very cordially, and expressed a hope that he
might soon have the pleasure of seeing her again.

"It's quite a treat, dear, to have you all to myself
once more," exclaimed Mrs. Pritchard, as she leaned
backed in her large lounge chair, with Hester
beside her in a similar chair. "I declare since
you came my head seems to have been in a whirl,
what with visitors and visiting, and the chicks, who
have taken up so much of your time; and one thing
and another, really I have had very little chance of
asking you anything about yourself. Now, tell me,
what do you think of Captain Sandon?"

"He seems very nice," answered Hester, and
speaking in a manner suggestive of her thoughts
being far off.

"Yes; and if I'm any judge, Hetty, he's smitten
with you already. He's a good fellow, a brave
soldier, and a member of a distinguished family. It
is said he will succeed to a very large fortune some
day."

Hetty laid her hand on her sister's. wrist. and said
in a tone of anxiety—

"Madge darling, don't let me sail under false
colours; and don't think me wicked or deceitful
when I tell you that not the least inducement for
me to come out here was the fact that the man who
has my heart is in this part of the globe."

Madge's face was a study in its expression of
surprise, as, half starting up, she turned towards

her sister, upon whom the full rays of the shaded lamp that stood on the little table fell, and ex- claimed—

"Hetty dear, why did you not tell me this before?"

"Because I have had no opportunity."

"And where is this man?"

"Alas! I know not. He is somewhere in Persia."

"That is vague. Persia is a large place. But what is he?"

"A soldier."

"Oh, that is another thing. He can be easily found then. I suppose he is an officer?"

"Yes."

"But how is it you don't know where he is stationed? Have you quarrelled?"

"Yes and no. But hush! I will tell you all by and by."

At this point Colonel Pritchard had come upon the verandah. He was dressed in his uniform, was booted and spurred, and the champing of a bit and the neighing of a steed told that his horse waited for him. Both the ladies started up, and his wife ex- claimed—

"Why, George, whatever is the meaning of this? I did not know that you had any regimental duty to-night."

"Nor did I, dear. But I have received some very important orders from the General in command, and I am to repair at once to his house, and hold myself in readiness for an immediate journey."

"What does this mean, darling?" asked his wife

with a little shudder, while her face paled, and, throwing her arms about him, she nestled to him.

"Why, nothing, I should say," laughed the Colonel in his habitual cheery way. "That is, nothing that you need alarm yourself about. These little surprises are incidental to a soldier's life, you know, and, having recently been appointed one of the General's staff officers, I am liable to this sort of thing."

"You will, of course, return here before you go away," said his wife, the anxious expression of her face in no way lessened.

"Well, yes, certainly; I shall if I can."

He kissed her, shook the hand of his sister-in-law, and, exclaiming that he had already kissed the children, he sprang into his saddle and galloped off.

CHAPTER X.

A SECRET MISSION.

For a little time after the departure of her husband
Mrs Pritchard seemed dull. She could not quite
dismiss from her mind an idea that there was something ominous in his being so suddenly summoned to
the commanding officer's presence. Dispatches of
great importance must have been received by the
commander, or he would not have called his staff
together, especially at such an hour. When the
children came on to the verandah to say good-night
to their mother and aunt, which they did soon after
their father's departure, she clasped them with an
expression of fervour to her bosom, and kissing them
again and again she murmured—

"God bless you, darlings; God bless you. How I
wish we were all at home again!"

"What is it, Madge?" asked her sister in a tone
of alarm. "What has upset you?"

"Oh, nothing, dear. A momentary weakness,
that is all. I am very stupid. I think I am getting
nervous in my old age. But it is only when I think
of the dear children," and she wiped the gathering
tears from her eyes. Then kissing the children, and
after their aunt had embraced them, she sent them
away with their ayah; and as it wanted yet half-an-

hour to the dinner, she settled herself down in the chair once more, and said to her sister—

"Let's see, dear, you were going to tell me about some lover of yours. A wild romance I suppose it is, especially as you say he was the sole inducement for you to come out here."

"Ah, Madge, that is not fair. I did not say that. I said he was not the least inducement."

"Well, Hetty, that is going very near the whole thing. But there, let me hear the story. I will judge you afterwards."

Hester did not like the tone in which her sister spoke. She knew that Madge had a tremendous opinion of her father's wisdom, and believed that he could not err. It was a knowledge of this fact which had made Hester somewhat reluctant to tell her story, for she could not disguise from herself that there was a probability of Madge siding with her father. But there seemed no getting out of it now, nor could she conscientiously suppress anything, so she told the tale in its entirety, omitting nothing.

Madge listened with a grave face, and said when the story was finished—

"I think, dear, you have been very foolish, and I don't see how I can give you my sympathy. You may depend upon it, our father's objection was based upon exceedingly good grounds. He would view the matter without bias, without prejudice."

"On the contrary Madge. He was as strongly prejudiced as he could be," cried Hester in anxiety, as she saw that her worst fears were realized, and her own sister was now arrayed against her in this love affair.

"Very well then, if that was so I am sure he was justified. He is not the man to do anything rashly, and you must not forget that he has your interests at heart. He is anxious about your future, and desirous of securing you welfare and happiness."

"But, Madge, Jack vowed to me on his sacred honour that there was nothing against him."

"Ah, dear, a man's vows are not always to be trusted," replied Madge, with a little cynical laugh, though cynicism was as foreign to her nature as it could well be. But she had something of her father's "hard-headedness," and his belief in the soundness of his own judgment; and having made up her mind on a given question, she was rather apt to think that she could not possibly be wrong.

"Did you not believe in George's vows?" asked Hester pointedly.

"Oh, yes, but that was different altogether. George is a treasure, and father approved of him.

"So is Jack a treasure, though father doesn't approve of him. But then, as I say, that is mere prejudice, and I believe Hallett to be the very soul of honour."

"Every woman, I suppose, thinks her lover the soul of honour," urged Madge, "but women are sometimes, ofttimes, in fact, deceived and betrayed, and the vaunted honour is found to be a delusion and a snare. But do not think me unkind, dear. I do not want to stand in the way of your happiness, Heaven forbid, and yet how can I encourage you to go against your father's wishes? I am sure, if he knew that you had come out to India on Hallett's account he would never forgive you."

Hester was silent and distressed, but she tried hard to conceal her distress. She knew now that she would have to fight her battle alone, though it seemed particularly hard that she should have all her house against her. The dinner-bell rang at this momemt, and Madge, rising, linked her arm in her sister's and kissed her, saying—

"Don't distress yourself, dearie. I will make inquiries about young Hallett But I do hope you will try to forget him. You know how unforgiving father is, and I am sure if you went against his wishes he would disown you."

Hester still remained silent. She felt it was no use giving vent to her feelings when she had only an unsympathetic ear to pour her woes into. But her hopes had certainly been dashed a little, though she mentally resolved that she would be true to Jack, unless he proved himself to be a thorough-paced vagabond, which she could not deem in the least degree possible, let alone probable.

The dinner was half finished when Colonel Pritchard returned hastily. His face was unusually grave, and this did not escape the notice of his wife, who exclaimed—

"What is it, dear? Is there anything seriously the matter?"

"No, Madge."

"You say no in a qualified way. Your face says yes."

"There is really nothing that you need alarm yourself about, Madge," he answered. "It appears that the Government has received some anonymous information that in certain districts there have been secret meetings of the natives, and resolutions threatening destruction to the Feringhees have been passed. A dispatch, therefore, has been sent to the commanding officers of all the stations requesting them to verify if possible or prove the information false. I may tell you, however, that General Hewett does not attach much importance to the report. At any rate, even supposing it's true, what then? We are strong enough to cope with any mutinous spirit that may display itself."

Madge shuddered as she answered—

"We think so. But should our native soldiers turn against us the consequences may be frightful."

"Tut, little woman," said her husband as he patted her cheek and kissed her. "Don't get such ideas into your head. Our native troops are staunch. I would trust them anywhere."

"God grant it may be so," sighed Madge fervently. "But sit down, dear, and have your dinner. I am sure you must be hungry."

"I am hungry," answered her husband as he took his place at the table and began his soup. "But I have very little time."

"What do you mean?" asked Madge quickly.

"I have to leave Meerut to-night."

"To leave Meerut!" exclaimed Madge, catching her breath.

"Yes. Now don't alarm yourself. There is no significance in it."

"But where are you going to?"

"To Bombay."

" To Bombay ! " echoed his wife, as the alarm she felt gleamed from her eyes and flushed her face. "That is a long journey."

" Yes, but I do not expect to be absent more than three weeks."

" But why are you going, dear ? "

" I am going on a special mission which I am not allowed to reveal even to my own wife. It is Government business ; but this much I may tell you —it has reference to certain Government stores."

Madge asked no further questions. She was a soldier's wife, and she knew that duty was the first consideration with a soldier; and when he was ordered to go anywhere or do anything, he must go or do it in spite of loved ones or home ties.

The Colonel made a very hasty meal the while his soldier servant was busy packing his clothes in his bedroom; and as he rose from the table he said—

" Well, Hester, I hope Madge will make you as comfortable as she possibly can. In fact, I am sure she will. You will find this is not half a bad place. There is good society, and you will have a jolly time. I saw Captain Sandon at the General's, and I asked him to look after you in my absence. He is a fine fellow is Sandon. I like him. He is a thorough gentleman, and has a most honourable record as a soldier. He will distinguish himself if he gets a chance ; I'm sure of that. I think, Hetty, old girl, you might set your cap at him. He is worth playing for."

Pritchard laughed, and Hester got up a little smile, though it was forced. Then her brother-in-law went in to kiss the children, and his wife followed him.

Both the little tots were asleep, looking sweet and bonnie beneath the mosquito curtains. Their father stooped and kissed them without disturbing them, and he murmured a scarcely audible—

" God bless you, sweet ones."

Madge clasped her husband's arm as he rose from his stooping position, and looking into his face with an expression of true wifely affection, she said—

" Hester has made a revelation to me to-night, George."

" Indeed."

" Yes."

" A revelation of what ? "

" That she is already deeply in love with a young fellow."

" Where and who is he ? "

" He is in Persia, or on his way there, and it is partly on that account that she has come out to us. His name is John Hallett. He is a lieutenant in the 20th."

" Why, the 20th are on active service in Persia."

" Yes. It appears that father strongly objected to Hetty keeping company with Hallett, and there was a row. She promised that she wouldn't see him again for a time, and went down to stay with the Judsons at Flodden. While she was there young Hallett started for foreign service, and it appears wrote to her before leaving, telling her he was going away. She jumped at my invitation to come out here, as she wanted to get away from home, and she assures me now that she will not give Hallett up."

" But what is your father's objection to him ? " asked her husband.

" Well, I don't exactly know, but I can't imagine dad taking a prejudice unless he had very good cause to do so, and I should be disposed to argue from that that Hallett is far from a desirable catch for my sister."

" Well, I will make some inquiries about young Hallett. Perhaps Hetty has right on her side when she says she won't give him up. Your father objected to me at first. He said some nasty things, you may remember, about soldiers and sailors not being fit to have wives. However, I haven't time to discuss the matter. Good-bye, old girl. Take care of yourself and the chicks. I will telegraph to you often."

When he reached the door the orderly was waiting, and holding the two horses. Hester was also standing there, and bade her brother-in-law an affectionate good-bye. And when he had once more kissed her and his wife, he sprang on to his horse, and, followed by his orderly, rode off into the darkness.

CHAPTER XI.

MISUNDERSTOOD.

THAT very night when Hester Dellaby retired to her own room she resolved she would make no further reference to Hallett unless her sister did so; for she was very painfully conscious that Madge by no means sympathized with her. But if she had wanted further evidence of this she had it during breakfast the following morning, when after a little preliminary conversation Mrs. Pritchard said, as she kissed her children and sent them off to their governess in company with their ayah—

"Hester dear, I have been thinking seriously of what you told me last night; and under the circumstances I really cannot encourage you in your clandestine love-making. In fact I do not think it would be right to father, who I am sure would never have taken such a violent dislike for Hallett unless he had been perfectly satisfied in his own mind that he was not worthy of you. But another thing, dear, I am sure you haven't known Hallett long enough to become so bound up in him that you cannot break the connection—a connection that you now see is decidedly objectionable to your family. It is very likely this young fellow is an adventurer. Lots of men who hold commissions in the army are only gentlemen by courtesy, and their careers won't bear looking into. Besides, if Hallett really loved you as he professed to do, do you suppose he would have gone off in the way he did, without so much as a word of explanation? The fact is he is a wild harum-scarum youngster, I suppose, with plenty of good fighting material in him, very likely, but with no stability, and not in the least likely to make a girl a good husband. You know, dear, a girl has to be so very careful, for she is so apt to be deceived. I do hope you will not do anything rash."

Hester remained dumb. These words coming from the lips of her sister for whom she bore such strong affection, and in whom she hoped to find an ally, seared her, and she would have wept tears of bitter anguish, had she not kept her feelings in subjection by the strong will which was hers. She was proud too, and her sense of dignity, which was very pronounced, enabled her to seem calm outwardly, while inwardly she was chafing with vexation and annoyance. One remark, however, that her sister made seemed to her to call for instant refutation. The remark was—

"Besides, if Hallett had really loved you as he professed to do, do you suppose he would have gone off in the way he did without so much as a word of explanation?"

To this Hester answered, when she had so far collected herself as to be able to speak with the most perfect self-possession—

"Madge, you are doing Jack" (she liked to speak of him affectionately as "Jack,") "an unconscious wrong. He did not go off without a word of explanation. If you will excuse me for a few minutes

I will let you see a letter he sent me." She rose from the table and went to her bedroom, returning in a very short time with Jack's letter; the letter he had penned to her when he was on the eve of leaving England. She handed it to Madge, saying—

"Read that for yourself, and you will confess that it is unfair to say he went off without any explanation."

Mrs. Pritchard perused the letter, and having done so she folded it up, and returned it to her sister with the curt remark—

"All I have to say, Hetty, is this—I cannot encourage you to keep up the connection with Hallett so long as father objects to him. For in my own mind I am sure that objection must be fully warranted. But I tell you what I'll do; I'll write to father, if you like, and ask him to let me know what his views really are."

A flush spread itself over Hester's face. It was a flush of suppressed anger, as she answered with a decisiveness which could not be mistaken—

"If you do that, Madge, I will leave you."

"Where would you go to?" asked her sister, somewhat alarmed.

"I don't know, and I don't care. Not back home that you may depend upon. But I will not be treated as a child. I am not a child, and I am not a fool; and rather than submit to what seems to me like parental tyranny, I will take my fate into my own hands."

Madge was very much upset. This spirit of insubordination, for so she regarded it, was to her terrible. She herself had been the most dutiful the most yielding of daughters; and her father had always appeared to her as the very incarnation of wisdom. To have gainsaid anything that he had said, to have opposed his dictum, would have seemed to her a sin calling for the very sternest and severest of punishment. Having less control over herself than her sister, her emotion betrayed itself in tears, and, rising from her seat, she twined her arms about Hester's neck, and, kissing her with the most devoted affection, said tenderly—

"Ah, Hetty dear, don't talk like that. We shall not always have our father with us, and it will be terrible if you feel you have anything to reproach yourself with when he is lying in his grave, and you can no longer seek his forgiveness. You *must*, for my sake, for father's sake, for all our sakes, forget Hallett; for how could you possibly reconcile your conscience to marrying him if your father did not approve of him? Poor father! He has been so good to us. He is so anxious about our welfare that it would be downright cruelty to cause him a moment's sorrow."

Mrs. Pritchard's deep affection for her parents caused her to overlook the possibility of error of judgment on her father's part. But Hester was clear-headed enough to see that there was nothing to be gained by argument, and in such a case silence on the subject was the wisest policy. Suspense was terribly hard to bear, but what could she do save wait for what time might bring forth? Callousness being no part of her nature, she was much moved by her sister's grief, and thus she answered her—

"There, Madge, don't disturb yourself, dear, or

you will make me bitterly regret that I came. We'll agree to sink Hallett for the time being. If it's my fate to have him I shall get him. If not—well, what does it matter? One's heart can only break once."

"You silly goosey, to talk about your heart breaking," said Madge, smiling through her tears. "You really don't know yet what love is. But come, don't let us continue this painful subject. The syce is waiting with the buggy. We must have our drive before the sun gets too hot."

Hester did not pursue the subject, but, returning her sister's warm embrace, retired to her room to prepare for the morning drive. The days slipped by very rapidly, and had it not been for the anxiety she felt about Hallett, Hester would have been perfectly happy. For her sister did everything she possibly could do to add to her comfort, while the children seemed never so delighted as when they could be with her. There was no lack of society, no lack of entertainment. Something was always going on: amateur theatricals, concerts, excursions, picnics. Time could not hang heavily in a military station of that kind. It is proverbial of soldiers and sailors that they know how to be merry and to enjoy life even under the most adverse circumstances. But in Meerut in those days there was plenty of bustle and stir, and if the daily round of life was somewhat monotonous it certainly did not lack interest; while flirtation, scandal, and gossip gave a piquancy to existence.

It soon became very obvious to Hester, no less than to her sister, that "Handsome Sandon" was particularly desirous of making himself more than agreeable to her. He was certainly a fascinating man; at least, he was so to ladies. But even amongst men he was regarded with great favour, for he had all the qualities of a fine soldier, no less than the distinguishing traits of a true gentleman and a punctilious man of honour. At mess, in camp, on parade, in private company, he was always the *preux chevalier*. Deferential but dignified to his superiors, courteous and kindly to his inferiors, tender and gentle to women and children; brimming over with animal spirits, and foremost in everything that could add to the amusement, the comfort, or the well-being of the garrison, there was no wonder he was a universal favourite.

Hester was not indifferent to the attention he paid her, nor could she help liking him. And she would hardly have been human—or, rather, she would have been a womanly phenomenon—if she had failed to experience a sense of satisfaction, even of pride, in having so distinguished, so handsome a man dancing attendance upon her, so to speak. Of course envy and jealousy were not absent in such a mixed community, and unkind things were said by those who would have liked to secure Sandon's attentions all to themselves. But if Hester heard of these things she did not allow them to disturb her, and while she enjoyed Captain Sandon's company and admired him for his many good qualities, she had no heart to give, for she had given it to Jack Hallett, and to Jack she was resolved to be true.

Of course Sandon knew nothing of the little episode in her life. She and her sister had mutually agreed that it should be a dead letter, and, in fact, Madge had come to think, judging from the external signs of happiness and contentment that her sister showed, that she was forgetting Hallett, and that in a little time she would laugh at what she would term "the folly of her calf love."

Whatever Hester's feelings of respect and regard for Captain Sandon were, they were fully reciprocated by him. He was evidently not given to mere tongue flattery, but he made it unmistakably plain that it was not merely a passing admiration that drew him towards her. But if his conduct had been open to doubt, the doubt was soon set at rest, for meeting Mrs. Pritchard one morning on the drive he spoke to her, for she happened to be driving alone, her sister having accompanied some young people on a picnic.

"May I come over to your bungalow this afternoon, Mrs. Pritchard?" he asked. "I want a little conversation with you."

"Oh, certainly, Captain," she answered with a laugh. "And pray what is the subject of the conversation to be?"

"You shall know this afternoon," he replied with a smile, as, bowing graciously, he rode on.

For some minutes after he had left she wondered in her mind what it was he wished to talk about. Then it suddenly dawned upon her, and she thought —"How dull I am to be sure! It's Hetty, of course. He is over head and ears in love with the girl, and she must have him. He is no less desirable as a brother-in-law than as a husband. My father, I am sure, could take no exception to him."

It will be gathered from this that Captain Sandon had certainly secured an ally in Mrs. Pritchard. He had timed his visit well, but he knew that Hester had gone off for the day, and it was an opportunity he could not let slip. He arrived at the Pritchard bungalow soon after tiffin, and, after a little beating about the bush, said—

"I wonder, Mrs. Pritchard, if you have any idea of what it is I wish to say to you?"

"I fancy I have," she answered with a smile. "Unless I am very much mistaken you want to talk about Hester."

"How do you know?" he exclaimed quickly.

"Why, surely, Captain Sandon, you don't suppose that I haven't made good use of my woman's eyes. I have noticed the attention you have paid to her; the sighs you have sighed, and the eager glances with which you have followed her movements."

"I am glad you have, I am glad you have," he said bluntly. "I think your sister is charming. She has quite captivated me."

"And have you captivated her in return?" asked Madge eagerly.

"No; I'm afraid not. It is that very point that has induced me to come to you. If you think I am worthy of her; if you think she would be happy with me——"

"I think you are quite worthy of her," put in Mrs. Pritchard, and encouraged him as he commenced to stammer a little, for, gallant soldier as he was, he lost his nerve somewhat when it came to the question of laying siege to a woman's heart. What honourable and conscientious man does not?

"I feel honoured and flattered," he replied, "and I infer from what you say I need fear no opposition from you?"

"No, Captain Sandon, I will help you if I can."

"Really this is an almost unhoped-for stroke of good luck," he answered, with an eagerness of expression that told how glad he was. "May I—may I venture to inquire if she has said anything to you that I might construe into—well—that is—has she ever uttered a word to you that would lead you to suppose I am regarded by her with any favour?"

"She has not, Captain; not in the sense that you mean." The Captain's face fell a little, and Mrs. Pritchard noticed it. "I know this, however," she added; "she thinks you are a very agreeable man."

"Is that all?" he asked, with a crestfallen countenance.

"Is that all! I really think, Captain, that is a good deal. When a young lady thinks a gentleman is agreeable it is almost his own fault if he doesn't ultimately prevail upon her to believe that he is indispensable to her happiness. Hetty is a somewhat reticent girl. She has been strictly brought up; and though she may not be lightly won, I am sure when she is won she will prove a treasure and the most devoted of wives."

The Captain looked delighted; but there was a touch of anxiousness in his tone as he asked—

"Then do you think I may hope to win her?"

"You may certainly try. My sister's heart I suppose is in her own keeping."

"But may I count upon your assistance?"

"If it is in my power to render any assistance, you may certainly count upon me. I have no hesitation in expressing my deliberate opinion that her happiness would be safe with you. My husband, I know, has a very high opinion of you."

"Mrs. Pritchard," answered the Captain, with a touch of solemnity, "if it should be my good fortune to win Hester, she will never have cause, if I can help it, to regret ever having become my wife."

With a few more well-chosen sentences, Mrs. Pritchard did her best to still further encourage him to win Hester. She was half tempted to tell him there and then the little story of her sister's connection with Jack Hallett, but somehow she could not quite bring herself to do so, for she had managed to persuade herself that that connection was rather a slur on her sister's dignity, and detracted from her self-respect, so she held her peace. A little later Captain Sandon took his departure, feeling elated with what he considered his success so far.

Mrs. Pritchard, on her part, regarded Captain Sandon in the most favourable light. She thought that in every possible way he was a desirable husband for Hester, and one of whom her father would highly approve. Every one who knew him predicted a future for him, and said that he would, if he got a chance, gain some of the highest prizes of his profession. Holding these views, she determined to speak to Hetty at the very earliest opportunity, for strangely enough she thought that, as Hester never now referred to young Hallett, she was ceasing to think of him. Before the opportunity she wanted occurred, the receipt of a letter from her husband, who was on his way home from Bombay, strengthened her hands very much—at least, that was her idea. That night she went to her sister's room, and the two sat together, and Madge said—

"I got a letter from George to-day, and there is something in it that will interest you—well, that is, it will painfully interest you."

"What is it?" asked Hester, with a catching of the breath, as instinctively she guessed that the "something" had reference to Jack; that it might even be news of his death, for he was on active service in Persia, and a soldier on active service necessarily carried his life in his hand.

"Well, dear, I'll read what George says in his letter. This is it.

"'I met a Major Tonkin in Bombay a few days before I left. The poor fellow has been invalided from the seat of war in Persia, and was waiting for a ship in which to return home. I asked him if he had come across young Hallett. He told me he had; and he also told me he had heard that on the passage out from England Hallett had been in disgrace. It appears from what I gathered from Tonkin that Hallett, having drunk not wisely but too well, quarrelled with a brother-officer, and unmercifully pummelled him. Of course an inquiry was held, and on the arrival of the ship at her destination the young fellow was reported to the Commander-in-Chief, and there was quite a scandal about the affair.'"

During the reading of this bit of information Hester closed her eyes, and her lips quivered with

the emotion she could not altogether stifle.
Mrs. Pritchard waited for her sister to speak,
but as she uttered no word the lady added—

"What a truly disgraceful thing, to be sure. It
is shocking to think that a young man on the threshold of his career should make a blackguard of
himself like that. I am sure, Hetty, you must
congratulate yourself on being rid of such a fellow,
and you will give father credit for having acted
wisely."

Hester made no comment or remark of any kind
in answer to what her sister had read, but said—

"Madge, I am so tired. I want to go to bed. I
wish you would leave me."

Madge was surprised, and even disappointed, but
she complied with the request, and kissing her sister,
she bade her good-night, and retired. Then the
poor girl turned the key in the door, and her forti-
tude giving way, she threw herself on the bed, and
wept piteously. It seemed to her as if a great
darkness had come into her life; as if the idol she
had worshipped had crumbled into the dust which
henceforth and for ever she must water with her
tears.

CHAPTER XII.

MAKING AN ALLY.

WHETHER this weeping was the result of sorrow, shame, a sense of degradation, disappointment, or what, was not then to be made manifest; for days passed, and she said nothing. It may be imagined that Mrs. Pritchard was more than surprised; she was annoyed and vexed. It was not pleasant to have to confess to herself that her sister was not disposed to make a confidante of her, and it was equally clear that she did not intend to ask her advice or take counsel with her in any way. That wounded the good lady's *amour propre*. As an elder and married sister, she considered it a duty on the part of her young unmarried sister to look up to her, to be guided by her; in short, to obey her. Mrs. Pritchard liked to be obeyed. In that respect, and in many other respects, she took after her father. She was somewhat self-opinionated, she was inclined to be dictatorial, and she had a very firm belief in the wisdom of her own judgment. Hester, however, had *her* views, and it was very apparent that in this particular juncture of affairs her views did not coincide with those of her sister. Nor was it easy then to find out what those views were, as she kept them to herself, and the only indication she gave that she was at all affected by the news of Jack's disgrace was in a certain thoughtful expression and a preoccupied air. Her behaviour to her friends and relatives in no way altered. She loved to be with the children, to romp with them, to listen to their childish prattle, to read to them, to display an interest in their toys.

Mrs. Pritchard, in spite of her annoyance and vexation, had the good sense to make no further reference to Hallett, and what she thought was, that Hester felt humiliated and ashamed at having been associated with the young fellow, and that silence under the circumstances was the wisest—in fact, the only proper course.

For some little time after his interview with Mrs. Pritchard, Captain Sandon had no opportunity of taking any means to strengthen his position with regard to Hester, for his regimental duties kept him actively employed; moreover, he was sent to Delhi in command of an ammunition escort.

In the meantime Colonel Pritchard returned from his mission to Bombay, to the intense delight and joy of his wife, though that joy was doomed to be but short-lived. Of course they had many things to talk about, and Madge lost no time in telling him that she had read to her sister that portion of his letter which referred to Hallett.

"How did she take it?" asked the Colonel.

"She received the news in silence."

"But did she make no remark?"

"None whatever."

"Surely she said something."

"Not a syllable."

"Well, upon my word, she is a queer girl."

"The fact is," pursued his wife, "I suppose she

felt so utterly ashamed that she thought it was wiser to keep silent. For what could she say ? "

" Ah, very likely ; and her idol having crumbled, she will soon forget him. It's astonishing how soon girls do become infatuated. But the infatuation just as soon wears off when they find they have been deceived."

" Of course it does," answered his wife, with an air of wisdom, " and I am sure Hetty is not a girl to go and throw herself at the head of a scamp."

" Well, it is to be hoped she is not," the Colonel remarked, also looking very wise.

"What I should like to see her do," continued his wife, " is to encourage Sandon, for there is no doubt he is quite gone on her."

" Well, she couldn't make a better choice. Sandon is an excellent fellow, and I shouldn't be at all surprised if he is able to write K.C.B. after his name some day. He's got the stuff in him, and if he gets the chance he will be heard of. He is the fellow to win the V.C. too. I know he is thought a good deal of at head-quarters, in spite of his strong prejudices."

This was all very pleasant to Mrs. Pritchard, in her self-assumed *rôle* of match-maker for her sister, and she had persuaded herself that Hester's ultimate acceptance of Sandon was only a question of time. But time often disarranges men's plans and proposals. And the time was then at hand when the call to arms, the din of strife, and the shock of battle were to give such an awful sternness to life in India, that love-making, courtships, and matrimony would form no part of it. But no living soul in Meerut at that moment had any idea that the long-threatening storm was on the very point of bursting, not even the natives themselves. It is true the mutterings had been growing louder of late, but those in command quite believed that if anything did happen it would be a mere flash in the pan, and that they were quite prepared to cope with it, and nobody surely believed that more firmly than did Lieutenant-Colonel Pritchard. This view was also fully shared by General Hewett, the Commander-in-Chief of the Meerut Division. Hewett was a brave man and a good soldier, but, like many others throughout India, he displayed a remarkable obtuseness with regard to the signs that were everywhere making themselves manifest. It was a fatal obtuseness, and terrible indeed were the consequences to be.

Captain Sandon returned from Delhi, bringing with him a large supply of ammunition from the enormous arsenal of that city. And that evening, as soon as he was off duty, he hastened to Pritchard's house, for he had heard that the Colonel had returned. Of course the two comrades greeted each other warmly, and it was but natural that the conversation, in the course of the evening, should turn upon Delhi. At that period the great city of the Moguls was the military storehouse for the whole of Upper India. But even this statement cannot convey an adequate idea to the mind of the reader of the incalculable quantity of ammunition, small arms, shot, shell, great guns, little guns, and all the instruments of destruction and warfare that had accumulated there.

"It amazes me," remarked Sandon, " that the authorities should be so supine about that tremendous arsenal. Why, if an attack in force was made upon it by the natives, Lieutenant Willoughby and his little band couldn't hold it for six hours."

"My dear boy, what a dreadful pessimist you are," laughed Pritchard, for he was always ready to ridicule his friend's fears. "Depend upon it, if the powers that be dreamed for a moment that there was any danger of the Delhi arsenal falling into the hands of the natives, they would not lose a moment in strengthening the garrison. But such a danger only exists in the heated imaginations of certain gentlemen who have persuaded themselves that there is a widespread dissatisfaction throughout the native army. For myself, I do not believe anything of the kind. A few malcontents have made fools of themselves, and a few more may continue to make fools of themselves, but you may rely upon it, Sandon, that we shall put them down with such a strong hand that we shall soon cease to hear any more grumbling."

Sandon was not the man to be lightly argued out of a position he had taken up. Less prejudiced in favour of the natives than his comrades in arms, he saw with different eyes, and the signs which those comrades were inclined to sneer at seemed to him very ominous indeed.

"Well, Pritchard, I tell you what it is," he answered, as he puffed the smoke from a choice cigar, and watched it curl upward in the languid air towards the brilliant stars that burned in the hazy Indian sky. "Unless I'm a veritable prophet of evil, we shall soon have an opportunity of determining who is correct, and it will then be seen what we Englishmen are made of. My visit to Delhi has rather opened my eyes. Why, could anything be more ridiculous than keeping an old puppet of a king there? The last of the once powerful Mogul rulers sitting in his marble palace in lonely state, presents the natives with a sentimental picture of fallen greatness, and his name will furnish them with a rallying-cry. And suppose the natives did make good their hold on Delhi, with its circle of fortified walls, seven miles in extent, how long would it take us to recover this old seat of the Mogul Empire, do you think?"

"I don't think it's necessary to work out that problem," replied Pritchard, in the light-hearted manner that was customary with him, "for the natives won't make good their hold on Delhi, or anywhere else. But as I'm going to Delhi, I'll study the problem on the spot if you like, and let you know my answer when I come back."

"You are going to Delhi!" exclaimed Sandon.

"Yes."

"When?"

"Well, in the course of a day or two, I expect."

"Am I at liberty to ask what takes you there?"

"Oh yes. It's no great secret. Hewett is desirous of being furnished with an accurate report of the ordnance stores in the arsenal."

"Does *he* anticipate danger there?" asked Sandon.

"Bless your soul, no. I believe it is simply to gratify a whim of the Quartermaster-General, who has asked for a return."

The conversation was interrupted at this point by the entrance of the ladies on the verandah. Captain Sandon sprang to his feet, and drew chairs up for them. But Mrs. Pritchard said to her husband, no doubt in pursuance of a little plan she had pre-arranged unknown to any one—

" I wish you would come to my room, George. I want you to read some letters I'm sending home. The mail goes out to-morrow, you know."

" So it does, by Jove ! " exclaimed her husband, as he sprang up. " I must write too, for I've got to give old Fenton some instructions about that bit of property of mine down in Devonshire."

" Will it be boring you, Captain, if I ask you to entertain my sister for a little while ? " said Mrs. Pritchard, addressing her guest.

" Boring me ! Oh dear, no," cried the Captain joyfully, experiencing an overwhelming sense of gratitude to the lady who had thus so cleverly managed to afford him the opportunity he had long been craving for. But, as if she saw through the little plot, Hester put in—

" But you know, Madge, I ought to write to the old folks as well as you."

" I've said all there is to say, dear," answered her sister. " You can send by the mail that goes out next week. Besides, we cannot leave Captain Sandon to smoke in solitude. Pray keep him company, and catechise him severely on the number of hearts he has broken in his time. Don't let him escape easily now, but just worm the secret out of him."

Hester recognized that, without being positively rude, she could not escape from the situation, so with a sigh she yielded, seating herself in the chair the Captain had placed for her. As Pritchard left the verandah, he said jokingly—

"I hope, Sandon, old fellow, you will survive the infliction of my sister-in-law. I'll send the khitmurghar out with some brandy-pawnee to keep your strength up."

"Infliction!" repeated the Captain, as he seated himself as near Hester as propriety permitted. "As though it could be an infliction to me to be alone with one so charming as you are, Miss Dellaby!"

"Oh, pray, Captain Sandon," she sighed, with something like a sneer, "pray don't flatter. I hate flattery. I always think it is a sign of a weak mind."

"Miss Dellaby," replied the Captain gravely, "acquit me, I beseech, of any desire to flatter. A man who sincerely admires a woman does not resort to the stupidity of paying her merely idle compliments. My admiration of you is not a thing of an hour's growth."

"You must not talk like that," she said. "You mustn't say you admire me."

"Why not?"

"Because I cannot listen to you."

"Is it a crime for me to confess that I have come to regard you with feelings of more than ordinary interest? For a long time you have occupied a large share of my thoughts."

"It may not be a crime, but——"

"But what?"

"It is distasteful to me."

"I am sorry to hear that—deeply and truly sorry."

"He spoke with such obvious feeling that she was quite distressed, and could not find it in her heart at that moment to interrupt him. Perhaps she was not altogether averse on that beautiful Indian night, with the brilliant stars watching, and the air heavy with the fragrance of a thousand flowers, to listen to a confession of love from one who was regarded as the handsomest man in the station. The situation was not without a touch of romance in it, and it might have accorded with her humour of the moment. Whether this was or was not so, she remained silent, and he construed her silence as a happy augury. "It is now a good many weeks since I first met you," he went on. "During those weeks I have been much in your company, and you have impressed me as no other woman has ever impressed me before."

"I wonder to how many women you have said the same thing?" murmured Hester, ironically.

"On my soul and honour I have never said it to any woman on earth," he exclaimed, with a display of sincerity.

"Perhaps all those you have vowed the same vow to have died off, then," she remarked, with a light laugh. "You may be what is termed 'a lady-killer.'"

"Miss Dellaby, pray don't trifle with me. I am serious. Up to my meeting with you I had never formed an attachment of any kind. It may seem strange, but it is true. In all my wanderings I have never met a lady who has made the same impression upon me as you have done. I am stating an absolute fact."

"Then I am unfortunate, Captain Sandon."

"Unfortunate! Why?"

"Because I cannot reciprocate your feelings."

"But perhaps you will in time," he answered eagerly. "I have the honour and privilege to enjoy the close friendship of your sister and her husband, and I have reason to think they would throw no obstacle in my way if you will only say that I may hope. I represent an excellent family. I have ample means, and could retire from the army to-morrow. I took up the profession of arms because it had a fascination for me, and not from necessity. I have hitherto endeavoured to so order my life that no man can honestly assail my honour; and I am vain enough to suppose I am not altogether deficient in those qualities which a soldier and a gentleman should possess. It is not good, perhaps, for a man to recommend himself even to the lady he is desirous of wooing. But——"

" Captain Sandon," exclaimed Hester, interrupting him, " I should be doing you a wrong, no less than wronging myself, if 1 listened to you any longer. I know that you are a man of honour, that you are a gentleman, that you are rich. My sister has told me these things. For the rest I have eyes to see, and sense enough to form an independent judgment. My friendship, my highest respect, if they are worth anything, shall be yours, but I cannot give you anything else. I am going now to try and enlist your sympathy; I am going to appeal to your honour. I am going to throw myself on your generosity. I sorely need a friend—you look astonished, but it is true—and I want you to be a friend to me."

She displayed more outward emotion than it was customary for her to do, and she had to cease speaking for a few moments. He took advantage of this pause to remark—

" Miss Dellaby, next to being something dearer to

you than a friend, I shall consider it the highest honour to be regarded by you as your friend."

"I want a friend," she said energetically; "for, astounding as it may seem to you, I feel at this moment friendless. At any rate those from whom I might expect sympathy and consideration show me none, and my sister and my brother-in-law—pray don't think me bold in what I am going to say, but it is far better the truth should be told than that there should be dissembling and deceit—they desire that I should allow you to make love to me, and I am bound to say this, it is because they are very fond of you themselves, and they believe that my happiness would be safe in your keeping."

Captain Sandon bowed, but remained silent. His face was thoughtful and grave, and he smoked with the air of one who was thinking deeply.

Having taken the plunge, having so far committed herself, Hester felt that retreat was now impossible, and as her position had recently become intolerable, she determined that the truth should come out.

"The fact is, Captain Sandon," she continued, "I am not free to listen when you speak of admiration for me, because my love is given to another man, to him I am pledged, to him I will be true."

Something very like a sigh escaped from Sandon's lips as this revelation was made, and a look of distress swept across his handsome face.

"I gather from what you say that you are engaged to him?" he remarked.

"I am."

"With the knowledge and consent of your people?"

"Not with their consent. They are all opposed to him."

"Including your sister and her husband?"

"Yes."

"Why?"

"For reasons it is not quite easy to explain without going into minute details, and I do not think it is necessary to do that."

"Where is this fortunate man?"

"In Persia."

"In Persia!" echoed the captain, elevating his eyebrows.

"Yes, he is an officer. He recently joined the 20th, which, as you know, has been sent out to Persia."

"Am I at liberty to ask his name?"

"You are. His name is Hallett—John Hallett, and I first met him in Edinburgh, where he was quartered with his regiment."

"And what do you wish *me* to do, Miss Dellaby?"

"I want you to understand what I mean when I say I am friendless."

"I think I do understand. Your friends do not approve of your connection with this young man, and they desire that you should give him up."

"That is so; but I cannot, I will not give him up. Therefore to you as a man of honour, as a gentleman, I appeal not to say things to me that pain me."

"So be it," exclaimed the Captain, with a sigh. "I cannot turn a deaf ear to that appeal, though it is very much like asking me to jump on my own heart, for—let me say it this once—I am desperately in love with you, and this disappointment, for dis-

appointment it is, will make a difference in my
life."

"But you will soon meet somebody who will be far
worthier of you than I am," remarked Hester.

"Ah, a girl always says that under similar circumstances, as though she thought all men are as fickle
as an April day. I have seen a good deal of the
world, and known many women, but never met one
before I met you who screwed herself into my heart
as you have done. I have dreamed you might be
mine. The dream is over. So be it; but believe me
something has gone out of my life. The world does
not appear to me in quite the same colour it did half-
an-hour ago."

He spoke so seriously, so mournfully, and withal
really looked so sad, that Hester could not help but
pity him. And she said in a kindly tone, at the same
time mechanically putting forth her hand—

"Poor fellow, I am so very, very sorry that I am
the cause of making you unhappy. But what am
I to do? It is not my fault. I cannot love two
men."

He took her outstretched hand, and held it between
his, nor did she attempt to withdraw it.

"No," he answered, "it is not your fault. You
are the innocent cause. Your beauty, your sweetness, your charming disposition have made me your
slave. But a slave cannot command; he must obey.
I will obey you."

He carried her hand to his lips and kissed it two
or three times, and that act was witnessed by
Mrs. Pritchard, who at that very moment appeared
in the doorway. She looked very charming herself,

clad as she was in white, and with the soft light in
the room behind her bringing her shapely figure
into relief. Hester caught sight of the white dress,
and turning, beheld her sister. Like one suddenly
detected in a wrong, she reddened to the roots of her
hair and drew her hand hastily from Sandon's grasp.
Mrs. Pritchard's first impulse was to steal silently
away again, but her presence being detected, she
laughed and exclaimed—

"I declare if you young people are not making
love to each other. How very romantic and sweet."

Captain Sandon rose and stammered out something,
and Hester said quickly—

"No, Madge, you are wrong."

"There, there, my dear child," retorted Mrs.
Pritchard, in her pleasant, laughing manner, "I've
got eyes, dear, to see with, I've caught you in—let
me see, what is that dreadful Latin sentence?—oh,
flagrante delicto. Is that correct, Captain?"

"Yes, I believe your quantities are right," laughed
Sandon.

"But why be ashamed?" continued the lady. "I
am sure it is very nice for you to play Juliet to
Captain Sandon's Romeo on such a delicious night.
The air is faint with the smell of flowers, and the
garden is jewelled with the fireflies; seldom have I
seen the stars so brilliant, while everything is
so still, so beautiful. These are the poetical acces-
sories to a love scene. It's really too affecting,
and makes me wish that I was a sentimental
girl again instead of an old married woman with
two children, and a big soldier husband to look
after."

"Really, Madge, how ridiculous you are. I tell you we were——"

What she was going to say was left unsaid, suddenly cut short by the report of a rifle not far off. This was followed by the fierce shouts of men, then there was another shot, and another, and another.

The laughter faded from Mrs. Pritchard's lips as the colour faded from her face, and flinging her arms about her sister, she murmured in nervous dread—

"God help us! what does that mean?"

Captain Sandon, who was in mufti, half started forward as Colonel Pritchard came rushing on to the verandah exclaiming—

"What was that? what was that?"

At that moment the clear, silvery notes of a bugle —a sentry call—rang out on the night air.

"I don't know what it is," answered Sandon calmly and collectedly, but with a significant glance at his friend; "I will go and ascertain what it means."

"Stay," said Pritchard, "you are unarmed. I will lend you a sword."

"No, thanks, I don't think it necessary," said Sandon, not wishing to alarm the ladies, and without displaying the slightest sign of trepidation, he descended the steps that led from the verandah to the garden and disappeared in the darkness.

CHAPTER XIII.

AT JHANSI.

For some moments after his friend had gone Colonel Pritchard stood irresolute. Then he said—

"I think I had better follow him."

"No, dear, don't," said his wife pleadingly, as she put her arms about him.

He laughed and patted her head.

"Why not?" he asked.

"Because—because—well, I feel quite nervous to-night. I don't know what has come over me." Then calling one of the native servants to her, she said—"Dundo, run along the road a little way, and see if you can ascertain what that firing meant."

The man salaamed, and went down the garden.

"Let us go in, dear, and look at the chicks," said the Colonel's wife as she took his arm and that of her sister, and led them into the house. But when the Colonel reached the room and had glanced at the sleeping children, his face became more thoughtful, and with a certain sternness of resolution he remarked—

"Madge, I have no right to stay here if there is anything wrong outside, and there is something wrong, or those shots would not have been fired and the sentry alarm sounded, though perhaps it is nothing more than a drunken row."

" Go then," she answered, with forced composure ; " I have no right to detain you."

He kissed her and left the room. He had scarcely got away from his own gate, however, when he met Captain Sandon returning.

"I am glad you are back," he exclaimed. "What is the bobbery about ? "

"Well, so far as I've been able to ascertain, it appears that two troopers of the 3rd Bengal Native Light Cavalry have been on the spree for the last day or two, and hiding in one of the bazaars. A picket of the 60th Foot were sent to find them and bring them in. Having discovered them, they were convoying them to barracks, when the ruffians suddenly sprang on their guard, seized two of the rifles, and tried to shoot some of the guard down. In this they failed, and were fired upon in return, with the result that one was seriously wounded. They are now, as I understand, safely lodged in gaol."

"I am glad it is nothing worse than that," re-marked Pritchard in his usual cheerful manner.

"It's bad enough in all conscience," returned Sandon. "It shows how strong the mutinous spirit is amongst the black rascals."

"Tut, man, what an alarmist you are, to be sure," answered Pritchard, with a scornful little laugh, for he so firmly believed in the fidelity of the native soldiers generally that he could not bear to hear even his best friend speak doubtingly of them.

"No, I am not an alarmist," was the decisive answer, "but I see without prejudice, and think without bias. I tell you, Pritchard, there is an evil day dawning for India. The black devils mean mischief. We want a man now at the head of affairs with the mind of a Wellington and the boldness of a Napoleon."

Pritchard answered his friend quite angrily.

"Really, Sandon, I am amazed that you should be so pessimistic. There is nothing, absolutely nothing, to justify the alarm you manifest——"

"Oh, pray, my friend, don't think I am alarmed," cried Sandon, interrupting the other. "Taking a purely selfish and personal view of the matter, I hope we may have an opportunity of teaching these natives a severe lesson. I have a murdered brother to avenge, and if the opportunity should arise for me to strike, you may make a bet I'll strike hard and sure."

"Well, you'll have to wait a long time, old man. But come, don't let us alarm the ladies."

"Trust me; I shall not do that," answered his friend.

The two officers entered the bungalow, and hearing their footsteps, Mrs. Pritchard and her sister rushed forward to learn the news, and plied Sandon with questions.

"A mere brawl, I assure you, ladies; nothing more. Such little incidents are part of the everyday life in a military station like this."

Captain Sandon spoke lightly, though he did not think lightly of the matter; and though his friend had dubbed him a pessimist, it would have been a good thing for India if there had been many more like him at that time. The "little incident" of that night was but the prelude to the great tragedy upon which the curtain was about to rise. It appeared that the two men who had been arrested as deserters were brothers named Chuna. The one who was wounded in the *mêlée* died the same night, and the survivor by some unaccountable means managed to break out of barracks again before the day dawned, and getting clear of the city he fled with all speed to Jhansi, where his people lived, and where we must follow him.

Jhansi was a singularly picturesque city, strongly fortified, and at that period was nominally ruled by the Ranee, who was then a widow. She was, however, a mere puppet, for Jhansi had really been annexed by Lord Dalhousie; but the Ranee was allowed to keep up some empty semblance of her former state, though the handsome money allowance offered her by the Government she indignantly declined, and in many ways she had shown that she was a bitter and uncompromising enemy of the British. Yet startling and strange as it seems, it is nevertheless true that the garrison we kept in her little kingdom was made up entirely of natives, with the exception of about half-a-dozen European officers or so, in addition to a "resident" and a political agent; but in spite of these two officials it is surprising how very little was known of the true state of native feeling in the deposed Ranee's dominions. The Ranee was like a tiger deprived of its young, but the white people believed she was a caged tiger, and therefore could do no harm. She was not, however, as harmless as was supposed. Her stronghold was a powerful place if she could but get control of it. The fortifications were armed with some com-

paratively heavy guns, and the natural advantages
of Jhansi as a place of defence were very great
indeed. What was wanted was a body of resolute
and trained troops and plenty of ammunition. Given
these and the fortress might have held out for a considerable time. But the Ranee was a shrewd, calcu-
lating creature, and she saw that even if she succeeded
in winning the allegiance of the native troops quartered in her town, it would be useless to attempt to
fight the British single-handed. If a general rising
could be assured, then Jhansi would play no unim-
portant part in the great struggle. All unknown,
of course, to the white conquerors, the dusky queen
had been sending out spies to different parts of the
country, and they were instructed to report to her
how the vast conspiracy progressed, and if the native
troops throughout India were unanimous in wishing
to throw off the British yoke. It will be understood
from this how ready the Ranee was to receive any
one who could supply her with reliable information,
and so when Chuna entered the city after his rapid
flight from Meerut, and sought an interview with the
deposed ruler, he had no difficulty whatever in gaining
admission to her presence.

Seated in a gorgeously-decorated room of her palace
the Ranee received the man, who, in accordance
with Eastern custom, prostrated himself before her.

" Your name is Chuna ? " said the Ranee.

" It is, your Mightiness, and in this city was I born,
and here for long have dwelt my people."

" Rise, Chuna. You have been a soldier in the
service of the Company Bahadoor ? "

" I have."

K

"And you love the service ?"

Chuna ground his teeth. His dark face was filled with an expression of intense hatred, and his eyes burned with the fire of suppressed passion.

"Great Ranee," he exclaimed, "I had a brother who up to a few days ago was strong and well as I am. We hated the white rule and wished to free ourselves of it. We met one of your emissaries and listened to what he told us. Then my brother and I vowed a vow by the sacred Gunga that we would devote our poor lives in trying to free our country from the oppressor. We went into the bazaars at Meerut; we spread the news that a great day was dawning for our land, and that the hateful British would be swept into the sea. We preached in our humble way the doctrine of defiance and revolution. We told our countrymen that we were slaves, but by a united effort we could be free, when from the Himalayas to the mouth of the Hooghly would go forth the great shout that the Company's Raj was over."

"You spoke well. You are a brave man. You will become a great one," answered the Ranee. "Proceed."

"While we were engaged in our mission," continued Chuna, "white soldiers were sent to arrest us. In shame and humiliation we were being conveyed back to the barracks, where we should have been loaded with chains and ignominiously treated. We exchanged signals together; we understood each other; we made a spring at our captors; we seized two of their guns and made a bid for liberty. Alas, alas, great lady, some evil spirit went against us.

My brother fell mortally wounded by the fire of the accursed Feringhees. They carried him in a dying state to the barracks, where that night Brahma claimed him. I had obtained permission to sit with my wounded brother. When he was dead, and as the morning broke, I managed to elude the vigilance of the sentry and get free. I have come hither because my people are here, and it is my native place, and to offer you my humble services."

"You are a hero," answered the Ranee. "You shall have riches, and your people shall be made rich, if you can succeed in stirring your comrades and countrymen here into breaking their shackles of serfdom. But tell me, what is the feeling amongst our people in Meerut?"

"They but wait a favourable opportunity and an assurance that they will be supported."

The Ranee smiled bitterly.

"We must see if we cannot give them our support," she said. "A spirit of fear has kept us down; but you shall tell the soldiers that the power we have feared is but a shadow that will flee before our fierce wrath. The bones of the accursed Feringhees shall strew our plains, and their blood shall fertilize our soil. Mata Singh"—she said to one of her attendants —"see that this man is well cared for. Then take means to get as many Sepoys here to-night as you can muster. Chuna shall address them. He shall tell them how weak the white Raj is, and how little effort is required to destroy it altogether. He is one of them, and they will listen to him. Like them he is a soldier under the Company, therefore his words will carry weight. If he wins the garrison here to

my cause he shall be loaded with riches ; and when
my power has been restored his people shall have
land and become rulers themselves.   See to it, Singh,
that my instructions are carried out, and if all goes
well here, messengers shall speed to Meerut, to Delhi,
to Cawnpore to tell them that we only await their
signal."

Singh, who was a handsome, grey-bearded old man
who had been in the Rajah of Jhansi's service for
more than a generation, made a low salaam, and
beckoning Chuna to follow him, the two went out
together.

CHAPTER XIV.

AMONGST the high-caste natives throughout India no one had been more active in propagating sedition and inflaming the passions of the people than the Ranee of Jhansi, and the British had no more dangerous enemy than this remarkable woman. The old puppet of a king at Delhi, who sat on his golden throne surrounded with mock state, and trying to cheat himself into a belief that he was still a ruler, although in his heart he knew full well that the mighty power once wielded by th Moguls had gone for ever, hated the British as strongly as she did. But he was an old man. His energy was dead, his hopes crushed, the grave was yawning at his feet, and in his senility he felt the uselessness of trying to subdue the conqueror. He was a king in name; the representative of a princely house which for centuries had been all but supreme in Asia; he lived in a palace; he had followers and a toy army; he was surrounded with luxury and the conditions of state. But it was all mockery to him. The theatrical monarch with his tinsel crown and foil-covered sceptre was not more powerless than he. Therein he differed from the Ranee of Jhansi.

Jhansi had ever been a small State, and the sway

of its rulers was as nothing compared to the Moguls. But they had been a fierce and warlike people, and when the last Rajah died, and his widow saw that the British had destroyed her royal house, she was too fierce, too energetic, too martial to submit tamely and uncomplainingly as the white-haired old King of Delhi had done. She chafed, she fretted, she raved; nor was she at much pains to conceal her feelings. But her fuming and raving were laughed at. She was regarded as a pigmy, and the white giant, conscious of his own might, treated her with contempt, and did not concern himself about her. It was one more of numerous fatal mistakes which the British had made, and those mistakes were to be paid for at a fearful cost.

As already stated, the garrison kept at Jhansi was composed entirely of native troops in charge of some seven or eight British officers. In common with the discontent which had shown itself in so many places, the Jhansi garrison had murmured and growled, but they had been afraid to take the initiative in any upheaval. They wanted the start to be made elsewhere, and as elsewhere entertained precisely the same idea, it seemed as if there was not likely to be any widespread outbreak. The Ranee had done her best to overcome this difficulty. She was wealthy, and was able to pay her emissaries well, and her restless, fiery nature would not allow her to remain quiet and submissive under what she considered a great wrong.

The arrival of Chuna seemed to her singularly opportune. She knew how a little leaven could leaven the whole mass. Here was a Sepoy, a fugitive, a deserter, whose life would be sacrificed if he were retaken. His brother had been killed, and he was burning to avenge that brother's death. Such a man, the Ranee saw at once, might prove invaluable, and help her to carry out her fell designs. So she resolved that the utmost use should be made of the instrument which fortune had thus placed in her hands. That night, owing to the exertions of her hirelings, she got together a large number of the Sepoy garrison. They assembled in the large hall of her palace, and every precaution had been taken to guard against surprise, while the fidelity of her servants was beyond doubt. The soldiers had not come in a body, but one, two, and even three at a time. This was done in order to avoid arousing any suspicion. But the British officers were enjoying their mess as usual, and never dreamed of danger. On the contrary, the commanding officer being a great shikaree, he and his comrades were planning a shooting expedition for the following day, and it was decided that a polite request should be sent to the Ranee for the loan of some of her elephants.

When all had assembled in the palace who were likely to come, Chuna was brought forward, and the Ranee, raising her voice, said—

"Friends and countrymen, behold here one of yourselves—a soldier like you; and up to a few days ago a slave like you. You wince. You don't like the word slave, and yet are we any better than slaves? This man's brother was shot down before his very eyes, and he himself escaped by a miracle. He has come here to his native place—to his people. He has sought safety and shelter with us. Say, shall he be dragged forth again to be butchered by these dogs of English ? "

Only a murmur answered her question. The spirit of fear still held the men in its thrall. They were in truth afraid of each other. Then the Ranee looked appealingly at Chuna, and he spoke. He was an imposing man—a true Sikh, with the fierce martial bearing of his countrymen. His voice was full and round; his manner impressive.

"Brothers," he began, "we are Oudh men, and our country has been stolen from us." *

The dusky faces around him lit up with passion at these words, and white teeth gleamed, as men were moved by an emotion they could not conceal. One powerful fellow, a duffadar (sergeant) stepped forward a few paces, and, biting his nether lip for a moment, he said, as he made a salaam to the Ranee—

"True, O brother; my people owned a little land, and were contented. But it was taken from them. Therefore they were robbed."

* The large province of Oudh, it is perhaps unnecessary to remind the reader, had been annexed under Lord Dalhousie, to the intense dissatisfaction of the land-owners and of the people generally. Four-fifths of the population of Oudh were Hindoos, and from this source the Bengal army was principally supplied. The Oudh-men, being a warlike race, made splendid soldiers, and were quick and apt at learning English drill. They were fearless riders, excellent swordsmen, and at first seemed to take kindly to the new condition of things. Up to the time of the Mutiny the native regiments were made up almost entirely of Oudhmen.

"And yet you serve the white Rajah, although your royal house was destroyed, your king deprived of his rights, and his subjects made slaves to a foreign ruler," remarked the Ranee, with a scornful curl of the lip.

"We serve the white Rajah because he conquered us," remarked the man sullenly.

"But the conqueror may be conquered," the Ranee said.

The men remained silent, but they looked at each other. Although they hated the foreign rule, the power of the British was to them incalculable. They were afraid of it, and yet the fire smouldered within them. It only wanted fanning into a flame. None knew this better than the Ranee, and hence her motive in utilizing Chuna to play upon their feelings.

"Brothers," said Chuna again, "the duffadar has spoken. He and his people were robbed. You have all been robbed, and in the old days we were wont to sally forth in our might, and smite those who robbed us into the dust."

"Aye, aye, it was so," murmured the soldiers with a certain sullenness, which seemed to indicate that they wanted very little more to stir them into fury.

"Think of it, men," put in the Ranee. "You have been robbed; we have all been robbed; and while we are as numerous as the sands of the sea, the robbers may be counted by scores. Oh, my dead ancestors, I blush as I think of it." She covered her face with her hands, and appeared to be overcome with emotion. She was a good actress, and no one knew better than she how to appeal to men's feelings.

" It is so," answered the duffadar, as he glanced round at his brother-soldiers. " The great lady speaks truly. We are many; our rulers are few. Yet do we remain silent and inactive."

" It shall be so no longer," murmured his listeners.

" Ah, you speak like soldiers and heroes now," said the Ranee. " Chuna, tell them what you know, and see if you can stir into a flame the fire that smoulders in their hearts."

" I have come from Meerut," said Chuna.

" And what report bring you? " asked several.

" A good report."

" Speak it then, that we may hear and act," remarked the duffadar.

" Our brothers there groan beneath the yoke as you groan here. But they await your help."

" And we wait theirs," put in the duffadar.

" It will be given when you have sworn to support them even to the death."

" We swear it; we swear it," cried all.

" A few nights ago," went on Chuna, " my brother was shot down before my eyes. His blood cries aloud for vengeance."

" And he shall be avenged," murmured the men.

" We want something more than words. We want acts and deeds," said the Ranee.

" But we wait on Meerut," answered the duffadar, speaking for his fellows.

" And Meerut will rise when it knows that it can count on Jhansi," said Chuna, growing more excited. " Let us make a start, and when once the fire catches, not all the might of the British will be able to

extinguish it. Go back at once to your barracks.
Tell your comrades that on them our freedom depends,
then seize your guns, and let not a white man or
woman or child escape. Do this thing this very
night, and when the Feringhees are butchered we
will hasten to Meerut; our arrival will be Meerut's
signal, and then woe betide all who carry a white
skin."

His dusky listeners had caught his excitement,
and they looked dangerous now, and as if they were
itching to rush off and put Chuna's suggestion into
execution. But that would not have suited the wily
Ranee's book. If the Sepoys went away who would
defend her kingdom? What she hoped was this,
that Meerut and Delhi would rise simultaneously.
Then the British would be too much occupied to
trouble her. It would be with them a desperate
struggle for their very lives. In the meantime she
could consolidate her position, extend her rule, and
organize a powerful native army of her own. But
to let the native garrison that then held the place go,
would be to lose what little she then possessed.

"Chuna speaks wisely, but counsels not well," she
said. "We must make no move until the Feringhees
are engaged defending their worthless lives at
Meerut, Delhi, and Cawnpore. We are not powerful
enough to drive these white devils into the sea.
But we can send to our brothers at those places our
oath of fidelity to the cause. What you have to do
is to stir up your comrades, and when to a man you
have sworn to stand by me, our secret messengers
shall go forth to the other towns, and through all the
bazaars, and amongst all the native regiments. They

shall spread the glad tidings that our swords will fly from their scabbards at their bidding. When they strike we will strike too. But my kingdom here must be built up. That which has been taken from me must be restored. The Rajahs of Jhansi have been all-powerful in the past, they must be still more powerful in the future. Say, my brave friends, shall this be so?"

"It shall, it shall," they exclaimed in chorus.

"Ah, now does my heart begin to beat true again," the Ranee said. "Chuna, we owe you much. Here shall you lie concealed and in safety. And since you must have many friends in Meerut, you shall send them secret messages by the fakirs. You shall tell them that we are ready and willing, and the first shot that is fired in Meerut shall be the signal for the death of every Feringhee here. Their doom is sealed, but they shall live on until their hour strikes. It is not just yet. Rashness will undo us. Like the cobra of our jungles we must move silently; like the tiger strike swiftly and crush at once. Say, good people, are we agreed on this?"

"We are."

"And you will carry out my instructions?"

"We will."

"You make me glad. I could cry aloud for very joy. And now, hearken; as earnest of what I intend to do for you, every man of you, before you leave here to-night, shall receive twenty rupees. That is nothing to what you may expect if you serve me well. The Company Bahadoor give you no more than will buy you rice, but I will make you rich, every mother's son of you. And now go. From this very hour begin to prepare the mine, but fire it not until I give the word."

The prospect of getting twenty rupees each, which to these men was a large sum, aroused them to such an extent that they rushed forward and struggled with each other to kiss the Ranee's hand. She got rid of them at last. Then she bade one of her attendants summon Rhabdool. In a few minutes a little, weazened old man entered. His hair was long and white; his beard and moustache like driven snow. He wore a long, loose robe of muslin, fastened at the waist with a piece of cord. He was ostensibly a fakir or mendicant priest, but in reality a spy and messenger in the service of the Ranee. Fakirs were privileged people all over India. No one thought of molesting them. No one questioned them as to whither they were journeying or whence they came. They were free as the winds, and, wandering as they did through the bazaars of the towns and villages they visited, they gathered up the news and bore it on. In the days preceding the Mutiny, all unsuspected by the British, these fakirs wandered from place to place, keeping in touch with all the budmashes (rascals) of the towns and stations, and secretly spreading the report that the British were to be driven from India in 1857, in fulfiment of an old prophecy. It can well be understood how such men would be made use of as spies and firebrands by those who had no other safe means of communicating with the people.

Rhabdool salaamed to the Ranee.

"You have work for me," he said.

"Yes. Behold this man. His name is Chuna. He

is a soldier. His brother has been butchered before his eyes, and he has fled hither for safety. You will journey to Meerut with messages from him. Speak, Chuna, and say who are your trusted friends there."

"I belong to the 3rd Bengal Light Cavalry," said Chuna.

"Yes," answered the weazened-faced little man, as he folded his hands on his breast and looked so mild and gentle that no one unacquainted with him would have suspected that he was one of the most insidious enemies of the English, and as bloodthirsty as the most ferocious Sepoy. "Proceed. I listen," he added.

"In that regiment I have many friends."

"Their names?" asked Rhabdool, as, laying his forefinger on his temple, and closing his eyes, he listened attentively. Like all his class, he had a most excellent memory.

Chuna mentioned the names of many men in the regiment, and as each name was uttered Rhabdool tapped his forehead, as if to impress the name indelibly on his brain.

"Tell these friends of mine," went on Chuna, "that if they remain in the Feringhee's pay they will be defiled, and cast out for ever and ever from Brahma's presence."

"What mean you?" asked the Ranee, displaying great eagerness as she guessed that there was something more in the man's remark than appeared on the surface.

"I mean that their caste is to be broken."

"How broken?"

"The cartridges served out to them for their carbines are to be greased with hog's fat, and since these cartridges must be bitten with the teeth, the biters will be defiled, since no true Hindoo can taste the fat of pigs and remain whole."

The Ranee shuddered. It was either a real or an assumed shudder.

"This is horrible," she murmured.

"Most horrible," added Rhabdool.

"And yet it is true," remarked Chuna, with a fierce expression and flashing eyes.

Rhabdool drew his little figure up to its full extent of inches. He seemed almost, as it were, to undergo some change. The mildness of his expression had given place to one of ferocity. He looked dangerous, and as if he were capable of performing any deed, no matter how bloodthirsty. He snatched from the folds of his robe a strip of dirty, greasy parchment, attached to a string that was round his neck. On the parchment were written some verses from the Hindoo bible. He pressed the parchment to his shrivelled lips, and said, with an angry snarl—

"Hereon I swear that I will rest not until I have informed these men of the devilish attempt to destroy their souls. An they be men and not cravens they will rise like a whirlwind, and sweep these damnable Feringhees from the face of the earth. Yes, Ranee; yes, Chuna! It shall be done. My old heart beats with youthful vigour as I enter on my task. Woe, woe to them, I say, who have attempted this thing."

"When will you go forth?" asked the Ranee, with a look of joy beaming on her dusky face.

"This very night; and I will sleep no more until

I have warned these poor children of the awful peril they stand in. With fire and sword they must purge the land of the accursed white man."

"Go," said the Ranee, "and may Brahma aid your efforts—sow the wind, so that the whirlwind will be irresistible."

She dismissed Rhabdool, Chuna, and her attendants; and when she was alone she laughed to herself and rubbed her hands gleefully.

"All goes well so far," she murmured. "With the coming of Chuna has come the dawn of a better fortune for me. Jhansi shall be mine again, and the power of its ruler shall be mightier than ever."

So dreamed the treacherous Ranee, and through the darkness of the night the fanatical fakir travelled on his way to Meerut.

When the morning dawned the few officers in charge of the garrison rose full of their hunting project, all unmindful of the danger that threatened them. A polite message was sent to the Ranee to say how much obliged the officers would be if she would lend them three of her elephants for two days' shooting, and she replied that it would give her unspeakable pleasure to comply with the request of the gentlemen, and the elephants would be prepared and sent forthwith.

And during the time that the officers were absent on their excursion, the lump of leaven was doing its work, and amongst the native regiments in charge of Jhansi and in the pay of the Company the ferment ran. Those who had been at the Ranee's palace told how handsomely she had behaved, and how she had promised to make them all rich. Then certain men in the regiment were secretly appointed to be leaders, and the others swore a sacred oath that they would stand by them to the death. It was next arranged that some morning, when the troops were assembled for general parade, and assuming that Meerut had taken the lead, a signal was to be given, and every officer shot down. Then the women and children were to be put to death. That done, the fortifications were to be strengthened, and the absolute rule of the Ranee restored.

Thus the plot was hatched, and thus was every white soul there condemned to death. The signal for their execution, or rather let us say murder, would come from Meerut. A week later the officer in command at Jhansi received a "service" letter from Bombay, of which the following is a copy :—

"A young lieutenant named John Montague Hallett, late of the 20th, now serving in Persia, having resigned his commission in that regiment owing to some scandal, has been sent down here in charge of a batch of invalids. As he has expressed a desire to join the Punjaub army, he is, by order of the Commander-in- Chief, to be posted to your regiment, and is now on his way up country. His abilities as an officer have been favourably reported upon, but he wants keeping in hand."

CHAPTER XV.

DIPLOMACY.

THE escape of the prisoner Chuna from Meerut was not regarded as a very serious affair, although the sentries on duty at the prison hospital where the wounded man lay dying, and where with unusual leniency and indulgence the other deserter had been allowed to be with his mortally-wounded brother, were at once tried by court-martial, and two of them sentenced to imprisonment. For it was perfectly obvious that these two men must have connived at the escape, or otherwise been singularly lax in their duty. In either case they had been guilty of a breach of military discipline, and so were made an example of.

The punishment awarded, however, was very mild, for up to then there had been a desire on the part of those in authority to treat disobedience lightly. It was thought that kindness and indulgence would have a better effect that severity. Never was a greater mistake made. The oriental mind looks upon anything in the shape of leniency or concession as a sign of weakness and fear. The past rulers of the East have ever ruled with a rod of iron. The word has been followed by the blow the moment there was the faintest sign of disobedience. Thus the people have been kept in subjection. They are used to it. It is the discipline they appreciate, the discipline they respect.

It is true that since the dark and sanguinary days of the Mutiny we have given the masses a freedom they never enjoyed before, but at the same time we have deprived them of the power for mischief. That one tremendous weapon which was turned against us with such awful effect, the native artillery, has been done away with. That arm of the service is now entirely in the hands of the British, and while the number of British officers in the native regiments has been largely increased, the number of the native officers has been as largely decreased. Profiting, too, by the bitter lessons which the Mutiny taught us, we no longer leave important stations to be garrisoned entirely by native troops, with only a handful of whites to look after them. And, moreover, we have succeeded in convincing princes, rajahs, and other high-caste natives that their interests are bound up in ours. But so far as the masses of the people are concerned, it is doubtful if they are yet reconciled to to our rule; but though they are numbered by hundreds of thousands, they recognize their weakness, for they have no arms, and no one to marshal them in battle array. Without arms, and without leaders, how could even their mighty numbers prevail against the relatively small British army stationed in India, and which, though small, is one of the best-drilled, best-trained, and best-equipped armies in the world, and not to be dislodged even by the might of Russia!

The exciting little incident of the death of one of the brothers Chuna and the escape of the other

having been got over, the every day life in the
station of Meerut resumed the even tenor of its way,
and the flirting, scandalizing, church-going, and
parading went on as usual. Mrs. Pritchard recovered
her spirits, which had been somewhat dashed, and in a
few days her husband started for Delhi on special service, expecting to be absent for a fortnight. During
that fortnight, however, many things were to happen.

Although Captain Sandon's suspicions concerning
the natives had not abated one jot, he resolved for
the moment to keep his views to himself, as the
weight of the white opinion in the station was largely
against him. And he also resolved not to relax his
endeavours to win Hester Dellaby, for he had really
spoken truly when he said no other woman had ever
influenced him as she had done. That he was
a gentleman in the best sense of the word was
certain, and it was equally certain that he was a
gallant and brave soldier, with all a soldier's
instincts, and he believed, as most soldiers do, that
all is fair in love and war.

Hester had appealed to his honour, and had asked
him to befriend her. He was not likely to jeopardize
that honour, which he prized so highly, and his
friendship had in a sense been pledged. But she
had told him her lover was in Persia, and that all
her people had objected to him. Being in Persia,
where a conflict was then going on, the chances were
she might not see him again. And even if he came
through the fortunes of war with a whole skin, there
were also strong chances that the objections of her
people would prevail, and she would give him up
Whichever way it was, Sandon decided that he was

justified in holding himself ready to step into the breach, and to be ready to do that was to so ingratiate himself in the girl's favour that she would readily change the friend into the lover. As a man of the world, he knew that girls in their youth believed that their love for some particular man could never change, but in a little while they found out that what they thought was love was merely infatuation, that died out with the absence of the object that produced it. He relied upon this occurring in Hester's case. He quite thought that time—and but a short time—would serve to disillusionze her, and she would feel annoyed with herself for ever having regarded her attachment for Hallett in any serious light.

On the understanding that had been arrived at between them, Hester was glad of Captain Sandon's attention, and her sister saw with silent pleasure what she believed was the commencement of an engagement, and she encouraged it in every possible way. She was fond of Sandon, and her husband was fond of him, and they both felt that if Hester would have him it would be an excellent match. Of course the affair soon came to be the talk of the station. Gossip of this kind was a toothsome morsel for the ladies as they met at their respective tea-fights, and such remarks as the following were freely indulged in :—

" I wonder if there is anything serious between Miss Dellaby and Captain Sandon ? "

" No, I should think not," answered a certain Miss Clifton, daughter of one of the staff-surgeons, and who, it was notorious, had herself tried to hook the handsome Sandon. " The Captain is a frightful flirt, and as hollow-hearted as he can be. I pity the girl who gets him; besides, I should think a man like him would look somewhat higher than a girl of Hester Dellaby's standing. He is simply amusing himself, that's what he's doing."

"I think you are wrong, dear," remarked another lady, who was said to lead rather a cat-and-dog life with her husband. "The Captain's serious enough in my opinion, but, of course, if he married Miss Dellaby he would very likely tire of her in six months. He is not the man to remain true to any one long; in fact all men are deceivers. They are a bad lot. If I had my time to come over again, I wouldn't trust one of them."

"They are not such a bad lot if you know how to keep them in hand," remarked a big stout lady in spectacles, who was said to rule her husband with a rod of iron.

"Oh, I think men are just delightful," chipped in a pert miss of nineteen, but she was promptly frowned down and sat upon, and no doubt regretted that she had spoken.

Amongst the men generally the opinion was, "Sandon's a deuced lucky fellow," and that Hester was the handsomest girl in the station. Many of the young subalterns sighed their hearts out with envy that they had no chance of competing with the handsome Captain for possession of the station prize, for so Hester was regarded.

Of course, the talk that was so freely indulged in was not likely to escape the ears of Mrs. Pritchard, and that lady considered, as her sister's guardian, that it was her place to have a definite understanding with Sandon as to what his intentions were, and, with all the artfulness of her sex, she contrived to get the opportunity to do this, without seeming as if she was trying to force his hand or that of her sister. In fact, Hester had shown a determination not to give herself away, and, having every faith in the Captain, she determined that Mrs. Pritchard might form any opinion she liked.

The opportunity came about in this way. She persuaded Hester to accept an invitation that had been sent to her to accompany some friends on a day's excursion, and in the course of the afternoon Mrs. Pritchard drove to the house of the chaplain, where she happened to know Sandon was to be. After the usual tea and small talk, she rose to go, and asked Captain Sandon if he was going back to his quarters, volunteering to drop him on the way. Although he had shared a seat in the buggy of a brother-officer coming out, and would have returned that way, he gladly availed himself of the lady's offer.

After some preliminary conversation, she opened fire by remarking—

"I quite miss Hester now when I drive out alone, for I have got so used to having her with me."

"Yes, I suppose you do," he answered. "She's gone off for the day, I understand."

"Yes, but how did you know?"

"I heard it from the Richardson girls."

"There is not much one can do in the station without its being known," said Mrs. Pritchard with a little laugh.

"No, there is not indeed. Gossip is essential to the well-being of ladies."

"That reminds me, Captain, that the attentions you show to my sister have become the subject of common gossip."

"Oh, that is very likely. In a place like this the old women must have something to talk about. They would die if they had not."

"Yes; but it's not pleasant to have one's name made the subject of scandal at tea-fights."

—"My dear Mrs. Pritchard," said the Captain, with an air of unusual seriousness, "my idea of life is that it is too short and too interesting to fritter any portion of it away in listening to the mere tattle of irresponsible chatterers, who talk because they have nothing better to do. You and I can surely afford to be indifferent to paltry frivol."

"Oh, I quite agree with you, but still one should endeavour to avoid giving these chatterers opportunity to wag their silly tongues."

The Captain shrugged his shoulders.

"If one thought of that, one would have no time for anything else," he said sententiously.

"I am not so sure about that, Captain Sandon."

"But I am. Pardon me for differing from you. For myself, I care not what people say."

"But you are a man," she exclaimed, as though she thought she had scored a point.

"And you are a lady, and a very charming lady too," he answered, with his pleasant laugh.

"Oh, pray don't be ridiculous, Captain Sandon. You know well enough what I mean."

"A man who always knows what a lady means is a clever man indeed," said Sandon laughingly.

"Really you are most tantalizing. I must be

blunt with you then, and express a hope that you will respect the good name of my family."

"I trust I shall always do that, Mrs. Pritchard."

"Remember that I am Hester's sister."

"She is to be congratulated on having so excellent a sister."

"I shall certainly have to take you to task, sir, if you prevaricate in such a way. You know quite well what I am alluding to. You mustn't talk a lot of silly nonsense to the girl, and turn her head."

"Mrs. Pritchard," answered the Captain, with that decisiveness of tone which he adopted when very much in earnest, "I leave the silly nonsense to be talked by the gossips of the station. As for turning the girl's head, I don't believe I could do that. She is too strong-minded."

"I am glad that you think so. But what I want to understand is this, have you any serious intentions about Hester?"

"My intentions are always serious, Mrs. Pritchard. I am a serious man."

"You are a most tiresome one," she cried.

"I am sorry that *you* think so."

"You know you are, and you are just playing with me. Men always think they can play with women."

"That remark is not fair to yourself and not just to me," he answered.

"Very well, then; to be perfectly frank, do you not admire my sister?"

"I have admired her almost from the first hour I saw her."

"And does she admire you in return?"

"Ah, that is a question that you ought certainly to

be in a position to answer much better than I can."

"No, that is not so, for my sister does not make a confidante of me; she tells me few or none of her secrets."

"Perhaps she has none to tell."

"Oh, yes, she has.   But what I want to know, Captain, is this, does she reciprocate the feeling you entertain for her?"

"I am presumptuous enough to think that my company and conversation are not altogether distasteful to her."

"Ah, now we are getting at it.   In other words, you are both falling over head and ears in love with each other."

"I can only speak for myself."

"Then you admit *you* are in love?"

"I do not deny it certainly."

"Come now, that's a confession.   And when a man falls in love with a woman, he hopes, I suppose, to ultimately win her for his wife."

"Well, I've generally understood that the goal of the lover is matrimony."

"Is it *your* goal, sir?   I have heard it said you are not a marrying man."

"That is another illustration of how often strangers know more about one's business than one knows one's self," answered Sandon ironically.

Mrs. Pritchard was annoyed, though she concealed this annoyance.   She was a good tactician in her way; at least, she had always thought so, but she had certainly been worsted on this occasion, and Sandon had parried her questions with great skill.

She was resolved, however, to make one last effort to draw him out, and, putting on her pleasantest smile, she said—

"I cannot help remarking, Captain Sandon, that my sister is a very impressionable girl, therefore I hope you will not trifle with her feelings for the sake of amusing yourself."

"Mrs. Pritchard, you can rest perfectly sure I will not do that."

This answer seemed to her more satisfactory than any he had yet given, and it encouraged her to go a step further. In a half-pathetic, half-confidential tone, she remarked—

"I think, Captain, under all the circumstances, I am justified in letting you into a little secret. My sister, it appears, has had some flirtation with a young fellow at home, of whom her father and mother strongly disapproved, and of course it could not be expected that I should oppose them, so when Hester told me about the affair I was quite angry with her, and said she must think no more of him. Of course, it has been a mere bit of calf love, such as occurs between an irresponsible girl and boy, but very likely at the time she thought it was all real enough. However, she has quite got over it by this time."

Captain Sandon evinced no surprise, as the lady expected he would do, and she had been watching his face narrowly to see how he received the information, but he said quietly—

"I have heard the story."

"You've heard it!" she exclaimed, there being no mistake about her surprise. "From whom have you heard it?" Then, before he could answer her question, she burst into a laugh, saying—

"Oh, why, of course, my sister told you."

"Yes; she related the incident to me."

"Did she tell you that the young fellow had gone to Persia?"

"She did."

"Then, if she has so far made a confidant of you, Captain, it is very certain you must have succeeded in ingratiating yourself very deeply in her favour, and I trust she will never have reason to think she has misplaced her confidence."

"I don't think she will," was the only answer the Captain made. However, Mrs. Pritchard was quite satisfied. She felt that she had scored a very good point, and that in a short time she might be able to announce a formal engagement between her sister and the gallant Captain Sandon of the 6th Dragoon Guards.

By this time they had entered the cantonments, when they became aware of some commotion going on. Mrs. Pritchard pulled up her horse, as the road was filled with a noisy, excited crowd of budmashes and a picket of carabineers, who were driving a strange-looking old man before them. He had a long white beard, and was garbed as a fakir. The expression of his weazened little face was one of supreme contempt, and his hands were folded on his breast, as if he felt he was a martyr, and he was trying to impress the crowd with his own views.

Captain Sandon jumped down to see what was the matter. In a few minutes he returned to Mrs. Pritchard, who had waited with the buggy.

" What is it ? " asked the lady a little anxiously.

" Oh, nothing serious ; it appears that the dirty little old fakir has been found two or three times in the native lines against orders, and when told to leave he spouted treason in the presence of one of the native companies. The General in command has therefore sent word that he is to be driven out of the town."

" I think that is a pity," answered Mrs. Pritchard. " These fakirs are very dirty and great rascals, but I think it is a mistake to take any notice of them."

" That's a lady's idea," smiled Sandon, as, shaking her hand and raising his topee, he bade her good-evening, as he was going to his own quarters, which were in the opposite direction to her bungalow. So she drove away, and he walked on, pushing some budmashes who stood in his path roughly on one side.

The fakir who was being driven from the town was Rhabdool of Jhansi. The date was the 23rd of April, 1857.

CHAPTER XVI.

A WARM DISCUSSION.

THAT evening Captain Sandon dined at his mess, at which there was an unusual gathering of officers, amongst those present being Colonel Carmichael Smith, commanding the 3rd Light Cavalry. The conversation in the course of the evening turned upon the incident of the fakir; and Captain Sandon, in his usual brusque and pronounced manner when speaking of the natives, expressed his views very forcibly. He did not hesitate to call a spade a spade where the natives were concerned.

"We are far too lenient with these blackguards," he said. "What ought to have been done with that wretched fakir was to hang him in the presence of a general parade of the native regiments. That would have taught them a lesson."

Colonel Smith laughed.

"I doubt it, Sandon," he said. "Violent measures do no good. Besides, I doubt if the fellow made the slightest impression on the soldiers who listened to him."

"And so do I," chimed in another officer.

"You see," began a third, "Sandon's a comparatively new comer. He doesn't know the natives as well as we do."

"Gentlemen, you are like the people who live at

the base of Vesuvius," answered Sandon quietly. " They view the mountain with contempt, and though they know it has caused havoc in the past, they don't believe it will ever do so again. Well, I confess that is a kind of fool's paradise that I've no wish to occupy."

His remark was greeted with laughter, and the iced champagne was circulated more freely.

" By the time you have been in the country another six months," Colonel Smith remarked, " you will have changed your views. You will have discovered by then that these natives are very much like children—humour them a little, and you will get a lot out of them."

" And give them the rod occasionally and they'll obey you better," Sandon replied. " The rod is an excellent corrective for children."

" Not a bit of it," put in a young medical officer named Parker, who was rather fanatical on matters of religion, and who had made himself somewhat notorious by his attempts to proselytize the natives. " Not a bit of it, Sandon," he repeated. " I've seen a lot of India, and a command of the language of the country has enabled me to understand the thoughts and feelings of the inhabitants better than men who cannot converse with them. I maintain that they are a noble-hearted people, and as truly Christian in spirit as we who are professing Christians are. In fact, some of us who call ourselves Christians act and speak as if we were the most violent barbarians. Some men seem to forget that all men are flesh and blood, and the same God made us all—black and white."

This was a severe thrust, and for a moment Sandon flashed an angry glance at the young fellow who had had the boldness to thus beard him, but breaking into a scornful laugh he said, with withering sarcasm—

"Well, all I've got to say is this, you pap-fed Christians have a lot to answer for, and when the tug comes, as come it will sooner or later, I hope you will not hide yourselves away in your feather beds. God helps the man who helps himself, and, for my own part, I have infinitely more faith in dry powder and conical bullets than in the effort of trying to permeate the dense mind of the native with a doctrine which to him must seem ridiculous. My own experience is that men who talk the loudest about their Christianity are generally the greatest cowards, and the least to be depended upon. We want fighting men in India, not preachers of twaddle. This country must be ruled by soldiers, not old women."

The young doctor fairly started in his seat, and a look of insulted pride swept across his pale, insipid, and characterless face. He seemed inclined to make some angry reply, when Colonel Smith interposed—

"Gentlemen, gentlemen, *gentlemen!*" he exclaimed, "we must have no personalities, if you please. "Whatever your respective views are, I think it is better that you express them calmly, otherwise do not express them at all."

"But a man and a soldier must defend himself, Colonel, when he is attacked," replied Sandon in his old pleasant manner.

"I did not attack you, sir," retorted Surgeon

Parker, with a certain violence of expression, and feeling rather small, for he was conscious that he was no match in any way for the burly, handsome Sandon, who was universally admitted to be a magnificent soldier.

"No; your attack was only a fizzle," answered Sandon. "I apologise for having taken you seriously."

"Gentlemen, *gentlemen!*" cried the Colonel again, and holding up his hands as if to deprecate any further discussion on the subject, "this contention really must not go on. Pray restrain your feelings. We all have our own particular views, and each man has the right to think as he likes."

"That is precisely the privilege I'm sticking up for," said Sandon, nothing abashed; "but I like to mete out the measure that is meted to me. However, to go back to the incident of the fakir——"

"No, no, pray let the subject drop," cried several voices.

"As you will, gentlemen; but I was only going to make one remark which may rather astonish you."

Sandon paused, as if disposed, now that he had roused their curiosity, to punish them by keeping them in suspense, but the Colonel said—

"What is it, Sandon? It strikes me we are not easily astonished."

"Do you know what it was the fakir had been telling the soldiers?" asked Sandon.

"No," "No," "No," came as a general answer.

"Well, it was—at any rate, this is what I gathered—that the cartridges served out to the troops here were greased with hog's lard."

M

A roar of laughter ran round the table.

"And do you suppose the natives believed it?' asked Parker somewhat timidly, and yet in a manner that seemed to indicate he thought he had scored a point.

Sandon did not condescend to answer the question direct, but addressing himself to the company said—

"Now, I hold that when the fanatical mind is inflamed with treasonable statements of that kind there is no telling what the result may be. Therefore, I maintain we should have hung the rascal in the presence of all the regiments. It's no use fighting with kid gloves on. When you've got to fight, strip to it, and show your muscle."

"I certainly do think, Sandon, that you take rather an exaggerated view of the situation," said Colonel Smith in a kindly way. "For my own part, I don't believe if all the fakirs in India preached that nonsense that they would get half-a-dozen soldiers to believe them. Of course, we have heard it before, and some dreadful things have been predicted, but the predictions have fallen flat. All the Sepoys know perfectly well that the cartridges have been made regimentally, and that the lubricant used is nothing more dreadful than beeswax and clarified butter."

"In theory that is all right, sir," answered Sandon; "but you must admit that strange murmurs have been heard."

"I believe those murmurs were originated by the pessimistic whites," replied the Colonel.

Little Surgeon Parker laughed loudly, and mumbled

"Hear, hear," for he thought that thrust must lay the dogmatic Sandon low. But not a bit of it. The gallant officer came up smiling again, and still ignoring the very presence of the doctor, he addressed himself to Colonel Smith, and asked—

"Are you disposed, Colonel, to put that to the test?"

"In what way?"

"By having a special parade of your regiment."

"To what end?" asked the Colonel.

"You shall speak to them about the cartridges."

"Yes."

"Point out to them that the fakir lied to-day, and that all the stories they have heard about greased cartridges are lies."

"All right. I follow you."

"Very well. Having read them a sermon, you shall order them to load their rifles with the suspected cartridges."

"And what is likely to come out of that?" asked the Colonel, with an air of scepticism.

"That remains to be seen. If the men obey the order with alacrity, and bite their cartridges without manifesting any suspicion, I will frankly own that I am wrong. If, on the other hand, they refuse, you will give me credit for seeing better through a deal board than you do."

"All right, dear boy," exclaimed Colonel Smith in a genial, laughing way. "This matter shall be put to the test. There shall be a special parade of my regiment to-morrow for platoon exercise, and I am prepared to bet that when we assemble at mess to-morrow evening we shall have the laugh of you, Sandon."

"All right, sir. I shall take my defeat as a man should, but you must not forget that at Dum Dum Barrackpore, and one or two other places, the native soldiers have already shown a mutinous disposition with regard to the rumoured hog's fat in the cart ridges."

"Well, yes; there have been some bobberies in those places, but I believe that the legend about the hog's fat was simply made a peg on which to hang other grievances," replied the Colonel.

"It may be so," returned Sandon, "but you can now put it to the practical test."

"Yes, and I hope you will prove a false prophet,' the Colonel replied, as he sent an order for the orderly officer on duty to come to him, and when the officer arrived the Colonel gave him some instructions and that done, he turned to his brother-officers, and said—

"That bit of business is settled. Special parade to-morrow morning at five o'clock for platoon exercise. And now, gentlemen, what do you say to a final peg? and then I think we may retire, for it's already past ten."

Brandy-and-soda being voted for all round, the khitmurghars proceeded to supply it, and half-an hour later the mess was deserted; and the native servants—who had overheard the conversation, for many of them understood English—collected in little groups, and discussed the prospects of the fateful morrow.

CHAPTER XVII.

THE EIGHTY-FIVE.

THE 24th of April dawned on Meerut with all the splendour of Indian sunrise. Soon after reveille parade was sounded in the quarters of the 3rd Light Cavalry; that was the regiment commanded by the gallant Carmichael Smith, who, in putting his faith in the goodwill of the natives to the test, never dreamed for a moment that evil would come out of it. When the order for the parade had been circulated the night before, none of the men had any idea as to what the object was, nor was it generally known in the station. It was noted that when the men assembled on the parade-ground they did not look cheerful; in fact, in many of the dusky faces there was a sullen, hang-log expression. Captain Sandon, who was present, was quick to observe this, and it seemed to him also that he particularly was an object of fierce looks on the part of some of the men. He was well aware that he was not beloved by the natives. He had been told that by his white soldier servant, who had heard it as common gossip. He had even been anonymously warned that his life was not altogether safe from poison or the assassin's dagger. It testified to his undoubted courage that he was not troubled about this. He had been heard to say that no man could guard against the secret assassin, especially in India, but that if they only gave him a chance he would be able to account for some of his enemies, and it was known that he never went anywhere without being armed with a revolver, which, however, he carried concealed.

"I should say," remarked the gallant Captain, as he and the Colonel rode down the lines together, "that these rascals must have been apprised of your intention."

"What makes you think so?" asked the Colonel.

"The expression of their faces indicates it."

"You are a remarkable fellow for reading signs," remarked the Colonel good-humouredly. "But I don't see how the men could have become aware of my intention unless some of their wonderful seers have warned them."

"Oh, it needed no seers. You forget the servants were present last night during our discussion."

"True, true," muttered the Colonel thoughtfully. "One ought to be more careful."

"Yes, for every native servant is a spy."

"Come, come, that is very severe; I don't quite believe that."

"Well, Colonel, we must agree to differ. Events sooner or later will decide whether I am a true or false prophet."

"I hope you will be proved a false one for all our sakes," said Colonel Carmichael Smith with a laugh, for he really thought, as a good many of his colleagues thought, that Captain Sandon was particularly hard on the natives.

Now, whether it was due to some peculiar instinct, some keener powers of observation than those possessed by his brother-officers, or some other faculty which could not be named, it certainly was a fact that Captain Sandon had for a long time insisted that trouble was coming for India, and he had even gone so far as to advocate the strengthening of all the garrisons. When he last returned from Delhi he loudly censured the laxity which placed the tremendous collection of arms and ammunition in the charge of nine white men only; for he had found that young Lieutenant Willoughby, two other brother-officers, and six non-commissioned officers and privates practically formed the only garrison of the great arsenal. His views, however, were ignored. The usual cry of " Pessimist " was raised, and there the matter ended. But he had given it as his opinion, from what he knew of Willoughby, that that young officer would blow the arsenal to the sky rather than let it fall into the hands of the natives. For this he received an official hint that he was to be a little more guarded in his expressions, and he was told that such an extreme measure as he spoke of could only be justified by a concatenation of circumstances which it was almost impossible could occur in India.

Of course one can always be wise after an event, and it is easy to prophesy when you know; but it is beyond dispute that if more men holding Sandon's views had existed in those days the Mutiny would never have attained the proportions it did. As it was, he had to bear the brunt of a good many sneers, and even some ridicule. Not that men doubted his courage or his soldierly qualities, but he was regarded rather in the light of a chronic grumbler who viewed the natives with unmerited contempt.

He had held his ground, however, and in effect said—

"Wait. Time will prove me right or wrong."

Now, on this brilliant morning as he rode with the Colonel and inspected the men drawn up in columns, he was conscious that in a certain sense he was on his trial.

"You will admit that they are a soldierly-looking lot of fellows," remarked the Colonel after he had inspected his regiment.

"Oh, yes, in looks they are," replied Sandon, "but it must also be admitted they might prove ugly customers if they got the reins. To my mind their fierce looks do not indicate that their hearts are bursting with love for us."

The Colonel made no answer to this remark, but proceeded to put his men through certain exercises, having previously harangued them on the absurdity of the reports about the greased cartridges. Then came the crucial test for which every one in the secret had been waiting. The soldiers were ordered to load their carbines. All the men of the regiment complied with the command with the exception of eighty-five. These eighty-five stood sullen and silent. Again was the order given to them. Still they remained motionless. Their eyes glowed with excitement. Even their dark faces seemed to take on a certain paleness. Captain Sandon, who sat on his horse like a statue in front of the mutinous body of men, expressed no sense of exultation that it was at last proved he was no false prophet. Some men might have exulted, but he did not. He knew too well what a terribly serious business it was. Eighty-five soldiers on parade had refused to obey the orders of their superior officers. That was an open act of mutiny. It was really the first public display of the smouldering fire, at any rate in that part of India. If one or two or even half-a-dozen men had refused, it would have been a small matter, and regarded as having no special significance. But here were eighty-five of them, eighty-five troopers of an important cavalry regiment, a formidable body to show a mutinous spirit in presence of their comrades, the general spectators and budmashes, who had collected in unusual crowds, as if they had had some intimation of what was going to happen.

The face of Colonel Smith wore a look of anxiety that was quite foreign to it, and there was not an officer present who did not regard the business as serious.

A brief consultation of the officers took place. Then the recalcitrant eighty-five were ordered to ride forward twelve yards from the ranks, and form in line. For a moment or two they showed a disposition to disobey that order, until a few of the number complied. Then the others followed suit. The muster-roll was called, and as each man answered to his name it was written down. It was remarked that the native officers seemed inclined to keep in the background, as if they secretly sympathized with the mutineers. As soon as all the names had been taken the bugle sounded, the regiment was dismissed from parade and trotted back to quarters, and the parade thus came to an abrupt termination.

That evening when the British officers assembled at mess there was an absence of the convivial feeling which had distinguished them the previous night, and Dr. Parker did not put in an appearance at all. If Captain Sandon had displayed an exultant spirit he surely would have been justified, but he did nothing of the kind, and he made no allusion to the event of the day until the Colonel himself broached the subject, which he did when the dessert was placed on the table, and having first taken the precaution to send all the native servants out of the room, and place a sentry on duty at the door.

" Sandon," he said, " I think that in a certain way we owe you an apology. At any rate, we must give you the credit of having seen what we did not see ; and what, perhaps, we were even unwilling to see. But facts are facts, and cannot be winked at. This is a serious business whichever way we look at it. I honestly confess I did not think there was such a widespread spirit of discontent ; and, without wishing in any way to pose as an alarmist, I look with concern on this public display of disobedience. Of course, an example will have to be made of the eighty-five men, and I only hope that the matter will end there."

" I echo that hope," said Sandon, " but I also hope there will be no squeamishness, no Christian sentimentality, shown in this business. The slightest sign of weakness on our part at this juncture will be fatal. It must not be forgotten that we have to deal with an Eastern people, and in their case the French proverb *L'audace et toujours l'audace* applies with remarkable force. Nothing impresses Orientals so much as promptness in striking. We have our prestige to maintain, our honour to uphold. But we have to do even more than that; we have to let these native soldiers see that though they outnumber us twenty to one we have no fear of them; that behind us are all the resources of the Company; that behind the Company is the tremendous power of England. Gentlemen," he added solemnly, "we stand face to face with a crisis. It remains to be seen how we shall deal with it."

"Although it is serious enough," remarked the Colonel, "I don't think that all the resources of the Company will be called for; and certainly England will not be required to put forth her might. These mutineers will be punished, and the punishment will prove salutary."

"Yes, if you publicly hang every one of the black-guards," answered Sandon, with a look of stern determination flashing from his eyes.

"Oh, come, come, Sandon; that would be carrying severity to an extreme," exclaimed one of his brother-officers.

"Not in the case of Orientals," replied Sandon firmly. "It might seem so in the minds of arm-chair-and-carpet-slipper politicians, who sit at home at ease, and are as ignorant of the world generally, and human nature in particular, as sucking babes; but we are soldiers. Soldiering is a stern business. The many conflicting elements of our armies are held together and wedded by discipline. Once relax discipline, or once let any number of the atoms composing the great whole think they can set it at defiance, and then fire, slaughter, and chaos will come. If I were in command I would hang every one of these rascals who have disobeyed orders to-day. Then, while they were still swinging on their gibbets, I would assemble all the native regiments, and say—'Now then, do any more of you want to be hanged? If so, just step forward, and we will accommodate you.'"

This remark was greeted with laughter; and yet somehow the laughter did not seem spontaneous; certainly it was not hearty. Perhaps every man present felt at that moment that for once he was inclined to agree with the pugnacious Captain.

"You may laugh, gentlemen," said Sandon, with something like a sneer on his handsome face, "but depend upon it that though the remedy I propose may seem drastic, it is the proper one. I will tell you rather a curious thing. When I was in Cawnpore last year I was Nana Sahib's guest at Bithoor. He had given a *fête* in honour of something or somebody, and, of course, as all his *fêtes* are, it was a very swell affair. In a conversation I had with him he referred to the Crimean War, and he said he had been credibly informed our power had been so weakened by the struggle with the Russians that it would be years before we could recover. I did not attach much importance to the remark at the time, but thinking over it afterwards it made a great impression on me, and I thought if that idea was held generally by the natives of India it might mean trouble for us. Now, I am one of those who have never bowed the knee to this wealthy Nana. He gave me the impression that he was a wily serpent, who some day might turn and sting his benefactors. And my own belief is, when he gave utterance to that remark the wish was father to the thought. I feel sure that Nana Sahib wears a mask, and that in his black heart sits a devil."

There was a general dissent from this view, and as the discussion seemed likely to wax warm, the Colonel put an end to it by suggesting cards, which were indulged in until an early hour of the morning, when the company broke up. On the following day Captain Sandon took the first opportunity to call on Mrs. Pritchard. He found her, Hester, and the two children in the drawing-room. With shouts of delight the children rushed forward to greet him, for they were very fond of him, and he was fond of them. On one occasion some brother-officers who had dropped in unexpectedly found him down on all fours in the verandah, with a string in his mouth, and the two children sitting on his back shrieking with delight, as they made believe he was a horse. No wonder, therefore, that he was a favourite with them, and no wonder that their proud mother was fond of him, for if you want to win your way into a woman's heart, show kindness to her children.

Both Hester and her sister were very glad to see the gallant Captain now, and Hester was full of the picnic and the way she had enjoyed herself, and presently when the conversation on this and sundry other commonplace topics had exhausted itself, Mrs. Pritchard said—

"This is very serious news, Captain Sandon, about the mutinous conduct of the men of the 3rd Light Cavalry."

"Yes, it is rather serious," he answered smilingly, as he allowed the children to rifle his pockets.

"What is to be done, do you know?" queried the lady.

" Oh, yes ; there is to be an inquiry held."

" And they will be court-martialled, I suppose ? "

" Without a doubt, I should think."

" And what then ? "

" Ah, that remains to be seen."

" I don't think they would have much chance if you were their judge, Captain," said Hester slyly.

He laughed as he answered—

" I don't think they would, Miss Dellaby." Then, as if he wished to turn the conversation, he began to whistle a lively air to the children, who were sitting straddle-legged on his knees.

" I wis, Taptain Sandon," said little Amy, " that you and papa wouldn't be nasty soldiers, but always stop at home and play horses wiff us."

" Oh, oh, oh," he laughed. You call me a nasty soldier, do you ? Now, I won't come and see you again."

" Oh, yes, you will," said the boy, " because Auntie Hester's here, and you'll come to see her, because you like her."

" Don't be rude, Freddy," exclaimed Mrs. Pritchard, while Hester's face reddened a little. " If you make remarks of that kind," continued his mother, " you will have to go to bed."

After a little more romping, which Sandon seemed to enjoy quite as much as the youngsters, Mrs. Pritchard said—

" Hetty dear, would you mind giving the chicks a run in the garden ? "

Now, whether Hester was really glad to get away, or whether she guessed that her sister wished to have some private conversation with the Captain or not, she jumped up with alacrity, and exclaiming,

"Come on, Babs," she took the children's hands and ran off with them to get their hats.

Then Mrs. Pritchard dropped some needlework she was doing, and, looking her visitor full in the face, said—

"Captain Sandon, I think I must have become nervous of late, and it takes very little to upset me. This affair of the parade has given me quite a shock. Now, I want you to tell me honestly if you think there is any danger of a general rising? If so, I would at once send Hetty and the children off to our friends the Sutcliffes, in Calcutta."

"And why would you not accompany them?" he asked.

"Because my place is at my husband's side. I am a soldier's wife."

"Nobly spoken," he answered, and his face was unusually thoughtful. "But really, Mrs. Pritchard, you place a terrible responsibility on my shoulders. Supposing I advised you to adopt that course, and nothing happened, I should be laughed at all over the station as an alarmist; and supposing I say stay, and an outbreak occurs, you would severely blame me for having counselled you. I do wish you had not put the question to me, but as you have done so, this is my answer—you should be guided entirely by your husband's advice."

"But I want to know what you think," she urged, with womanly persistency.

He remained silent for some moments, and played with the tassels on the hilt of his sword in a pre-occupied way. Then suddenly jumping to his feet, he exclaimed—

" I confess, Mrs. Pritchard, you have cornered me ; but I will not take the responsibility of advising you one way or the other. I would suggest, however, that if you are really nervous, you might send your sister and the children away until after the mutineers have been tried, and their sentence, whatever it may be, has been carried out. If there is to be a rising, it will be when the fellows are sent to prison. But once the shackles are on them, and the prison doors have closed behind them, I think all will be well. Nevertheless, I must repeat I think your husband is the person whose advice you should seek."

" But he is away."

" Yes ; but I suppose he will be coming back soon ?"

" I had a letter from him yesterday, and he said he thought he might be detained somewhat longer than he anticipated, and that probably he would not be able to get back until the end of the first fortnight in May."

The Captain rose to go. Mrs. Pritchard also rose, and said in an appealing way to him—

" Of course, Captain, you won't say anything in the station about my fears. Very likely they are groundless and foolish, but I am a mother and have a mother's anxiety."

" You can rely upon my not doing so," he answered as he shook her hand.

As he went through the garden towards the road he came upon Hester and the children. The latter rushed to him at once, and clung to his knees, saying they didn't intend to let him go. After affecting to have a desperate struggle with them, he got free, and spoke a few words to Hester, and as he held her hand, and thinking he was unobserved — for Freddy was trying to kill with a piece of stick he had a small centipede that was crawling across the garden path, and Amy was looking on—he pressed her fingers to his lips. The act did not not escape the sharp eyes of little Amy, who shrieked after him as he ran away—" Oh, I saw oo kissing Tantie Hetty's hand."

CHAPTER XVIII.

OF course the mutinous conduct of the eighty-five troopers was the subject of general conversation throughout Meerut, and the opinions expressed were many and varied. It is a fact, however, that amongst the officers, from General Hewett, commanding the division, down to the humblest sub., the feeling was that while in a military sense the rebellious disobedience of the troopers was serious enough, it was not seriousness from a political point of view. It need hardly be said here that Captain Sandon was not included amongst those who thought in that way.

As soon as the affair was officially reported at headquarters, a court of inquiry was ordered. This was composed of all the principal Europeans and some of the native officers. This court at once got to work. Every man of the eighty-five malcontents was separately examined and questioned as to his motives for refusing to use his cartridges. The answer was almost the same in each case. He believed that hog's fat had been used as the lubricant. The men were reminded, however, that over and over again had they been assured that there was not the shadow of foundation for the suspicion. But to this they replied that they did not believe those

tatements, for they had been told by fakirs and
thers that the English intended to destroy the caste
f the natives, and degrade them all to one common
evel. These fellows were pressed to give in the
ames of the fakirs and others who had spread the
eports, but they resolutely declined to do so, and as
hey had no better excuse to offer for their conduct,
hey were ordered for court-martial, and were con-
eyed to prison.

It is a singular commentary on the way things
vere managed in those days that the prisoners were
ommitted entirely to the care of native guards.
And it is no less singular that the guards should
ave consented to have acted in that capacity
vithout taking advantage of it. But the fact is,
here was a want of cohesion amongst the natives
hen. They were burning and chafing to rise and
trike a mighty blow for their freedom from the
oreign yoke, but fear of the consequences held them
 back. The shadow of "The Great White Hand" *
oomed over them, and if the authorities had shown
nore judgment, more sternness, if there had been
nore Captain Sandons, there would have been no
nutiny; but it was when subsequent events drove
he men to madness, and subsequent folly gave them
he game into their own hands, that an electric thrill
an through their ranks, and with a roar their swords
eapt simultaneously from the scabbards, and the
eign of blood was inaugurated.

* The natives were in the habit of describing the power
f the British as " A Great White Hand " that stretched
orth and grasped everything.

No time was lost in getting the court-martial into working order, and that done the trial of the mutineers commenced. A feeling was manifested at first that it would be better to endeavour to single out four or five, or even more, of the men as ring-leaders, and make an example of them. But it was found impossible to do this, for no man had made himself more prominent than another. Either they were all innocent or all guilty in equal degree. There could be no nice shade of distinction drawn. If number one was pronounced guilty, then number eighty-five was just as guilty. It was on this basis the court-martial proceeded, and with all the solemnity of a military tribunal constituted to try men for as grave an offence almost as any that a soldier could commit. The Court heard the evidence against the prisoners. Nothing could have been clearer; and against it there was no evidence to oppose save the ridiculous contention about the fat; and when everything had been urged that could be urged in favour of the mutineers, the Court considered its verdict, and when the president had addressed them with all the weight of powerful argument and warning admonition, he pronounced upon them a sentence of ten years imprisonment.

The sentence was received in hushed silence. The culprits looked surprised, and they exchanged glances with each other, but not a man spoke. As condemned felons now they were marched back to gaol, still under native guard. But the formalities were not yet completed. The finding of the Court before it could become law had to be confirmed by the commanding officer—that is, General Hewett. When it came before him that officer did not hesitate to say he considered the punishment too severe. The argument that most other European nations would have shot the prisoners had no weight with him. His sympathies were clearly with the natives, and he did not attempt to disguise the fact. The result was, he reduced the sentence in the case of many of the younger soldiers to five years.

There for the moment the matter rested, as before the actual punishment could begin the sentence would have to be read out to the prisoners before the whole of the assembled garrison. And the date for doing that was fixed for the 9th of May.

Opinions as to the sentence were very much divided. While some said it was too lenient, others said it was too severe, and others were found who entirely agreed with it. It is not difficult to guess upon which side Captain Sandon ranged himself. He was bold enough to say that the sentence was ridiculous. He denounced it as a namby-pamby one, and he argued that it wasn't by such grandmotherly means that our forefathers had won India.

During the days that intervened he was frequently at Colonel Pritchard's house, and he made anxious inquiries as to when his friend the Colonel was likely to return. Mrs. Pritchard's fears, whatever they were, had evidently been allayed, for her spirits had recovered their usual buoyancy, and she was full of plans for the future. She was one who considered that the sentence passed upon the mutineers was adequate, and that it would deter any malcontents from following suit. In common with her husband, she had great faith in General Hewett. She believed that his judgment could not err, and that he was equal to any emergency that might arise.

Hester, of course, was too new a comer to feel any concern. That is, she did not understand the matter and, like all people who are ignorant of danger, she had no fear. Her views were best expressed in the following remark which she made when she heard what the sentence was—

" What a dreadful punishment, to be sure, for such a simple thing as some soldiers refusing to put bullets in their guns when they were told. Why, I should have thought that a week's imprisonment would have been quite enough."

This view was, of course, the result of inability to appreciate the gravity of the offence, and its significance as a sign of the times. Nor did she understand that an open act of mutiny either in the navy or the army was considered to be a very heinous thing while the slightest toleration of anything approaching disobedience to just orders would soon make discipline impossible, and that enormous bodies of men banded together for a common cause, and subject to the commands of their leaders, could only be kept in hand by the very sternest discipline.

It was well, perhaps, for her that she did not view the matter just then in any graver light, for she was saved a great deal of anxiety. It may be supposed Captain Sandon did not say anything to alarm her. He became more assiduous in his attentions, and though he did not talk to her in the language of love, he manifested in the most unmistakable way that she occupied a large share of his thoughts. On one evening, however, as he sat alone with her on the verandah, while Mrs. Pritchard was engaged in seeing her little ones tucked snugly in their beds, he allowed his feelings to so far carry him away, that he exclaimed impulsively—

" Hester, I am getting awfully fond of you."

" But you mustn't get fond of me," she answered quickly. " I belong to another."

He sighed, and was silent for some moments ; then asked—

" Have you ever heard from him since you have been here ? "

" Never a word," she answered sorrowfully.

" And you have no idea where he is ? "

" No, except that he is in Persia."

" Yes, I know that ; but Persia is as vague as if one said I have a friend in India. India is a vast place."

" Well, I can tell you no more," Hester remarked sadly. " He wrote and told me he was going out with his regiment."

" Is it not just a little strange that he has never communicated with you ? "

This question was put in such a pointed way that the girl was quite startled. She had written to him, and told him she was going to her sister at Meerut. If his love for her was as strong as he had wished her to believe, why had he not sent her a few comforting lines ? Then suddenly she accounted for his silence by the probability that he had not received her letter; but that again begot the dreadful thought that he, still thinking her false, had recklessly exposed himself to danger and had thrown his life away.

Although by no means unduly sentimental, she ould not restrain her emotion as these things flashed through her brain, and tears flowing down her cheeks, she used her handkerchief in a way that indicated to Sandon that she was weeping. Otherwise he would not have known, as for some reason or other the usual verandah lamp had not been lighted.

"Why, you don't mean to say these are real tears, Miss Dellaby?" he said, as he leaned forward and laid his hand on her hand.

"Oh, it's nothing," she answered peevishly, as if ashamed of herself. "A stupid sentimental fit, I suppose. Pray excuse me for a few minutes."

She rose with the intention of going into the house, but he rose at the same moment, and clasping her wrist, he murmured—

"Love does make us sentimental. I know it makes me so. Ah, Hester, if you would only give me some hope! Why should you sigh for a shadow when the substance is at hand?"

She released herself from him with quite an angry gesture, and said warmly—

"You must not talk to me like that, sir. I won't listen to you. You are betraying the confidence I repose in you, and it isn't fair."

Mrs. Pritchard arrived on the verandah just in time to witness the last of this little scene, and as Hester swept by her into the house she said in astonishment to Captain Sandon—

"I hope you young people have not been quarrelling?"

"Oh dear, no," exclaimed the Captain. "It takes two to make a quarrel, Mrs. Pritchard, and I am not in the least likely to quarrel with your sister."

"Then I suppose Hetty is in one of her tantrums. But you must take no notice of that, Captain. It's the privilege of girls, you know. It's a kind of mental tonic to them, and they are all the better for it."

Sandon laughed, and after a little more desultory conversation he took his leave, saying he had promised to dine with some friends.

Later on in the evening, Mrs. Pritchard said to her sister—

"Hetty, you are a stupid girl. I declare you treat Captain Sandon as if he were a school-boy. I do wish you would make yourself agreeable."

Hester was hurt at the tone her sister adopted, and she could not help answering—

"It seems to me, Madge, that you are disposed to treat *me* as if I were a child. The fact is, all the family seem to misunderstand me. I dare say if you will leave me and Captain Sandon alone, we shall get on very well together; but, pray, don't nag at me. I can't stand it."

"There, forgive me, dear," said Madge tenderly. "I didn't mean to hurt your feelings, but you know poor Sandon is dreadfully spooney about you, and you ought to have some regard for his feelings."

Hester sighed, but held her peace, and Madge thought to herself—

"Things are going on well, and Sandon may congratulate himself."

Two days after this conversation between the sisters, a letter came for Hester. When Mrs.

Pritchard opened the mail bag that morning she found this letter, and she was struck by the fact that it bore the Jhansi postmark. The address was in a man's handwriting. When Hester appeared at the breakfast-table, Mrs. Pritchard asked—

"Who do you know in Jhansi, Hetty?"

"In Jhansi? I don't know anybody in Jhansi."

"Well, here is a letter for you from that place any way."

She handed the letter across the table as she spoke, and as soon as Hester's eyes lighted on the super-scription the blood rushed into her face, for she recognized the handwriting of John Hallett. She seized the letter in a confused way, and thrusting it into her pocket, hurriedly stammered out—

"Oh, yes ; I know who it's from."

Madge's suspicions were aroused, but she deemed it prudent to say nothing at that juncture. She watched her sister narrowly, though. She saw that she was absent-minded, that she ate no breakfast; and as soon as she could do so Hester made an excuse and hurried away to her room.

"This is strange," mused Mrs. Pritchard. "Can it be possible that Hetty is deceiving me? I must look into this matter."

The date of that day was the 8th of May.

CHAPTER XIX.

As soon as Hester was alone she sank down on to a chair, and for some moments held the precious letter without daring to open it. Her heart beat violently, her temples throbbed; she was feverish with excitement. This letter was far more to her at that stage than all the burning questions that were vexing the souls of natives and Europeans alike throughout India. The one she only understood as a vague and abstract principle; the other, that is, her lover's letter, was a concrete and solid fact. If there should be a tendency to condemn her for what may be considered frivolity and selfishness in the presence of momentous imperial matters, let it not be forgotten that we gauge things by our own sensations, and that our views of life are determined by the circumstances which more directly affect us. For months poor Hester had been able to think of little else save the love episode which had exercised such a powerful influence upon her, and had changed so thoroughly the current of her life's stream. But for that episode she would never have been in India; and, being in India, she now, after weary waiting and sickening suspense, held a letter in her hand from the man in whom she had built up her faith—in whom she had placed her trust—and who seemed to her, from her woman's standpoint, her heaven-appointed destiny.

That letter, by the postmark, had been posted in Jhansi, and Jhansi was within three days' ride of where she was then.

At last she opened the letter, and with greedy eyes read what follows :—

" *The Fort, Jhansi,*
May 3, 1857.

" MY BELOVED GIRL,

" Your letter, which overtook me at Alexandria, was like a reprieve to a man cast for death. Physical death, especially on the field of honour, I do not think I have much fear of—but to suffer a living death, just as one has commenced to live, to see one's hopes crushed, one's ambition mocked, is more than I could stand ; and when I left England it was with a heart as heavy as lead, and full of a great recklessness that made me indifferent to everything. But your letter showed me that I had misjudged you, that I had been blind and foolish. I had allowed my faith in you to be too easily shaken. I had jumped to a conclusion which might have been averted had I paused to reflect, had I taken the trouble to inquire. The consequence was, that when far away from you I learnt what a mistake I had made—learnt it when the ocean rolled between us. You remember what you wrote. These were your words—' You have deemed me false ; you shall prove me true. I am going to India to my sister, who is at Meerut. Perhaps, as time moves on, we shall meet. Don't think me weak. Don't despise me when I say you have carried my heart off, and since I cannot live without it I must seek it.' Such were your words, Hetty. You were going to seek your heart which I held. It was a romantic quest, perhaps, but love led the way; and yet our paths lay widely apart. It was true we were both journeying to the East, but I was going to a land where a fierce struggle was being waged, and by the fortunes of war I might never see you again. Up to the moment of receiving your brief note I had been burning with enthusiasm; I was filled with martial ardour; I wanted to be in the thickest of the fight, to seek a reputation even at the cannon's mouth; I was stirred by the recklessness begotten by wounded pride and unrequited love. Your letter, however, changed all that, and I resolved to go where you were, even though I compromised my good name to do it. I carried out that resolve, and to some extent my good name was compromised. But love overruled every other consideration, and though in a sense I placed myself in a terribly false position, it has been the means of bringing me within a short journey of you, and in a few days I hope to hold you in my arms again. A few days! What a short space of time in reality, and yet how long to a lover! Think kindly of me, dear one, and should you hear me spoken ill of, hold your peace, but rest assured that what I have done I have done for your sweet sake. In a few days I shall apply to the commanding officer for a week's leave, and run over to Meerut to see you. In the meantime dispatch me a few lines to tell me that your heart still yearns for me as I yearn for you. With all the love that a true man can give to a woman,

"I am, yours always,

"JACK HALLETT."

If Hester had been excited before reading this letter, her feelings afterwards may be better imagined than described. She well understood now how Jack had " disgraced " himself on the passage out. It was part of his scheme to get to her, and whatever others might do, she was prepared to condone everything for the sake of the love he bore her and she bore for him. She agreed with him that a few days seemed a long time when love was yearning for its object, but she consoled herself that the time would speed, then would come the great reward for the misunderstanding and the weary waiting. And she made a resolution that when Jack came, if her sister did not choose to make herself agreeable to him, she would go away. She knew not where she would go to, nor what she would do. She was content to leave that knotty point for Jack to settle. At any rate he was lord of her heart, and every other consideration and every one else must give way to him. If her friends and relatives refused to see him as she saw him, that was their affair, and they must settle it with their own consciences. She was fully prepared and no less determined to take her fate in her own hands, whether it was for good or ill. She was her father's daughter, and her father was a man of iron will when occasion required. She had come thousands of miles in the carrying out of her purpose, and now that her lover was within hail of her—and she knew that he was true—she was not going to be baulked of her triumph.

However, in a few days she would know what course to take. If her sister acknowledged Jack,

well and good. If she did not, then whatever
rupture occurred would be due entirely to her own
perversity.

In a few days!

Little did Hester dream what momentous events
were to happen in that brief space of time, and how
blood, fire, and slaughter would fill the land, and how
the man who was her life and hope would be in the
hands of a pitiless foe.

All unconscious of the great shadow that was
already darkening the sun, she filled page after
page with love's burning language, and when she
had finished her letter, she sealed it, and addressed
it to Lieutenant Hallett at Jhansi, and afraid to
trust it to any other hands, she went forth herself
and dropped it into the post. She quite anticipated
that she would have to submit to a rigid catechising
on the part of her sister, who would not rest satisfied
until she had found out who the mysterious correspondent was at Jhansi. But, as a matter of fact,
Madge was so fully occupied with other things that
it quite slipped her memory. She had heard from
her husband at Delhi, who told her that he expected
to return in the course of a week, and incidentally he
added—

" I find the people here are rather excited about
the cartridge business at Meerut, and some uneasiness
is expressed as to the probable consequence of the
punishment inflicted on the mutineers. I have even
heard an opinion expressed that the whole of the
eighty-five malcontents should have been hanged
outright, after the formality of a drumhead court-
martial. I really have no patience with people who

express these views. To endeavour to rule the natives with a high hand is a mistake. Gentleness, forbearance, and brotherly love are what are required. My own view is that the sentence passed upon the stupid fellows who refused to load their carbines is outrageous, and I am glad to learn that General Hewett has had the courage to reduce in many cases the sentence of the court-martial.

"By the way, I met a man here the other day—a Mr. Griffith, who is something in the department of the Chief Commissioner, and is up here in connection with some property dispute—who knows Sandon's family very well. He says the Sandons are excellent people, and there is a great deal of money in the family. He speaks very highly of Captain Sandon, and quite anticipates that he will distinguish himself. I hope Hetty is treating him kindly, and that he and she will utimately pair off. I like the fellow, although there are a good many things we do not agree upon. Say kindly things to him for me, and tell Hetty to be a good child."

Apart from this letter, Madge had also been asked to take her sister that evening to an informal gathering of friends at the house of Mrs. Sandling, the wife of Major Sandling, of the 6th Dragoon Guards. Mrs. Sandling had a friend who had come over from Lucknow for a day or two; this friend was a very brilliant musician, and Mrs. Sandling thought that a musical evening would be a treat to her acquaintances in the station, hence the gathering, and in sending the "chit" of invitation to Mrs. Pritchard, she added, with womanly artfulness—

"I have asked Captain Sandon to look in. He is

such an awfully nice fellow, that I think half the unmarried girls in Meerut are wild about him."

Madge smiled as she read this. She could take a hint as well as most people, and she knew that Mrs. Sandling had noticed the attention the handsome Captain had paid to Hester. Therefore the reference to him in the note was not without meaning.

"I've got an invitation for you for this evening, Hetty," said Madge, as they sat at tiffin. "It's quite an informal affair. There is to be a little gathering at Mrs. Sandling's house. She has a lady staying with her from Lucknow who is a wonderful musician, I believe. I understand that Captain Sandon is to be there."

Hester was not slow to gather the meaning of this reference to Sandon, but she made no comment. She deemed it better until her lover came from Jhansi to allow the little deception to be kept up. It did no harm, so far as she could see, and it saved her some annoyance. She didn't dislike Sandon, and he enjoyed his mild flirtations with her. Therefore she didn't think it worth while to set people by the ears and cause unpleasantness. She recognized very clearly now that she must play her own cards, and that the game was a waiting one if she wished to win.

Mrs. Sandling was one of those small-minded busy-bodies to be found in every community. She had time for everybody's affairs, but none for her own. When a stranger came to the station she made it her business to find out all about him, and with that petty feminine spite peculiar to some women, she seemed to take delight in setting scandal rolling.

The most trivial bit of gossip was sufficient for this lady to make a mountain out of. Hardly any reputation, in fact, was safe from the venom of her foolish tongue. But she erred more with her head than heart, for she was a generous creature enough, and had been known to display acts of heroic self-devotion in cases of sickness and trouble. She could not resist, however, "poking her nose," as the saying is, into everybody's affairs, while tittle-tattle and scandal were as the breath of her nostrils to her. She had noticed the flirtations, or what she considered the flirtations, of Sandon and Hester, and she felt it was time she had a say in the matter, hence the reason she had invited the young couple to her house that evening.

Mrs. Sandling was a commonplace woman. Pretty enough as far as mere looks went, but it was the prettiness of a wax doll. She hadn't an original idea in her head, and her conversation was always mere chatter. Dress, jewellery, and parsons were her weakness, and she was in the habit of telling her friends with a sigh that she had made a mistake in marrying a soldier, for she was sure she was intended for a clergyman's wife.

Although she was by no means on familiar terms of acquaintance with Hester, she kissed her gushingly when she arrived, and exclaimed—

"I *am* so glad, dear, that you have come. It would have been so dull without *you*. And I was *sure* you would be glad to meet Captain Sandon, so I have asked *him* to be here. Of course I *suppose* it will come to an engagement, if there is *not* one already. But take my advice, dear, be careful. A girl with a reputation cannot be *too* careful. Mind you, I know *nothing* against the Captain, though I have been trying to find out *all* about him. These handsome fellows, you know, are generally *devils*. I used to be quite afraid of handsome men when I was a *girl*. They are so run after by the girls that they become perfectly *heartless*. However, I dare say Sandon will turn out all right, but take *my* advice, dear, do not marry him until you are *perfectly* satisfied there is nothing against him."

Thus the silly woman rattled on. She had a peculiar habit of emphasizing certain words, and she always spoke with the air of one who considered herself an oracle who couldn't go wrong.

Miss Dellaby was disgusted. She could hardly fail to be so, and, without wishing to enter into any discussion, she deemed it necessary to say emphatically—

"I assure you, Mrs. Sandling, you are wrong in supposing that there is or is likely to be any engagement between me and Captain Sandon——"

" My *dear* child," cried the lady, with an expression of injured innocence on her face, " I *have* eyes to see with."

" But I am afraid you do not always use them," answered Hester severely, though she regretted having made the remark as soon as it was uttered.

"Oh, well, perhaps *not*," returned Mrs. Sandling, with evident annoyance. " Still I am not so blind as *some* people *might* imagine. All I've got to say is *this*—if *you* are not gone on Captain Sandon the *Captain* is gone on *you*. But take *my* advice, Miss

Dellaby, don't *pledge* yourself to him until you know *all* his history. Men *are* such deceivers."

"I am not likely to pledge myself; at the same time, I am bound to say I believe Captain Sandon to be a perfect gentleman, and the soul of honour."

Mrs. Sandling burst into laughter, and tapping Hester's shoulder with her fan, she said—

"There *that* remark settles it. You've lost your *head* to the Captain, and, of course, your *heart* will follow. But *do* be careful, dear. Men are *all* alike. They are as *dangerous* as cobras."

With these words the fussy little woman ran away to attend to some of her other guests, much to the relief of Hester, who would infinitely have preferred to have been alone with her thoughts, and to have read and re-read again that precious letter from Jhansi. The people who were generally found at Mrs. Sandling's social gatherings were not the most interesting people in the station, for her propensities to tattle caused her to be rather shunned. The men voted her a bore, and the women were severe enough to say in confidence to each other that she was a mischief-maker, and nobody's reputation was safe where she had to do with it.

Hester was not sorry, therefore, when later on in the evening Captain Sandon came to her and asked her if she would care for a walk in the garden, which was illuminated for the occasion with Chinese lanterns. She readily complied with the request, for the night was torrid, and the heat of the rooms intolerable. The cooler air of the garden was most refreshing, and the brilliancy of the moon and the stars that glittered in the cloudless sky imparted a marvellous, almost weird beauty to the scene. Myriads of fireflies scintillated amongst the foliage, and somewhere from a clump of palms came the delicious liquid notes of the bul-bul.*

"It's a glorious night for a walk," said the Captain, as he offered his arm to his companion, "and a perfect night for love-making."

"It is," answered Hester absent-mindedly, her thoughts being then at Jhansi, and she clasped her hands about the proffered arm.

Sandon interpreted this in his own favour, and he laid his hand on her hands, and for some minutes they strolled in silence along the garden paths. He was unusually quiet, unusually thoughtful, but at last he spoke, and his words indicated the channel of his thoughts.

"Do you know, Miss Dellaby, I had a curious dream two nights ago."

"Indeed! What was it? Pleasant or unpleasant?"

"I thought the natives had risen against us, and we were beleaguered in this place. My whole anxiety was about you. There was some desperate fighting, and I succeeded in cutting my way out, and carrying you off on horseback. In return for this you promised to become my wife, and at that point I woke."

Hester laughed, and answered—

"Dreams always go by the contrary, you know."

"I have no faith in dreams," he returned, "but I confess frankly I think there is trouble brewing for

* The Indian nightingale.

us. I am a soldier, and my duty is here, and I must take my chance amidst the fortunes of war. In your case, however, there is no reason why you should be exposed to peril; and if there is danger, why not avoid it?"

"How?" she asked, showing a lively interest.

"By going away for a few weeks. Your sister told me that you have some friends in Calcutta. Why don't you go down to them, and take the dear children with you?"

Hester shook with an involuntary little shudder as she replied—

"Captain Sandon, I am sure you are not the man to lightly hint at danger. Your words, therefore, alarm me. It would be an awful thing if anything should happen to the darling children, and if I thought there was any real peril I would go for their sake; but you know, Captain, what they say about you in the station. You are called an alarmist. Now, are you *quite* sure that your fears in the present instance are justified?"

He shrugged his shoulders, and laughed lightly.

"It is not pleasant to have that reputation. I know what people say about me, but the fact is, I have not been here long enough for my faith in the natives to grow. I have been betrayed into speaking to you to-night as I have done, from no concern for myself. I only hope I may have the chance of avenging my brother's murder; but I am concerned for you because I—I—love you."

"Hush, you must not say that. You mustn't say you love me."

"Well, call it by any name you like, but it is love

all the same. Now, will you consider my suggestion?"

"Yes; and if in a few days you still hold the same
views, and there are any prominent signs of danger,
I will speak to my sister. But to-morrow, as I
understand, the eighty-five mutineers are to be
publicly manacled, and sent away to fulfil their
sentences. After that is done we may hear no
more of discontent amongst the native soldiers."

"No, perhaps not," replied Sandon thoughtfully,
"if we carry out our duty firmly and sternly. But I
am afraid we shall not do that. There are too many
jelly-headed people in the station. The natives don't
love us, and yet the jelly-heads want to make us
believe that they do. Some spirit of great unrest
is at present at work, and I am convinced that if we
show signs of weakness we shall be in for a fight. I
am speaking plainly to you because I wish you to
thoroughly understand the situation. And the very
love I bear you induces me to wish that you should
not be placed in any risk by remaining here. In
Calcutta there is safety. Here there may possibly be
danger."

Hester did not reply, but her mind was agitated.
She was troubled with many conflicting thoughts,
and while this man had risen largely in her esteem,
she was thinking of, and concerned about, her lover
at Jhansi.

They had approached the house, and as they
ascended the steps to the verandah Mrs. Sandling
confronted them. She had missed them, and had
come out to look for them.

"You *dreadful* young people," she exclaimed, with

a laugh of triumph, "can you not reserve your *spooning* for another time, and give us the benefit of your company."

Hester blushed deeply red, for she divined what was passing in Mrs. Sandling's mind. That lady evidently thought that she had found her out in a falsehood. She saw Hester's confusion, and added—

"There, there, child, don't look so sheepish. Love is a very natural thing, you know. Captain Sandon, I congratulate you. Miss Dellaby is one of the most *charming* young women I have *ever* known."

Hester was indignant and the Captain furious with this meddlesome woman, but they had no chance of giving expression to their thoughts, for a number of ladies and gentlemen came on to the verandah to enjoy the beauty of the night and the cooler air, and Hester left her companion to go and talk with the ladies.

CHAPTER XX.

THE 9th of May dawned hot and sultry on the Meerut station. It was a day big with the fate of an empire, and even those persons who affected to have no concern secretly wished that the day was well over, and the condemned eighty-five safely interned. Then it was thought one would be able to breathe freely again. At a very early hour the bugles began to speak, and when breakfast was finished parade was sounded, and the whole garrison turned out to witness the remarkable event. History was to be made that day, and the most confirmed optimist knew it.

The 3rd Bengal Light Cavalry—the offending regiment—dismounted on this occasion, were marched to the parade-ground with the eighty-five prisoners amongst them. Only ninety men in this regiment had been armed with the muzzle-loading carbines, and eighty-five of those ninety had mutinied. It was a tremendous percentage. The other five probably had funked at the last moment; and the faith of the rest of the men not having been put to the test, it was impossible to say whether they would have remained staunch or not. At any rate they were now sullen and silent as they saw their comrades going to that scene of degradation and humiliation. Next came the rest of the two native infantry corps—the 11th and the 20th—and the precaution was taken of massing all the native troops together on one side of the parade-ground. Facing them were the artillery with loaded guns, and her Majesty's 60th Foot, together with the 6th Dragoon Guards or Carabineers. All these men were supplied with service ammunition, and they opposed a tremendous force to the native regiments, who, at the slightest sign of disobedience or attempt at rescue, would have been mowed down by the big guns and the rifles of the white troops.

It was a somewhat strange commentary on the opinions of those who vowed that the natives were staunch, that such preparations should have been taken to guard against surprise or attack. It will be said that they were only the ordinary precautions, which any nation would have adopted under such circumstances. That may at once be admitted, but let it not be forgotten that most of the European officers believed that the natives had been maligned, that they were as staunch as steel, and that though a few of their number had foolishly yielded to a spirit of disobedience, the rest were quite willing to see those few punished, and would express their loyalty by aiding in every way to carry out the sentence of the Court. Nevertheless, when it came to the test, this belief was backed up by shotted guns and loaded rifles. Guns and rifles and determined soldiers are often very strong arguments for enforcing a display of loyalty, and on this occasion— on this historic 9th of May—all the white troops had been informed that they were to be on the alert, to exercise the keenest vigilance, and be ready to instantly obey the orders of their superior officers. What those orders were likely to be was well known. If occasion arose the guns would belch forth their storm of shot and shell, and the rifles would rain iron hail, and the native regiments massed in front would have been swept off the face of the earth.

Apart from the military element, which was so strongly represented on the parade-ground, nearly all the civilians of the place seemed to have turned out. The scum of the bazaars was there. The bud-mashes gathered in full force, and no doubt hoped that a *hulla-goolla* (riot) would take place, so that they might have an opportunity of looting the bungalows. If these wretches had been able to secure arms they would have had to be reckoned with. As it was they were a mere rabble, but latently ferocious and thirsting for blood. They were not to be feared, however, unless the whole of the native troops broke into open insubordination; then the rabble, like a hornet's nest disturbed, would prove dangerous. Strings of vehicles of all kinds, containing the European civilians, the wives and daughters of the officers, were drawn up just outside the British lines, but in such a position that they commanded a full view of the parade-ground, and the occupants could see all that was to be seen.

Miss Dellaby was there with her sister and the two children. Hester had expressed a desire to remain away, but the night previous Captain Sandon had urged her to go, saying that it would be one o those historic scenes which one would talk about in the future, therefore it should not be missed. Mrs. Pritchard had taken her children, because she thought that in the event of an outbreak they would be safer with her than at home with their nurse in the bungalow. Perhaps that was so, but no one who thoroughly understood the native temperament would have ventured to say an outbreak was likely to occur in the face of a formidable array of white troops massed in their strength with their heavy guns and loaded rifles. It is not too much to say that if that show of strength, that display of resolution, and those precautions had been maintained, there would have been no Indian Mutiny. But the fatal belief in native loyalty was allowed to obtain, and lulling the British into a false sense of security, it was responsible for all the dreadful consequences that ensued.

And now all being ready the stern lesson commenced. The drums rolled forth their impressive tattoo; the bugles sounded, and the eighty-five disgraced troopers were marched forward in double columns, then they faced about and formed into single line. That done, General Hewett, surrounded by his staff, and supported by the other European officers, read out the sentence. This was followed by the appearance of a number of native blacksmiths carrying the tools of their trade and a quantity of leg-irons. The order being given, the smiths fell to work to rivet on to the ankles of each convict the galling chains of degradation. Slowly of necessity and methodically were the shackles hammered on. Motionless stood the troops, their nerves strung to the highest tension. The hot sun blazed down and glittered on guns and bayonets. The Sepoys were silent, but the expression on their dusky faces indicated clearly enough the feelings that agitated them as the convicts called on them to save them, and in violent language abused the British generally, and all the Meerut garrison particularly. Cries of despair and yells of desperation went up to the burning sky from the eighty-five condemned mutineers. The budmashes became restless; the native regiments displayed uneasiness. But what could they do, confronted as they were with those guns and rifles, and the small but splendid body of British cavalry and infantry ready on the sign being given to instantly spring to action? and had they done so scarcely a native would have lived to have told his kinsfolk the tale.

For nearly two hours—two dreadful hours—the scene lasted. Seldom were troops called upon to have their nerves tested, their sympathies evoked, their *camaraderie* tried, their endurance stretched, to such an extent as these troops, native and British, were on that fateful Saturday in Meerut.

At length the last shackle was fastened—the last rivet hammered home. Then forth rolled the drums once more, once again the shrill bugles sounded. The chained felons, surrounded by a guard of native infantry, were marched to the gaol. The swarming crowd was pressed back by the white troops, the long string of vehicles moved off, the guns rumbled, the horses neighed and champed their bits as if expressing their thankfulness that the strain was over, the blinding dust arose in clouds as the troops returned to quarters, and in a little while the parade-ground was deserted. The prologue to the drama was over, but after a very short interval the curtain would be rung up on more stirring scenes.

CHAPTER XXI.

WHAT HAPPENED IN THE BAZAAR.

THERE was one man at least in Meerut—there might have been many more—but one certainly who did not believe that the last had been heard of the mutinous eighty-five ; that one was Captain Sandon. He did not hesitate to openly express his astonishment that the shackled eighty-five degraded troopers should have been placed under the care of a native guard only. Of course the subject of the day's doings was the one common topic of conversation throughout the station on Saturday night. At the canteens, at the messes, in the bungalows it was discussed. Captain Sandon did not dine at his mess that night, but sallying forth in mufti, he resolved to go into the native quarters and hear what opinions were expressed. He had for some time been applying himself most diligently to the study of Hindoostanee, and being a clever man, with great aptitude for the acquisition of languages, he had made such rapid progress that if he didn't speak it fluently he at least understood all that was said.

Now, in taking the course he did that night, and it was one by no means free from risk, he was actuated by motives different to those he might have openly confessed to. His zeal as an officer and his loyalty as a soldier could not for a moment have

been called into question, but, under the circumstances that then existed, he was not compelled by
any regulation order to play the part of the eaves-
dropper in the native quarters. Nor could his act be
construed even in to a fulfilment of duty. His position
as an officer did not impose upon him just then any
such work. But there was another motive perhaps ; a
vague one it might have been, and he might even have
declined to have confessed to himself that it had any
existence at all. The motive was some anxiety for
Hester Dellaby and for Mrs. Pritchard's children.

He was—to put it in absolutely plain language—
desperately in love with Hester, and he was unmistakably fond of her nephew and niece. When a
man is in love with a woman she influences his
actions and motives to a much greater extent than
he is ever aware of. In this instance, believing as
he did that there was a lurking danger threatening
the station, he was anxious for the safety of those
who were dear to him. As a soldier he would have
been the first to have exclaimed—

"Though these natives are as the sands of the
sea-shore, and we are but a handful, we will fight
them and pulverize them, or, failing that, die with
our faces to the foe as British soldiers ever do."

But the reason of his anxiety was the astonishing
supineness of those in command. He saw with the
far-seeing eye of a tactician that too much faith was
being placed on native loyalty. The little puffy
upheavals that had taken place here and there—at
Madras, Dum Dum, Barrackpore—impressed him
deeply with the idea that there were internal fires
at work, and at some unlooked-for moment the

volcano would burst forth with a roar, and in the first outpouring many innocent victims would fall a. prey to it.

It really is an astonishing thing that he stood almost alone in this view. At any rate, he was all but alone in his boldness in expressing it. The fact is, that for some inscrutable reason those in high authority did not like to lay themselves open to a charge of being "alarmists," and for a long time in India that cant word had come trippingly off the tongues of sycophants and place-seekers as soon as any one ventured to express distrust. Of course when the rulers preserved silence the subordinates were sure to follow suit. And so people had con-- tinued to live in a fool's paradise; and in some of the most important stations in India the garrisons had been allowed to fall off to a ridiculous smallness. Particularly was that so in Delhi, where the enor- mous arsenal, from which all Upper India drew its supplies, was left almost unguarded. The defence of that arsenal by nine men only, when the mutiny did break out, is one of the grandest heroic episodes in the history of the tremendous story.

As Sandon left his quarters the first man he ran against was little Surgeon Parker. There had been considerable coolness between the two since that night of the rather heated discussion at the mess- table. Parker was unmistakably clever as a doctor, particularly as a surgeon, but as a man he was lamentably small-minded, narrow in his views, and paltry in his ideas. Since that evening he had never lost an opportunity of speaking snubbingly of the Captain, and at a tea-fight some time after he heroically denounced Sandon to a number of ladies as "a firebrand," and by way of a small joke, as he considered it, and hoping to raise a laugh at the Captain's expense, he added that it was his deliberate opinion there should be a regulation order passed compelling such firebrands as Captain Sandon to wear muzzles during the time they were suffering from "Indian-mania."

As he now unexpectedly encountered Sandon, he thought he saw the chance to have another quiet dig at him, and so exclaimed—

"Hullo, Captain. Well, you see we've got through the day all right, and I think even *you* must admit that we have made a very good display of authority. The almost barbarous severity with which we have dealt with these misguided men must have taught them a lesson they are not likely to forget."

"Yes," answered the Captain sternly, "you may depend upon it they will *not* forget it. But there is a lesson that some of our own people want sadly to take to heart—it is, that the English did not conquer India by the display of maudlin sympathy and rotten sentiment."

Having delivered this volley the Captain hurried on, giving his opponent no time to reply, and if Surgeon Parker did not feel that he was squashed, he must at any rate have been conscious that he had not scored anything.

Captain Sandon made his way direct to the main bazaar, for there the business of the day was over. The bazaars were the favourite resorts of stragglers, idlers, and gossipers, and it was there the pulse of opinion might be felt. The narrow lanes and streets of the bazaar seemed unusually crowded on this particular Saturday night, and Sandon noticed that there were numbers of Sepoys amongst the crowds. Many were the scowling looks directed towards him as he elbowed his way along, and it was clear to his mind that the natives were in a state of great excitement, and the way he was jostled, scowled at, and treated with disrespect showed him that very dangerous elements were present, and very little was required to cause an explosion.

With great forbearance and self-command he tolerated impertinences that at any other time he would have been quick to resent, but coming to a corner where a passage struck off at right angles to the main thoroughfare a large crowd had assembled, and were evidently greatly interested in something that was going on. By cautiously pressing forward he gathered that some orator—whom he could not see—was the object of the attraction, and listening intently he heard these words :—

" If we submit to this last indignity we shall be worse than pariah dogs ; and well, indeed shall we deserve all that these hated Feringhees can inflict upon us. But we must not suffer further. We are a mighty people, and in our might we must sweep these devils away even as the simoon's blast sweeps away all that obstructs it. The hour is ripe; indeed, it has been struck, my friends ; and our revenge and our triumph must not be delayed. The white garrison is weak ; their officers trust us ; we must take advantage of that trust. At Delhi our brothers await us ; and our king, the old Mogul, pants for the moment when throughout the land shall be raised the shout of death to the Feringhees. Blood alone can wipe out our wrongs, and blood must follow."

These treasonable remarks were received by the auditors with every sign of approval, and the crowd became very excited. Captain Sandon pressed forward with the plucky but rash intention of seizing the speaker and dragging him before the authorities. His movement attracted the notice of the crowd. Up to that moment everybody had seemed so eager to catch every word that was said that he had not been observed; now, as he tried to push his way through there arose a cry of—

"A Feringhee, a Feringhee; *maro, maro*" (kill kill).

Instantly he was hustled roughly, and an attempt was made to beat him down; but fighting his way clear from the press of the mob he got his back against the shutters of a shop; and whipping out his revolver he exclaimed—

"Have a care how you molest me, or there will be bloodshed. Stand away and let me pass."

The sight of the weapon and his resolute and determined air had their effect upon the cowardly rabble, and, nobody having the courage to take the initiative and raise a rallying-cry, the people began to fall back. But at that moment a wild-looking Hindoo, who, from his ferocious expression and bleared eyes, was probably half intoxicated with bhang, sprang forward brandishing a long and formidable knife, with which he made a desperate lunge at the Captain. He was not quick enough however. Simultaneously with the fanatic's move 'ment the Captain covered him with his revolver and fired. The fellow leapt up, then fell like a log on the ground, and his knife dropped at Sandon's feet. With a rapid sweep of his arm the Captain picked it up, and thus armed with knife and revolver he stood on the defensive, his back still to the shutters. There could be no mistake about the fatal result of his shot. The Hindoo lay motionless on the ground; the bullet had struck him full in the heart. Instantly there arose a mighty yelling and shouting, mingled with the peculiar and mournful wail with which the natives expressed their sorrow. Captain Sandon fully recognized his peril, but he was prepared to sell his life dearly, and there is no doubt several of his enemies would have given up the ghost before he himself had gone under, had they attacked him, as they fully intended to do; but they were so excited, they pressed so much one upon the other, that no one could get a fair blow at him, and the sight of a determined Englishman armed with revolver and knife would have made even a greater crowd than that hesitate. In the end, however, numbers must have prevailed, and the gallant Sandon's career would have come to an untimely finish. But in the nick of time a powerful Sepoy in full uniform rushed forward and scattered the surging crowd. He had recognized Sandon, and exclaimed—

"Fools, fall back. I will protect this Sahib, and the first one who raises a hand I will smite him to the ground." The crowd gave way, but there was a sullen roar of angry voices and deep menacing murmurs. Then the Sepoy addressing Sandon, said—

"Captain Sahib, go. I cannot keep them in check long."

Coolly and collectedly, without the slightest trace of being flurried, Sandon moved from his position of vantage, and wary and alert walked away, thanking the Sepoy as he went. The voices of the crowd now went up in a furious roar again, and there were indications of a rush being made for the officer, but once again the stalwart Sepoy interposed himself, and fiercely cried—

"Cursed dogs of evil things, would you undo us? If you bring the white troops upon us now, our plot will be frustrated, and our chance will have gone for ever."

These words were not intended for Sandon's ears, but he heard them, and, feeling that it would be the height of folly to run any further risk which could serve no purpose, and might precipitate an outburst that would only be suppressed after much bloodshed, he hurried off, and in a few minutes got clear of the bazaar. He then made his way straight to headquarters and reported the affair. It was between eight and nine o'clock. He stated that he had shot a native in the bazaar in self-defence, and that he had heard a man inciting the mob to a riot. He knew that no official inquiry would be made then. It was Saturday night, and the hour was late; that is, late in an official sense. Of the part he had played in the matter he had no fear—he was quite prepared to take all the responsibility of his act and to amply justify the shooting. It is certain that if he had not fired he would have been cut to pieces. But it was not this incident that concerned him. What did concern him was the dangerous temper the natives were in, and he felt so convinced mischief was brewing, that he resolved to seek a private interview with General Hewett, but on arriving at that officer's quarters he was informed that the General had gone out to a private dinner-party. Under these circumstances nothing was to be done, so he strolled down to his own regimental mess. Dinner had been cleared away, and a little group of officers, looking almost phantom-like owing to the thick cloud of tobacco smoke that encircled them, for every man was smoking, were playing whist, and enjoying their after-dinner drinks. His entrance was the signal for a shout of welcome, for he was very popular amongst his comrades, and somebody called out—

" Hullo, Sandon, where have you been to ? Some pretty girl, I'll bet, has claimed your attention."

" No, not quite," Sandon answered. " You would lose your bet this time. I've been having a little scrimmage on my own account. I've shot a nigger."

" The devil you have," was the general exclamation, as the players paused in their game and looked up.

" Yes," continued the Captain, as he helped himself to a cigar from a box that stood on the table, and lit it. " Yes, he tried to knife me, so I went for him."

" Was he drunk ? "

" I don't know. Perhaps he was. Though that doesn't matter much, he meant business, but I got the drop and put a tunnel in him. If I hadn't, you fellows would have had to attend a military funeral."

" Have you reported the affair ? " asked the senior officer present.

" Yes."

" Oh, well, that's all right. You'll hear nothing more about it till Monday."

" Perhaps not then," remarked Sandon significantly.

" Very likely not," answered the officer, failing to note the significance. " But, come, sit down and take my cards. I want to run away for a quarter of an hour."

So the gallant Captain played whist, but his thoughts, in spite of himself, would revert to Hester Dellaby, and he wished she was in some safer place, for he was convinced now the natives were in a very dangerous frame of mind, and but little more was required to incite them to revolt.

CHAPTER XXII.

SUNDAY, the 10th of May, dawned in all the brilliancy
of an Indian morning on the doomed station. The
early morning ride or drive was taken as usual by
the Europeans, and the business of the day proceeded with its wonted regularity. In due course
the bugles sounded church parade, and soldiers and
officers turned out looking spick and span in polished
buttons, fresh pipe-clay, and brushed-up clothes,
while their highly-burnished accoutrements flashed
and scintillated in the dazzling sunlight.

Captain Sandon intended as soon as service was
over, or at any rate as soon as he could get away, to
go over to Mrs. Pritchard's bungalow. As chance
willed it, he met her and Hester and the children
coming out of church. They all greeted him very
warmly. They seemed to be in excellent spirits and
perfect health. Of course he had not heard anything more of the bazaar incident. On his own bare
report it was not a matter likely to be investigated
on Sunday. To the authorities possibly it presented
itself as a mere riot, in which a British officer had
been compelled to defend himself from the fanatical
attack of a drunken native, and the native got the
worst of it. Rows of the kind were not altogether
infrequent between the natives and Tommy Atkins,

but if Tommy Atkins or his superior officer slew a
native in piping times of peace the subject was one
calling for official investigation, but still it was not
so urgent as to necessitate dislocation of Sunday
routine in order that a court of inquiry should be
held.   Consequently Sandon knew perfectly well
there would be no steps taken until the morrow
morning, nor was the incident likely to be generally
known over the station until then. It was obvious
Mrs. Pritchard had not heard of it, otherwise she
would surely have made some reference to it.

Captain Sandon thought he had never seen Hester
looking so radiant, the children so bonnie, or Mrs.
Pritchard herself so charming as they did on that
eventful morning. As every one knows, in a military station like Meerut, Sunday partakes very
much of the nature of a show day.   Tommy
Atkins seldom appears to better advantage than on
Sunday, and it is the one day when the British
officer doesn't seem to be ashamed of his uniform.
Certainly Captain Sandon need not have been
ashamed of his.   He was a handsome man, but
never looked so handsome as when in his regimentals; and yet for some mysterious and inscrutable reason known only to the British officer, he,
like all his *confrères*, would never appear in uniform
when he could avoid it.

"I was intending to call upon you this afternoon,
Mrs. Pritchard," he said.

"Oh, I am so glad," she exclaimed; "but
why not come round with us and have tiffin?
We've got a favourite dish of yours — Madras
curry."

"I cannot resist that," he said, in a manner that was for him unusually grave, and as though he spoke words only, and was hardly thinking of what he said.

"Oh, yes, do tum," cried out little Amy.

"Yes, I shall make you come," put in the boy, as child-like he seized the Captain's dangling sword, and began to tug at it until his mother with a thunderous frown and in severe tones exclaimed—

"You naughty boy, how dare you do such a thing? Now, Sir, take your sister's hand, and walk properly in front."

"Poor little fellow," said Sandon, in his sympathetic way, "don't scold him."

"But he must be taught not to be rude," answered Mrs. Pritchard, with an assertion of her matronly prerogative to correct her children.

"Oh, Madge, you *are* sharp with the child," exclaimed Hester, as she noticed that tears were streaming down Freddy's face. Captain Sandon noticed them too, and in a voice of infinite tenderness, in striking contrast to the previous night in the bazaar when he held his life in his hand, and sternly ordered the clamouring rabble who were clamouring for his blood to "fall back," he said—

"Come here, my little man."

With a chuckle of joy the child flew to Captain Sandon's side, and the Captain grasped his small hand, while Hester took the hand of the girl, and thus the little party walked back to the Pritchard bungalow.

The Captain did full justice to the tiffin; nevertheless his face wore an expression of gravity altogether foreign to it, and it led to both ladies inquiring if he had anything on his mind. The fact was he had a good deal on his mind, and never before perhaps in the whole course of his existence had he found himself confronted with a more perplexing situation. His intention in going to the house was to utter a word of warning to Mrs. Pritchard, and urge her to send Hester and the children off to Calcutta as soon as possible. But now that it came to the point he was disposed to shirk the matter. Suppose he uttered the warning, suppose his suggestion was carried out, and suppose after all his fears proved groundless, what then? Would he not appear in a very ridiculous light? The word "alarmist" so frequently applied to him of late would then seem more than justified; and would his friend Pritchard ever forgive him for having needlessly frightened his wife and sister-in-law?

These conflicting thoughts disturbed him, as may be supposed, and he could not make up his mind decisively one way or the other. He thought mayhap that a smoke would help him to a solution of the problem, and he asked if he might be allowed to go out on to the verandah to enjoy a cigar.

"Certainly," answered Mrs. Pritchard. "You know you are privileged, Captain. Hester and I intend to have a short siesta. I've ordered the buggy for four o'clock, as I'm going to drive over to Mrs. Major Scott's. She wants to see me about something or other. Some feminine frivolities, I suspect; frocks and fashions and such-like nonsense, altogether beneath the notice of you lords of creation.

I can drop you at your quarters, you know, if you like. There will be room in the buggy, as Hetty's not going. She wants to write letters home so that she may save to-morrow's mail."

"Thanks!" exclaimed the Captain, looking more than ever perplexed and troubled. So marked was this that Mrs. Pritchard noticed it, and said—

"Why, Captain Sandon, whatever *is* the matter with you? I've never seen you look so miserable since I've known you." Then suddenly, as if some inspiration had struck her, she added, with a pretty, artful, and very womanly smile, "Is it all for love of my dreadful sister?"

Hester had left the room, as she had gone to see the children before they took their afternoon nap. The question seemed to the Captain to give him a keynote, and he answered—

"In a sense, yes, it is."

"Poor fellow," returned Mrs. Pritchard, with a comical sigh. "But your triumph perhaps will come, Captain. You know a girl before her marriage has the power. Afterwards she is simply a domestic slave."

"Even as you are," he answered, brightening into a laugh. "A slave who rules her master."

"If you are so dreadfully gone on Hester," pursued Mrs. Pritchard laughingly, for the subject was congenial to her, "why don't you propose to her in the orthodox way? Never mind about spoiling a pair of regimental trousers, you know. I am sure that the girl admires you, and *you* ought to know how to win a woman's heart."

"I think I do," he answered, "and perhaps when

the right moment comes I may sue for Hetty's heart and hand, without even risking the knees of the regimentals. But now I am going to make a request, if you will grant it."

"Of course I will, if I can."

"You can do so."

"Well, what is it?"

"Will you remain at home to-day?"

"What, do you mean not go to Mrs. Major Scott's?"

"That is precisely what I mean."

She looked at him in surprise, and after a pause said—

"Well, upon my word, you are a funny man. Why, do you know I was going to suggest that if you have no duty, and no better way of passing your time, you should remain here, and Hester will keep you company. I shall be back long before dinner-time. Then if you like you could share our humble repast, or betake yourself to your more sumptuous mess."

"Mrs. Pritchard," replied the Captain, growing solemn again, "you are too good, and at any other time I should have felt the lack of words to thank you for your thoughtfulness. Now, however, I must press my request and ask you to remain at home."

Something in his manner, something in his tone, must have struck a chord of alarm in her breast, for she turned a little pale, and an expression of nervousness gleamed from her eyes.

"Why do you wish me to remain?" she asked, with a certain peremptoriness.

"Mrs. Pritchard, have you ever had what is called a presentiment?"

"Yes, often."

"Do you believe in presentiments?"

"To some extent."

"Then I've got a presentiment to-day."

"What is it?"

"That it will be far better that you do not go out."

Mrs. Pritchard had become thoughtful now, and she clasped her hands before her as if some motherly fear had sent a pang through her heart.

"Captain Sandon," she said, looking him full in the face, "there is more on your mind than you care to show me. I have sufficient faith in your friend-ship and regard for us all to feel sure you would not unnecessarily alarm me. Remember, I am a mother. I have two darling children and a loved sister here. My husband asked you to look after us, therefore I feel constrained to some extent to be influenced by what you say. Consequently I shall remain at home, and when the chicks have had their sleep I shall spend the afternoon in reading the Bible to them."

"Your decision to remain is wise," he answered, "and I feel relieved. Now, go and take your own siesta. Pray don't let me deprive you of that. Leave me to enjoy my cigar, and when you reappear I *may* perhaps tell you why I have asked you not to go out. Next week, no doubt, you will have a fine laugh at me; but never mind, I will stand your chaff. It's better to err on the side of caution, and when your husband comes back you can tell him that I am a regular old washerwoman."

He laughed and tried to resume his usual gaiety, but somehow he felt the trial was a failure, and Mrs. Pritchard was not deceived: but her heart was so full, her emotion caused her such a choking sensation, that she could make no reply. She merely pressed his hand, though there was a world of thankfulness, a world of trust and confidence indicated by that pressure. Then she hurried from the room, and flew to her darlings; he adjourned to the verandah and ensconced himself in a lounge chair.

For some time it seemed as if he was indulging in dreams. He lay back and watched the filmy smoke from his cheroot slowly dissolve itself into invisibility. Yet his mind was very active in spite of his seeming listlessness, and he could not quite console himself with the idea that he had done right in uttering a note of warning to Mrs. Pritchard. Presently he sprang up into a sitting position, and drawing forth his notebook he scribbled a few lines on one of the leaves, tore the leaf out, screwed it up, and calling one of the native servants he bade him convey the " chit " to the address he indicated.

The note was written in French. It was to the Colonel of his regiment, and the object of it was to make known his whereabouts to the Colonel. The motive which prompted him to take this somewhat unusual course was the same motive which prompted him to come to Mrs. Pritchard's house. He had a feeling which he could not possibly shake off that something was about to happen. It might not be anything more serious than an attempted rescue of the imprisoned eighty-five. But that would mean alarm, a struggle, bloodshed. If the prisoners had been in charge of a guard of white soldiers, Captain Sandon's misgivings would not have been called into play. But to him, entirely lacking as he was in faith in the native loyalty, it seemed an act of madness to entrust the prisoners to their own comrades, their own countrymen. Blood is thicker than water, and if the native guard chose to fraternise with their prisoners, what then ?

This was the view that Sandon took, and it was this view that caused him so much concern on account of those whom he had come to regard with more than ordinary friendship. In a sense, the Pritchard family were under his charge, and he felt responsible for them, while the love he bore for Hester made him more than ever anxious.

Precisely at four o'clock, the buggy Mrs. Pritchard had ordered drove up to the door of the bungalow. She had forgotten to countermand the order before retiring. Sandon went to the syce (the groom) as he stood at the horse's head, and said to him—

" You can take the buggy back to the stable. It's not wanted."

" But my mistress ordered it," answered the man haughtily.

" And what if she did? The order is now cancelled, and you can go back."

" But I prefer to see the mem Sahib," said the man, with an insolence of tone that was well calcu-lated to cause surprise. " You've no right to order me," he added.

This was too much for Sandon, who seized the fellow by the back of the neck and shook him.

Q

"Now, then, return to the stable as I order you to do."

At this moment Mrs. Pritchard appeared upon the scene, and the indignant and excited syce exclaimed with abundance of gesture—

"The Sahib has ill-used me. He is not my master, and I won't obey him."

Captain Sandon explained the situation, and Mrs. Pritchard commanded the man to take the horse back. Sullenly he mounted into the buggy, and as he clutched the reins and flourished the whip he hissed—

"Our time is coming."

Mrs. Pritchard was necessarily upset, and she said—

"It is truly remarkable. A little while ago a fellow like that would no more have thought of disobeying the order of my friend than he would have thought of flying."

"No, and it shows how the current is flowing. These rascals should be cowed into subjection, or they will subject us."

"I hope they won't," murmured the lady, with a little shudder which she could not suppress. Then she added with genuine sincerity—"They would not if all the garrison was as keenly alert as you are. Oh, dear me, it is dreadful to think of the possibilities of an outbreak. I do wish George was back. For a long time now I have noticed that the natives have not been as submissive as they used to be, and latterly they have got very much worse."

"Well, there is one thing," said the Captain, with a laugh, wishing to reassure her if possible; "if these black beggars mean business, we are strong enough to give them such a thrashing that they will think twice before they try the game on again."

In a few minutes Hester entered the room, looking particularly charming in a dress of gauzy muslin trimmed with pink ribbon, and the conversation became general. Mrs. Pritchard gave orders to her chief khitmurghar that tea was to be served on the verandah, and while it was being prepared she suggested a walk round the compound, and she, Hester, and the Captain strolled among the trees, feeling thankful that the heat of the day had passed. Presently the tea was announced, and they returned to the verandah, where the children joined them, and they sat there until the sun had quite gone down, and the short Indian twilight began. Suddenly they were aroused by the beat of horses hoofs as some rider tore along. Then they heard the gate of the compound clang, and a moment or two later a young English officer rode rapidly up to the bungalow. He had evidently been riding hard, for he himself was covered with dust and perspiration, while his horse was panting and was flecked with foam. It was Lieutenant Felbey, of Sandon's own regiment; he was a fine young fellow, and one of the few men who had the courage to uphold Sandon in his opinions about the natives. He and the Captain had been very friendly, and Sandon was fond of him.

As he leapt from the saddle he bowed to the ladies. Then, saluting his superior officer, said—

"Captain Sandon, I have a message for you, sir."

The Captain went forward, and Felbey delivered his message.

"I was ordered by Colonel Preston to ride out here with all speed, and request you to return to quarters at once."

"Why—is there anything wrong?"

"Yes. There is a great riot going on at the gaol. It appears the prisoners have broken loose with the aid of their guards, and all the native regiments have mutinied. Some portions of the station have already been set on fire."

The lieutenant, with considerable tact, in order not to alarm the ladies, had spoken in a low voice, but Mrs. Pritchard had caught some of his words, and, with face bloodless and eyes filled with tears, she rushed forward excitedly, exclaiming—

"What is it, Lieutenant Felbey, what is it? Tell me, I beseech you, is anything wrong?"

Captain Sandon took her hand, and now that the suspense was over, and the supreme moment had come, he was light-hearted again, for he was one of those who believe it is infinitely better to know the worst than live in constant dread of the sword of Damocles falling upon them.

"Calm yourself, my dear lady," he said kindly. "It appears that some of the gutter rascals are creating a disturbance, and have set fire to a house or two. That is all."

CHAPTER XXIII.

AN IMPROVISED FORT.

WITH a cry of fear, and an appeal to heaven for protection, Mrs. Pritchard threw her arms about her children and sobbed, while Hester, catching the alarm, inquired anxiously what the news was that Felbey had brought.

"A riot is going on," answered Sandon, "and some houses have been set on fire. That is all the news at present."

At this moment the ayah (the children's nurse) rushed on to the verandah, and falling down at the feet of her mistress, she moaned out—

"Mem Sahib, the servants have deserted. They have gone off to the bazaars. They say that all the white people are to be killed."

"And you, are you going to remain faithful, Sada?" demanded her mistress, with a fierceness that was begotten by her maternal anxiety for the safety of the little ones, and looking as if she were about to seize and shake the nurse.

"Oh, yes, mem Sahib, your poor Sada will be faithful," cried the ayah, as she shrank away and cowered with fear.

"But I won't trust you," exclaimed Mrs. Pritchard, clutching her now frightened children to her breast.

"Oh, mem Sahib; oh, mem Sahib, don't be cruel," pleaded the ayah, her hands outstretched in appeal. Then suddenly—still kneeling—she raised her right hand towards heaven, and said solemnly —"My people may torture me, they may hack me to pieces and kill me, but may Shiva smite me with leprosy and condemn me to be an eternal outcast if I am not faithful to you."

Captain Sandon heard these words, and, coming forward, he said—

"Mrs. Pritchard, I am sure you may trust this woman. While all your other servants desert you she remains. Trust her, I say; she will be useful."

The poor mother seemed terribly distressed and half dazed with a dread anxiety, but she was evidently encouraged by the Captain's words, for she caught the ayah's hand, and said in a voice choked with emotion—

"I will believe. I will have faith in you."

Captain Sandon and Lieutenant Felbey had been holding a consultation while this little scene was being enacted, and at last Felbey said—

"I must return, Captain. Will you accompany me?"

"No; we cannot leave these ladies and children by themselves," answered Sandon decisively.

"But I am under orders, sir," replied the young fellow, with an anxious expression.

"Your duty both as a soldier and a man demand that you should help to protect these woman and children," said Sandon somewhat sternly. "First of all, ride out to the road and reconnoitre, and report to me if you consider it safe to convey the children and the ladies to the European cantonments. In the meantime I will go to the stables and prepare horses."

Felbey at this command sprang on to his horse, and galloped down the compound, while Sandon ran to the stables, intending to saddle a horse for himself, and harness another to the buggy. Mrs. Pritchard was an excellent driver, and the buggy would hold the children, the ladies, and the ayah, while he and Felbey would ride as escort. But he found when he reached the stable that the syce had gone off with every horse, and he returned to the house to report this to Mrs. Pritchard, whose anxiety, as may be imagined, was greatly increased. But Sandon cheerily encouraged her to keep her spirits up, saying that he did not think the riot would swell to any great proportions. "The white troops," he added, "will sweep out of their cantonments like a whirlwind, and scatter these dogs as the wind scatters chaff."

Although he spoke thus he did not believe what he said, for he was convinced that if the native troops had revolted there would be dreadful carnage, and wherever it was possible for them to do so the mutineers would resort to pitiless massacre.

Let it not be supposed that during the occurrence of these little incidents Miss Dellaby remained unmoved, though outwardly she displayed no manifestations of alarm. Of course, she did not realize to the same extent that Mrs. Pritchard and Captain Sandon did, what an uprising meant. She had taken Freddy on to her knee, and was soothing him, for he, more than his sister, had been frightened by his mother's excited manner, and was sobbing bitterly.

"I think," said Captain Sandon, "that you ladies had better go inside." Then addressing Mrs. Pritchard with special emphasis, he added —"On you, Mrs. Pritchard, depends a good deal, and I trust for your co-operation. Although possibly there is danger it may not be formidable, and we can ward it off."

At these words up rose Hester, with Freddy in her arms, and speaking with steady voice, and looking calm and collected, said—

"Pray don't ignore me altogether, Captain Sandon. I am only a woman, it is true, but I am not going to sit still if I can be of use."

"I had no intention of ignoring you, Miss Dellaby. I am glad to hear you speak as you do, and I am perfectly convinced you will act up to your words."

"Forgive me for having lost my head," put in Mrs. Pritchard, as she dried her tears away, "but I could not help being the mother first. Now I am a soldier's wife. Give your orders and they shall be obeyed."

"Well and bravely spoken, both of you," answered the Captain in his cheery, hearty manner. "My suggestion is, then, that you all retire into the house now. Gather together such valuables as you can carry. Have some wraps ready, and we will endeavour to reach the cantonment on foot."

In compliance with this request the ladies, the children, and the ayah retired. As they went Sandon called out—

"By the way, Mrs. Pritchard, can I go to your

husband's room? I may find something there that will be of use." Of course the answer was "yes." He knew that Colonel Pritchard kept a large stock of arms, for he was a keen sportsman, and had quite an armoury. Mrs. Pritchard divined the Captain's object, and she came after him with a bunch of keys in her hand, saying—

"There is the key of my husband's cupboard where he keeps his ammunition. I know that he has a large quantity of both sorts, service and sporting. And remember, Captain, I am an excellent shot both with a revolver and a gun. A mouse will do battle for her young. A human mother is not less than a mouse."

"You are a brave woman," answered the Captain; "but I hope for your sake it will not come to fighting. It is well, however, to be prepared." He selected two army revolvers that were in the rack. Then from the ammunition in the cupboard he loaded both the weapons. One he thrust into his own belt; the other he laid upon the table, saying—"I will leave that one there for the present. I am going as far as the gate, but shall not be absent many minutes."

For a moment Mrs. Pritchard's face paled again at this announcement. Then she remarked firmly and pointedly—

"Remember, Captain Sandon, my husband left us in your charge."

He laid both his hands upon her shoulders, and looking full into her face, said, with the calmness and decisiveness of a brave and gallant man—

"My dear lady, I wanted no such reminder. I

have but one life; that life, however, will have to be extinguished before I am unmindful of my charge."

"God in heaven bless you, and may He protect us all," she murmured, as she went back to the other room where her children were, while Sandon left the bungalow, and hurried across the compound to the gate, where he strained his ears and eyes for some signs of Felbey's return. But what he heard and what he saw was this—the sky was lurid with flames, and from afar off came a roar like the roar of the surf on a rock-bound shore, swelling and sinking with a certain rhythmical cadence. It was the roar of fierce human voices, and mingling with it was the sharp crack of rifles.

"The devils are loose," he murmured.

The situation he was in was a terribly trying one. As an officer it was his place to go forth and join his comrades; but, as a man, how could he leave those helpless women and children? Even as he stood there, chafing with restlessness and wondering if Felbey was one of the victims, the roaring grew louder and seemed to be coming nearer, while a great burst of flame dyed the heavens blood-red, bringing trees into bold relief, and making the road visible for a long distance. And peering along that road he caught sight of a flying horseman, and a minute later there reached his ear the beat of hoofs. He drew his revolver, and stood on the alert. But his suspense was soon relieved, as Felbey dashed up with his drawn sword in his hand.

"We are cut off," exclaimed the lieutenant as he

reined in his panting steed. "The natives are swarming over the road. They are burning everything and are coming this way."

"We must hack our way through them," said Sandon coolly, "and get Mrs. Pritchard and her sister and her children into the cantonment somehow." He held the gate open while Felbey passed into the compound, and the two went to the house. Felbey dismounted, and held the bridle of his horse. "Have you a revolver?" asked Sandon.

"No."

"Take this then and remain here on guard."

Sandon handed him his revolver and then mounted the steps of the verandah and went into the bungalow. In an inner room he found the women and children, calm but anxious.

"We must leave here, Mrs. Pritchard," he remarked. Then to the ayah, "Sada, you carry Amy. Freddy can walk." He hurried to the Colonel's room again, where there were two or three more revolvers in the cupboard, which he proceeded to load. But now the roar of the multitude increased. It could be heard distinctly even from the interior of the house. Felbey had fastened his horse to the railings of the verandah and came running in.

"I am afraid, Captain Sandon," he said, "it will be too risky to leave this place now with the ladies and the children. Without them you and I could cut our way out, but with them we can do nothing. Will it not be better to do our best to defend them here?"

"Yes; perhaps it will. Stay, there is the godown.*
We will remove them into that. We can hold it possibly till help arrives. We have no time to lose.
Drag off the sheets from the bed and bundle in all
the ammunition from this cupboard, together with
the guns and swords. We are well off for arms, any
way."

Felbey set energetically to work to carry out the
order. An English bull's-eye lantern stood on a side
table. Sandon seized it, struck a match, applied it
to the wick, which lighted readily, then returned to
the room where the ladies were.

"Mrs. Pritchard," he said, "I think it will be
better on consideration that we repair to the godown
until daylight dawns."

"Do you know, I was going to suggest that too,"
she answered, wonderfully collected now that the
crisis had come. "I will get the keys."

She ran to her own room, returning in a few
moments and handing the keys to Sandon. Followed
by the three women and the children, who were
cowed with fright and did not even whimper, he
hurried across the compound, lighting the way with
the bull's-eye. He got the door of the storehouse
open; he sent the ayah and the children in, and,
leaving them the lantern, he asked the ladies to help
him to bring over some things from the house. As
they returned they met Felbey struggling along

* A godown is a storehouse always found in connection
with all Indian houses. In this instance it was an isolated,
oblong building on one side of the compound, and protected
from the road by a high wall.

under a huge bundle which he had slung over his back.

" This reminds one of a moonlight flitting," remarked the young fellow gaily.

The din and uproar now were dreadful, and the glare of flames could be seen in all directions, while the incessant roll of musketry told how fiercely the struggle raged. But there was one sound Sandon listened for in vain—the sound of big guns—and he wondered why the artillery had not been let loose against the mutineers, for the howls and cries, the lurid flames, and the report of the rifles made it only too painfully clear that mutiny of a terrible kind was going on. " It couldn't be possible," he thought, " that the European troops had been overawed and rendered powerless. Why then did they not make the big guns speak ? "

He and Felbey and the two ladies worked with such will and energy, that in an almost incredibly short space of time they had carried over a great quantity of things, including all the ammunition and arms ; the Colonel's papers and business books ; bedding for the children and the ladies ; food, water, candles, and other necessaries ; and a considerable amount of fodder from the stable for Felbey's horse, which was taken into the godown.

This place was by no means ill adapted for a temporary place of refuge. It was solidly built, as most places of the kind were. It was oblong in shape, one storey high. Access was gained to it by a large doorway. The door was divided into two halves—one half fastened by bolts shooting up and down into the frame-work · the other by a stout lock.

Over the doorway was a small window about fifteen
feet from the ground. It was protected by three
stout iron bars. Along each side of the building
were three or four slits not unlike loopholes; their
principal use was to admit air. Each slit was protected by an iron bar solidly let into the masonry.
Not that anything human could have got through
the slits, but small animals might. One side and
one end of the place abutted on the high garden
wall. It was, in fact, poked up in a corner so to
speak, and there was a narrow alley-way between
the godown and the wall about three feet wide. It
was choked up with rubbish, principally broken cases
and boxes. Inside were a number of cases of wine,
barrels of beer, casks of flour, two or three bags of
rice, a bag of sugar, and domestic stores of that
kind, besides a number of garden tools and a great
quantity of empty boxes and barrels, and some
spare domestic utensils. The horse was placed in a
corner; then the door was barricaded with boxes,
and a platform raised so that the window could be
reached, for that window practically commanded the
garden in a military sense. Next, bedding was laid
on a platform of boxes at the end farthest from the
door, and the ayah proceeded to put the children
into bed, without undressing them, however; and,
squatting beside them, she crooned Indian lays and
lullaby songs, and tired out as the little ones were,
they speedily dropped off to sleep.

All the fire-arms were loaded, and the ammunition
so placed that it was fairly well protected from
chance ignition. Amongst the arms were two of the
new pattern Enfield rifles, four or five old smooth-

bore Brown Bess guns, several sporting rifles, and a heavy double-barrel rifled tiger gun, which carried a very formidable ball. This gun was placed on the platform for use at the window. In addition the little garrison were provided with four revolvers.

With this by no means inconsiderable arsenal at their disposal, Sandon and Felbey felt confident of being able to hold the improvised fort until help reached them, and they talked cheerfully and chatted pleasantly in order to keep up the spirits of the ladies. All the preparations were carried out in a shorter space of time than it has taken to describe them, but none too soon, for from the glare that fell through the window and the openings in the walls, it seemed as if the whole station was a roaring furnace of flame, while the sea of fire was rolling nearer and nearer. From out the clear sky the stars looked down—looked down on a scene of carnage and hellish wrath that must have made the very angels hide their faces in horror at the sight.

CHAPTER XXIV.

In choosing Sunday night for their outbreak, the mutineers showed that they had calculated their chances
with almost mathematical precision. Most of the Europeans were at church or on their way to church, and a
larger number of soldiers were allowed out of barracks
than on a week-day night, and these men were not
allowed, of course, to carry arms. The fool's paradise,
against which Captain Sandon had so often railed, was
never more clearly indicated than on that memorable
Sunday. The authorities apparently had given themselves no concern about the desperate prisoners in the
gaol, and their sympathetic and no less desperate guard.
Yet, as is now well known, from the moment when the
manacled troopers were marched to the prison, solemn
vows were made that ere the moon had risen and set
twice they should be liberated; and two native bearers
were dispatched with all haste to bear that resolution to
the native troops in Delhi, who were warned to be on
the alert and ready to rise when the mutineers from
Meerut came in sight of the royal city.

Throughout the Meerut bazaar the signal ran that
when the white people were at their place of worship
on Sunday evening the gaol was to be attacked, the
prisoners liberated, and the streets were then to run red

with blood. During the night secret emissaries moved about inciting the population to deeds of atrocity, and all through the calm hot Sunday, when the whites thought that the natives were basking in the sun like lotus-dreamers, the emissaries were at work; and from the most unheard-of holes and corners arms were secretly brought forth, and other preparations were made for the great work. At last the hour struck and all was ready. A little army of native blacksmiths made their way to the gaol. The prisoners were liberated, and the black-smiths proceeded to strike off the irons they had so recently riveted on. Two or three British officers, who were apprised of what was taking place, fearlessly rode to the gaol, thinking their very presence would still the storm. But they were confronted by the gaol guard of native infantry, who received them with a volley, though owing to the darkness and wild firing not a single shot took effect, and the officers galloped back to the canton-ment with the news.

And now, with a mighty shout that seemed almost to rend heaven and earth, dense masses of natives poured forth, many armed with blazing torches, and in a brief space of time the flames of burning houses were licking the sky. Soldiers, mounted and on foot, joined the infuriated mob of yelling demons; women and children were massacred with a hellish pitilessness, and isolated European soldiers, wherever caught, were hacked to pieces. In one case, a veterinary surgeon and his wife were both ill in bed in their house suffering from small-pox. Startled by the yells, shrieks, and crackling of flames they sprang out of bed and rushed to the verandah, the surgeon snatching up a loaded gun that stood in a corner of the dining-room. The crowd

R

surged into the compound, and the unfortunate surgeon
in the excitement of the moment discharged his gun
full at them, and two or three of their number went
down.   Instantly he himself fell riddled with bullets.
Then the poor frantic wife, in her night-dress, appealing to heaven for mercy, might have moved the heart
of a statue, but those black demons were dead to pity.
They knew she was suffering from small-pox, and,
afraid to go near her, they flung lighted tow saturated
with tar and turpentine at her.   Her night-dress caught
fire, and she met with a terrible death.   Next the house
was set in a blaze, and on swept the wretches in their
mad fury.   Children were dragged out from their
homes and literally cut in twain from the head down-
wards.   Delicate ladies were treated with revolting
savageness which makes one's blood curdle even now to
think of it.

Frightful as the massacre was, it would have been
still greater in point of numbers had it not been for
rather an extraordinary circumstance.   On that very
Sunday a new military regulation had come into force.
It was that church parade should take place half-an-hour
later than usual on account of the increasing heat and
lengthening days.   This change had not become known
to the mutineers, and they rose a little to soon.   As it
was the custom then for British soldiers to go to their
respective places of worship with only their side-arms,
had the troops been assembled at church, there would
have been a holocaust.   As it was, they were just about
to march to the churches when flying scouts brought
the dreadful news into the cantonments, and so they
were not as *lachar* (helpless) as the natives thought they
would be.   Soon the bugles pealed out from all quarters

as they sounded the "assembly," and instantly the soldiers sprang to their arms. And yet, strangely enough, these British troops, panting with eagerness to go, were not let loose, but many of their officers rode forth thinking they could quell the fierce passions of the aroused natives. Amongst those who went out was Surgeon Parker—he who had always treated Captain Sandon's misgivings with such irony—he thought that if any one could still the storm he could. He went boldly among the 11th Native Regiment. He called upon them in the name of the Company, and in the name of the Queen of England, not to disgrace their profession of arms by acts of violence and mutiny. "Remember," he exclaimed, "we have helpless women and children amongst us who look to you for protection. You are human, and in your human hearts let the voice of pity obliterate your feelings of bitterness. Remember the same God watches over us all; the same God will judge us all."

He meant well, but his self-imposed task could not have been more hopeless had he attempted to stay the hurricane's wrath. A mighty trooper swept down upon him for answer, brandishing a naked tulwar, and with a sweep of his giant arm he severed poor little Parker's head from his body, and the headless corpse pitched from the horse into the dust, while many other British officers also fell, riddled with bullets.

From every quarter of Meerut rose heavy columns of smoke illuminated with many-coloured flames. The sight was awful; while the rolling of the musketry, the crackling of the burning timbers, the shrieks of the dying and the wounded, the cry for help of defenceless women and children, the piteous neighing of horses that were scorching to death in burning stables, the yells and frantic shouts of the cowardly demons, made up a night of such dramatic horror that it has not often been surpassed in the world's history. From every street and corner, from every hole and alley, from every bazaar and suburb, poured forth streams of maddened natives, bent upon plunder and murder, and howling at the top of their voices, "Death to the Feringhees." Like wild beasts from their lairs came the hordes thirsting for blood, and as the civilians and officers rushed from their bungalows they were cut down or riddled with bullets.

And what, it will be asked, was the force available to deal with such an emergency as this? It was a mere handful of British troops, and yet this handful, under the command of an officer possessed of an energy equal to the occasion, might have intimidated the fanatic horde and quelled the revolt; but, unfortunately, the command of the troops was in the hands of a man who, though not deficient in personal courage, was yet lacking in tact and decisiveness. For such desperate work a man of action was required, and it was an unfortunate circumstance that gallant soldiers like Captain Sandon found themselves, by the strict rules of military service, fettered in their enterprise by an infirm and enfeebled commander.

All the prisoners in the gaols had been set at liberty by the Sepoys, and miscreants and felons of the worst type were taking an active part in the work of destruction and plunder. These men fought like demons, for they owed a grudge to the British who had put them in prison, and the first use they made of their liberty was to wreak a terrible vengeance on the administrators of the law.

With true oriental barbarity these gaol-birds massacred every European they met without respect to age or sex, and applied their torches with shrieks of exultation to the bungalows of the English residents.

As for the Sepoys, they no longer displayed any religious scruples regarding the greased cartridges, the alleged excuse for the mutiny. On the contrary, the new ammunition was handled with perfect freedom, and without a thought of caste.

Inflamed with success and fanatical fury the tide of revolt rolled on. While the British commander was wasting precious moments in considering what was to be done, the rebel army swelled in numbers. From adjacent villages and hamlets the budmashes came pouring in, eager to share in the plunder, and to take part in the hideous scenes of bloodshed.

It was a scene that words fail to give any adequate conception of. From the burning houses there belched forth on the sultry air of the Indian night great pinnacles and pyramids of flame, while every now and then the piteous shrieks of women, the frantic cries of children, mingled with the explosion of ammunition barrels and the roll of musketry.

Colonel Pritchard's house escaped the first blast of the storm owing to its position. It was somewhat out of the main track. The Colonel had built it himself, and he had chosen the spot on account of its picturesqueness, and because he rather liked to be isolated. But bent as they were on the destruction and plunder of every European house, and on the killing of every European they could lay their hands on, the natives were not likely to forget the Pritchard bungalow and its occupants, and a great mob, headed by frantic savages with flaring torches, swept towards it. Down went the iron gates of the compound in the furious rush, and some of the wretches losing their foothold were trampled to death. The house was in darkness, the doors and windows shut. Baulked of their living prey, the cowardly wretches battered in the doors and swarmed over the place. Everything of value was appropriated, and they fought amongst themselves for possession of it. With insensate fury they hacked the pictures on the walls to pieces. A large and massive family Bible that stood on a table in the dining-room was seized, and there was a tremendous struggle for it. It was torn to shreds, and the shreds were danced upon and spat upon. Then the ladies' drawers and boxes were burst open, and their dresses and other apparel dragged out amidst ribald shouts and execrations. A large waxen doll which Hester had brought from home for little Amy, and which had been the poor child's pride and joy, was tossed into the air, caught upon a sword-point, then dragged limb from limb by the cowardly brutes, who were disappointed that it was not a living child.

Amongst the mob was the syce whom Captain Sandon had chastised in the course of that afternoon, and of course he knew the run of the house and where most of the things were. As soon as the door was burst in he was one of the first to enter, and he rushed to the Colonel's room, hoping to get the arms and ammunition which he was aware were stored there. When he found they had already been removed, he shrieked with baffled vengeance—

"Brothers," he yelled to those who crowded about him, "I hoped to have been revenged on the dog of a white man who shook me this afternoon, the Captain Sahib Sandon. But he has escaped, though only for a time, for we will have him, and when he is in our power we will mangle him to death inch by inch. The guns and the ammunition have gone too; we have lingered too long on the road; we have given the foul dogs time to get away. But not a stone of their abode shall be left standing. When we have sacked and plundered all that is worth taking, then the flames shall burn the place to ashes."

And so the sacred *lares* and *penates* of the once happy household were desecrated by these sacrilegious hounds, and the work of destruction went merrily on. Then from several places at once the flames shot up. The lamps that were filled with oil were dashed against the walls so that the oil might feed the fire—not that that was needed. So rapidly did it spread that some of the mob had a difficulty in making their escape, and as it was, three or four of them were actually scorched. Had it not been for the treacherous syce, the chances are the detached godown would have escaped the notice of the plunderers. But the syce knew there was a goodly store of wine and beer there, and in their half-maddened state the natives craved for drink, though at other times they would not have touched it.

" Here, the godown, the godown," roared the syce, as the crowd was swarming out of the compound, which was now brilliantly lighted up by the flare of the burning building.

" Aye, aye, the godown," answered many voices, and the stream began to stop its flow outwards.

" I have oft been in the place," yelled the syce.

" There is plenty of stuff there.   Ho! a battering-ram, a battering-ram."

Pell-mell, headlong rushed the mob towards the godown, tumbling over each other, and struggling frantically to be first. A young tree was drawn up, and five or six men holding it advanced, crying as they went—

" Clear the way, clear the way for the battering-ram."

Suddenly from the window over the door belched forth a blinding flame ; there was a loud report, and three of the crowd rolled over into the dust, dead. Before the cowards could recover from the temporary panic this utterly unlooked-for event threw them into, there was another spurt of fire, another report, and two more fellows pitched over, never to rise again.

It was the tiger rifle that had spoken, and its deadly messengers had smitten five of the enemy to death.

CHAPTER XXV.

THE great crowd that like any angry sea rose and fell, and moved now this way and now that around the godown, seemed for some moments to be paralysed by the unlooked-for outpouring of flame and death. It had taken them so utterly by surprise, and five of their number lay dead, while one or two others who had been wounded were writhing on the ground. The syce had escaped owing to the fact of his being close to the door, and its defenders could not so depress the muzzle of their heavy tiger rifle as to pour its leaden messengers on the men who were immediately beneath the window. But the execution done in the direct line of fire was relatively great, and the moral effect for the moment was tremendous. The mob fell back from the dark and deadly building with an instinctive feeling of horror. Nothing affects an undisciplined rabble so much as to be menaced from unexpected quarters and by an unseen enemy, and something like a panic seized many of these budmashes, who fled to shelter, while some threw themselves flat upon the ground. This served to increase the general fright, as it was thought the death-roll was much larger than it was. The syce, who had constituted himself the leader of that section of rascals who had attacked Colonel Pritchard's bungalow, was no less panic-stricken than his fellows, and hastily dropping the improvised battering-ram he fled to the nearest tree. Meanwhile, the defenders reloaded their deadly tiger rifle, and were once more ready for the assault should it be made.

When the natives had recovered from the first shock, and the reaction set in, they gave vent to a fierce outburst of passionate execration, and there arose a great cry for vengeance. The courage of the syce returned, and divining that Captain Sandon and the ladies must have sought shelter in the godown, he thirsted for the life of the man who had that very day treated him so roughly. Stepping from behind the tree where he had sheltered himself, he yelled—

" Brethren, shall we stand calmly by and see our friends shot down as if they were pariah dogs ? "

" No, no, no," answered the excited mob.

" Shall we exact a deadly reckoning for this slaughter of our comrades ? "

" Yes, yes."

" So be it. In this godown some of the accursed Feringhees have sought shelter. Shall we allow them to escape ? "

" No, no. Death to them."

" Let us batter the door down then, and drag the wretches out," cried the syce.

This suggestion was answered by another furious yell, and a desperate rush was made for the door of the godown. Weirdly picturesque and horribly suggestive was the scene. The burning bungalow threw a blood-red light over all the surroundings. The flames roared, the timbers crackled, and dense masses of sparks shot up every now and again, and floated far and wide on the night wind. Excited to a state that was little short of raving madness, the rabble charged the godown, but a volley of bullets tore through their ranks, and several of their number bit the dust. On the door blows were rained with sticks and stones, and the sapling which had been dragged up for a ram was brought into play, but without producing any material effect. Wild with rage, yet baffled, the crowd once more fell back just as the roof of the burning bungalow collapsed with a tremendous crash, and a huge column of sparks rose up to the very sky, while dense, suffocating volumes of smoke filled the grounds and temporarily obscured everything. Taking advantage of this the crowd made a rush for the godown once more, and furiously attacked the door with sticks and bars of iron, which some of them carried. The woodwork was splintered and cracked, but the door did not yield, for it had been well barricaded from within. At this juncture of affairs cries and shouts were heard, and another band of insurgents came rushing up, many of them carrying fire-arms, and amongst their number were several Sepoys armed with muskets and tulwars. The new-comers were hailed with a roar of delight, and the position of matters was soon explained. Then a storm of bullets fell upon the door of the godown, and it was answered by a volley from the defenders, who felt, however, as if all hope had gone.

Sandon had watched from the godown window the angry mob break into Colonel Pritchard's house, and he saw it given to the flames. So incensed was he, that had it not been for the two ladies, the children, and the native nurse under his care, he and his young comrade Felbey would have sallied forth and run amuck against the mob. They were both excellent swordsmen, and though they might ultimately have been overpowered by numbers, there is no doubt they would have given an excellent account of themselves, and would have done terrible execution before they had fallen. But the defence of the little building was in their hands, and as men and soldiers they could not desert their post. During the sacking of their house Mrs. Pritchard exhibited great alarm. It was terrible to see her once happy home desecrated by a brutal and fanatical mob, and little odds and ends that were endeared to her by a thousand and one associations destroyed or trampled in the dust. The anxiety and fear she suffered on account of her children may be left to the imagination. For her precious darlings to fall into the hands of the tigerish wretches who were thirsting for blood was horrible to contemplate, and she shuddered again and again, and bent weepingly over her children with the passionate devotion of a fond mother. Both the children had gone to sleep, soothed with the lullaby of the faithful nurse; but the yells and cries of the insurgents roused them. With an expression of fear Freddy leapt up and flung his arms about his mother's neck, while she strained him to her bosom and moaned out a prayer to the Father of all mercy, that He would protect her lambs. For some little time Amy remained quiet, her eyes wide open and turned to the slits in the wall, through which fell the lurid glare from the burning house. Then presently she uttered a half-suppressed cry of alarm, and stretching her hands out to the nurse murmured—

"Nurse, me so frightened, take me," and the ayah lifted her up and soothed her as best she could.

After the first rush of the mob on the godown, Mrs. Pritchard called Captain Sandon to her side, and, dismounting from the little platform under the window, he went to her. He had stripped off his coat and his waistcoat; his shirt-sleeves were rolled up; his arms were bare. His sword was buckled round his waist, and two revolvers were stuck in his belt. He looked now the stern, determined soldier that he was, and one who would be dangerous while life lasted.

"Captain," said Mrs. Pritchard solemnly, and speaking in low tones so that the others might not hear, "you have been a good and true friend to us, and my poor husband had a great faith in you. I for one do not expect to leave this place alive, but I am resolved that neither I nor my beloved children will fall into the power of the demons who are thirsting for our blood. Give me one of your revolvers. When all hope has gone my little ones shall die by my hand."

"Come, come," he answered cheerily, "I don't think our position is so desperate as that. We have heaps of ammunition, and Felbey and I can keep a horde at bay for hours. When the first panic that has seized the station has passed, the troops will sweep the town clear of those devils. The 6th Dragoon Guards, the 60th Rifles, and the Horse Artillery Batteries are within a mile and a half of us. Generals Hewett and Wilson cannot remain inactive, and it is impossible to imagine that all the white troops have been destroyed. No, it cannot be. In a little while we shall hear the boom of the big guns and the rattle of the sabres as our men are let loose. But if the worst comes to the worst, I will cut my way out and bring succour."

She shuddered and caught his arm, as she said—

" No, no, you must not leave us. All my hope is in you. But though I and my children should perish, you must save my sister. She loves you. She will in happier times be your wife."

" I will save you all," he answered, " or perish."

" You are a brave man, and I know that all that mortal can do you will do. But we must not forget the fearful odds that are opposed to us. These infuriated people will find some means of getting in. They will pile fire around the building and smoke us out. Please give me the revolver."

Sandon, although he displayed no misgivings, knew that she did not exaggerate the seriousness of the situation, and he was well aware the danger she spoke of was a very real one. Failing by other means to reach the occupants of the godown, the natives would kindle fire against the door, and then it would only be a question of the time the fire would take to eat through the wood-work. But still he spoke to her in his usual cheery and self-confident manner.

" It is far too early to despair," he said. " Young Felbey and I have a lot of fight in us yet, and two determined Englishmen are a match for any number of such wretches as these. But take the revolver. You are one of our little garrison, and should be armed. As I have often reminded you, you are a soldier's wife. For your husband's sake be brave and true to yourself."

" Yes, I will be brave," she answered with forced calmness, as she took the weapon and laid it on the top of a case within reach of her hand.

At this moment Felbey shouted out—

" The beggars are making a rush for the door again, Captain."

Sandon sprang on to his little platform and dealt out execution with the deadly tiger rifle, while Felbey and Hester blazed away through the loopholes. It was little short of wonderful the way that Hester had risen to the occasion. Whatever her real feelings were she gave no outward signs of fear or nervousness, and she had said to Sandon—

"I am not going to remain idle; show me how to hold a rifle and I'll undertake to fire it."

He placed her at one of the narrow windows or slits, and told her to depress the muzzle of her weapon so as to fire low, and only to fire when he gave the order. She was an apt pupil, and soon showed that she had the stuff in her that true Englishwomen are made of. It was a desperate fight for life and all that made life dear. She was perfectly well aware of that, but Captain Sandon and his young comrade were both so cheery, and spoke so hopefully of the succour that was sure to come to them in a little while, that she did not give way to despair.

Looked at from any point of view, it was an unequal struggle, but Sandon knew that sheltered as they were and with plenty of ammunition, they could certainly hold their own for a time, but if the enemy built up fires around the place escape would be next to impossible. When the insurgents were reinforced, Sandon was bound to admit to himself that the situation was likely to become intolerable. And when the bullets rattled against the walls and the door, he felt that unless succour came soon they were all doomed. Nevertheless he relaxed no effort; and the terrible gun which he handled so effectually made the enemy reel again and again, and he was ably seconded by his lieutenant,

young Felbey, who was full of pluck and spirit. Nor
was Hester's help to be ignored. She was a factor in
the sum, as the natives knew to their cost, for the bullets
from the rifle she handled found their billet. Felbey
did the loading for her, and in order that she might
have more command of the weapon, a couple of cases
had been placed for her to stand on ; but she had been
particularly cautioned not to expose her face at the loop-
hole more than she could possibly help. As a matter of
fact she need not have exposed herself at all, for she
made no pretence of taking aim, but fired when she was
told to fire. Suddenly, however, she uttered a half-
muffled cry. Her rifle fell from her grasp ; she threw
up her arms and pitched heavily to the ground. Her
sister and Sandon rushed to her simultaneously, and the
Captain lifted her in his arms. She was unconscious,
and blood was streaming down her face from a wound
in the forehead, where it seemed as if a bullet had
struck her. Sandon carried her to the bed that had
been made up for Freddy, and laid her tenderly down,
and manifested by his manner the keenest anguish and
distress. Fortunately they had water, brandy, and
other appliances at hand. These were speedily secured,
and Mrs. Pritchard and the ayah said they would attend
to the wounded girl.

"Our garrison is too small, Captain, to be able to
spare you from the ramparts," remarked Mrs. Pritchard, as she proceeded to sponge the blood away from
her sister's face. He did not reply, his heart was too
full ; but the anguish that shone from his eyes touched
Mrs. Pritchard deeply, and laying her hand on his arm
she said fervently—"We are in God's keeping. He
knoweth best."

Still speechless, the Captain returned to his platform, and there he saw that the rebels were hauling out the lumber—broken cases, and such like—from the narrow alley-way running between the godown and the wall, and were piling it up against the door with the intention of setting fire to it; while the Sepoys, with their tulwars, were lopping off branches from the trees. The fire from the still glowing bungalow lit up the scene, making everything perfectly distinct. Sandon laid his gun, covering two of the Sepoys who were hacking the branches, and taking deliberate aim he stretched both men upon the ground. It was a signal for another furious yell and rush for the building, but Felbey poured the contents of two rifles into the crowd, and once more they fell back, execrating their unseen foe. Sandon stepped down from his platform, and calling his young comrade to his side he said, speaking almost in a whisper—

" Felbey, it is impossible we can hold out till the morning Indeed, it is doubtful if our position will be tenable for another two hours, for the enemy is determined to make a bonfire at the door. But before that is done one of us must embark on a forlorn hope, and ride forth for succour. Which of the two shall it be ? "

" I beg that you will let me go," said Felbey.

" Good; it shall be so. Your chances of getting to the cantonments are small; and unless succour comes to us who remain within an hour, we are unmistakably doomed. But while there is life there is hope. For the sake of these dear women and the children we will do our best; no man can do more than that. Look to your horse and arms, and when you are ready we will

s

remove the barricade, fling open the door, and you must make a dash and hew your way through this damnable rabble of human brutes."

" I will do it if mortal man can do it," answered the young fellow, with an air of quiet but dangerous determination which clearly indicated that though he might fall the foe would suffer. It was not in the least likely he would yield while he had a weapon to wield and an arm to wield it with.

CHAPTER XXVI.

THE SUPREME MOMENT.

WHILE Felbey adjusted the saddle and tightened the girths of his horse, which was a well-trained troop-horse, and had shown but little restiveness during all the firing and the yells and cries, Sandon went to where Mrs. Pritchard and the ayah were attending to Miss Dellaby, who had recovered consciousness, although she looked dazed. She was deadly pale; and high up on her forehead, on the left-hand side, was an ugly, livid, starred gash, from which blood was still gushing. Captain Sandon sank the lover now in the stern soldier.

"Mrs. Pritchard," he said, "I want you. Leave Hester to the ayah. Come with me."

She followed him to the door. Felbey was standing by his horse ready to mount, and the intelligent animal, as if it understood that some important business was on hand, was champing its bit and showing impatience to be off.

"Felbey is going to ride for succour," said Sandon curtly. "You must help me to open the door quietly, and, as soon as he has dashed out, we must close the door again before the enemy recovers from its astonishment. Take this revolver, and do not hesitate to blaze away if one of the wretches shows his nose in the doorway. We must keep them at bay until troops are sent to release us."

"You can depend on me," she answered with a resolute air of unnatural calmness, as she grasped the revolver sternly.

She was very pale, and her eyes were a little bloodshot, but she bore the appearance of a woman who was not to be trifled with. She had removed her dress so as to afford herself more freedom, and her long hair was hanging loose down her back.

"Much depends upon our quickness," added the Captain. "The astonishment of the rabble will be great as a mounted man dashes out of the godown. It will seem like an apparition to them, and before they can draw their breath and recover, we must have closed and barricaded the door again. It will not be necessary to fire unless it is to shoot down any one who may try to force his way in."

"I understand," replied Mrs. Pritchard quietly; but her eyes were brilliant with a dangerous light.

"All right. Now, Felbey, help me to remove these boxes."

With right good-will the two men set to work, and, in a few minutes, had cleared the cases from the half of the doorway, making no more noise than they could possibly help. This done, Sandon shook the lieutenant's hand with that firm, significant grip which men give when in the moment of supreme danger they part, knowing that in all probability they will never meet again on earth.

"Now, old fellow, mount, and God speed you."

Felbey leapt into the saddle, his drawn sword in his hand, the reins gathered up, his heels ready to dig the spurs into the horse's flanks. One last look to see that nothing had been forgotten, and then Sandon gently turned the key in the lock.

" Are you ready? " he whispered.

" Yes," came the firm answer.

" Go then."

The half of the door was flung open. Felbey lay straight along the animal's neck to avoid striking his head against the beam of the doorway. He dug his spurs deep in, gave his horse the reins, and with one great plunge the poor beast bounded out, scattering and crushing down the lumber that had been piled up. If an apparition had suddenly risen out of the solid earth, the rebels could not have been more thunderstruck than they were, when they saw a mounted horseman bound out of the godown into their very midst. But they quickly realized what it meant, and with imprecations and furious shouts they tried to seize the horse ; but Felbey dug in his spurs, and slashing right and left with his sword he got free, leapt his horse over the compound wall, and gaining the road went at breakneck speed towards the cantonments. The heavens seemed filled with fire, and the air palpitated with shouts and cries from all quarters.

The passion of the mob rose again to fever heat when they found themselves outwitted. The business had been cleverly managed, but as the horse dashed out some of the rubbish fell in the doorway, and for a few moments it seemed as if Sandon would be unable to shut the door. The syce who had taken such a prominent part in leading the attack on Colonel Pritchard's house caught sight of the Captain, and with a frantic shout he sprang at him, aiming a blow with a tulwar which he had taken from one of the dead Sepoys. But ere the blow could descend there was a sharp report and a flash ; the syce staggered back, the tulwar fell from his grasp, he sank to the ground. Mrs. Pritchard had shot him dead. It seemed almost like the justice of heaven that this treacherous rascal should have met his fate at the hands of the lady whose confidence he had so shamefully betrayed.

Mrs. Pritchard's promptness in firing and accuracy of aim saved them. Sandon was enabled to close the door, and pile up the cases against it again. The fury of the baffled rebels seemed now to know no bounds. They hurled themselves like a storm-wave against the door, which happily did not yield, and again the tiger rifle poured forth its deadly contents. But the sight of their wounded, their dying, and their slain only maddened them, and on all sides arose fierce cries for fuel to pile up. Now to prevent them as long as possible from doing this was, as Sandon recognized, of the highest importance if his charges were to be saved. He could not do more than one man could do. He could not be in two places at once. The heavy tiger rifle was a terrible weapon, but its double barrels when empty had to be reloaded. Moreover, the crowd were not deterred by seeing two or three of their number bowled over. If they had had a small cannon they could soon have battered the place to pieces. But they did not possess one, nor did they know where to get one, so the next best thing was to burn down the door ; then when the barrier was removed the defenders, whoever they were, would be at the mercy of the pitiless foe. Sandon realized all this, and bold and reckless as he was, he was fully alive to the fact that

in the end he would have to succumb to superior force
—not that he had any intention of capitulating. There
was nothing to hope for from the wretches who were
thirsting and clamouring for his life. If the woman he
loved and the wife of his friend fell into the hands of
the rebels, they would meet with a fate worse than
death, while even the innocent children would be subjected
to the most fiendish torture. But he resolved that should
never be. He was too brave a man to dream of giving
in ; and serious as the position was, and terrible as was
the responsibility, he showed that he was equal to them
and full of resource. What had to be done was to hold
out until succour arrived, and that was dependent on
Felbey getting safely through. If he did not the morning would surely bring relief, for it was impossible to
suppose that the rebels would be allowed to retain their
ill-gotten victory when daylight came. The problem,
therefore, that Sandon had to solve was how to keep
the besiegers from setting fire to the godown. Although
he had lost two of his little garrison, he received a
reinforcement in the person of Mrs. Pritchard. She
recognised how desperate was the situation, and sternly
bidding her children to keep quiet, and not cry for her,
and leaving them and her sister in the care of the ayah,
she asked Captain Sandon to utilize her services in
some way. He thereupon placed her at the loopholes
with a couple of rifles, while he busied himself for the
time in carrying out a little scheme that had come
upon him like an inspiration.

Amongst the stores in the godown were seven cases
of brandy. Prising open the lids of some of these cases,
he took out several bottles, and knocked off the heads
with the back of his sword. Then he stood the bottles

in a row on his platform, so as to be within reach of his hand. He next got three or four tin pannikins from a stock which were hanging against the wall; he filled the pannikins with brandy, mounted the platform, and peered out. The rabble were piling up fuel against the door. Producing a box of matches from his pocket, he set fire to the brandy in the pannikins, and then hurled the blazing spirit on to the rascals below. The effect was marvellous! They had had several surprises that night, and this was another one. They scattered as if a bomb had burst in their midst, and those upon whom the burning spirit fell yelled and howled with rage and pain. A storm of missiles was hurled at the little window, but they did no harm. Then a band of volunteers was called for to place fuel against the door and fire it, but when a number of the rabble started to do this, both Mrs. Pritchard and Captain Sandon emptied their revolvers at them, and while the lady reloaded, Sandon hurled forth the blazing brandy again. The natives began to realize now that, small as the defenders must be, they had the advantage. A hasty council was therefore held, and was decided to try stratagem. While some of the mob made feints against the door, others were to steal round, and with the aid of ladders —two of which had been found in the stables—they were to mount to the roof, and pull the roofing off, so that burning brands might be hurled into the interior of the godown. The wonder was this had not been thought of before, but on such occasions a rabble, worked to a pitch of fury and thirsting for revenge, does not pause to think calmly. But now, after so many ineffectual attempts to dislodge the defenders of the improvised fort, and when the death-roll of the mutineers had become appallingly heavy, the cooler heads of the disciplined Sepoys prevailed, and so, while the attention of Sandon was kept occupied by apparent attempts to make a bonfire in front of the door—though the rascals took good care not to expose themselves to the burning spirits nor the bullets—a number of men planted the ladders on the wall and against the side of the building, and mounting they began to tear the roof away.

Sandon had become aware, by the tactics of the enemy in front, that some new plan was being tried, though he could not determine what it was. But presently the ayah crept down from her perch amongst the boxes, where she was attending to Hester and the children, and moving noiselessly over the ground with her bare feet, she went to Sandon and whispered—

" Captain Sahib! they are on the roof."

This warning was full of terrible meaning, and though he did not like to think that all was quite lost, yet it was difficult to hope. With the coolness which had characterized him throughout the trying hours, he loaded every gun and revolver, and while he did not relax his vigilance at the window, he kept a sharp look-out above. The sounds that were heard made it now only too evident that the wretches were pulling the roof off. Showers of dirt pattered down inside, and two or three small cobras, which had found snug harbourage amongst the dusty beams, fell to the ground and hastened to secrete themselves in the interstices formed by the piled-up boxes. Then a great mass of the roof fell in, leaving a gap through which the lurid sky and the glow of the still burning bungalow could be seen, while a triumphant roar from the natives announced their success so far. Dusky faces appeared at the gap looking demoniacal in the malignant hatred and fierce passion they displayed, but they were quickly withdrawn when Sandon blazed away at them. Then the work of tearing the hole larger was proceeded with, and a shout was raised for inflammable material to fling down.

Poor Mrs. Pritchard felt now that the supreme moment had come. Her face was ashen; her eyes blazed with a terrible purpose; her voice was husky as she spoke to Sandon, and grasping the revolver said—

"All is over. God will bless you for your noble struggle to save us. You are a brave man, but further defence is useless. Farewell, we shall meet in heaven."

He knew what she meant. He seized her arm and took the revolver away from her.

"Not yet," he answered. "There is still hope. But rest assured we will never be taken alive."

Even as he spoke there burst through the hole in the roof a great spurt of flame, and a shower of burning paper, leaves, dried grass, and other things was hurled down, scattering fire about the place, and filling the godown with dense smoke, while a mighty shout from the mob outside expressed their joy. Then Mrs. Pritchard, with a pitiable moan of anguish, broke away from the Captain, and rushing to the corner where her children were, she kissed them frantically, while they in their terrible fright clung to her, and Amy wailed out—

"Oh, mamma, mamma, save us."

Her woman's heart was rent and torn by that appeal of her beloved child. Falling on her knees she clasped the two children to her breast, and turning her unnaturally brilliant eyes to the hole in the roof, from whence mocking cries and laughter came, she hissed fiercely between her clenched teeth—

" You ferocious and accursed wolves, you shall not have my darlings."

CHAPTER XXVII.

FROM THE JAWS OF DEATH.

As poor Mrs. Pritchard gave utterance to this defiant expression, she made a dash for a revolver which lay upon the top of a box near where Captain Sandon was standing, rifle raised ready to fire at the first head that appeared at the hole in the roof. He guessed her object, for, half distracted as she was, she was not responsible for her actions. He therefore seized her arms, but it was only after a struggle that he succeeded in getting the weapon from her.

" I pray you be calm," he said sternly. " All is not yet lost."

As if to give contradiction to his statement, another mass of flaming material was at that moment hurled through the hole in the roof, some of it absolutely falling on the little stock of ammunition, but he seized a large can of water they had brought over from the bungalow, and dashed it on the flames, and then he beat out the smouldering embers with his jacket. Frantic with fear and anxiety for her little ones, Mrs. Pritchard shrieked hysterically, and tried again to obtain possession of one of the revolvers; and alarmed more perhaps by their mother's manner than the danger that menaced from the outside, the children screamed, and as they clung in horror to the ayah they called out piteously—

" Mamma, mamma, mamma, come to us."

From without came the roar of the rebels as they realized now how near they were to their prey. Any one who has ever heard the yelling of a savage mob infuriated to a pitch of madness can never forget it, while those who happily have not had that experience cannot imagine it. The roar of a wounded tiger in the jungle as he sees his destroyers bearing down upon him is one of the most appalling sounds in savage nature, and yet it is nothing to the roar of men thirsting for the lives of their fellow beings. That angry, desperate mob around the godown seemed with their cries for vengeance to rend the very air, and shake even the solid building itself.

" Drag them out, drag them out," they shouted. " We'll cut them slowly to pieces, and the Captain Sahib shall be roasted alive. Bring them out, bring them out. Take them alive that we may torture them."

These cries rose and fell like the sounds of tumultuous waves beating against iron rocks; and the mob surging like a wind-tossed sea, swept now this side, now that, and dashed themselves against the godown; recoiling with the shock, but rushing on again till many of their number were trampled down and crushed to death.

Captain Sandon, although he realized that hope was all but dead, manfully, bravely, heroically did his best to keep the host at bay, but his movements were terribly hampered by Mrs. Pritchard, who seemed to have become quite distraught. The very desperateness of the situation, on the other hand, restored Hester to consciousness and activity. Looking ghastly in her pallor, which was enhanced by the blood that still trickled from the wound in her forehead, she suddenly rose up from where she had been lying, and throwing her arms about her sister, said sternly—

" Madge, for shame. Be calm. Our protector will save us. Even now I hear the thunder of galloping horses. Succour is coming to us."

" My children, my children, save them," shrieked the unhappy mother, whose intense horror, engendered by the prospect of her little ones falling into the hands of the tigerish horde, had literally made her mad.

" They will be saved," answered Hester, speaking with strange calmness, and as if prompted by some prophetic instinct. " I tell you I hear the sounds of beating hoofs. The troops are coming."

Uninfluenced by this assertion, Mrs. Pritchard, with a wail of agonising despair, tore her hair, and breaking from her sister's restraining grasp, rushed to her children and clasped them frantically to her bosom, wailing out the while—

" God, God, why have you forsaken us?"

With this outpouring of her great agony nature succumbed, and a blessed unconsciousness suddenly seized her as she fell forward in a swoon. Then the ayah once more took the children to her arms and crooned a lullaby to them in her attempt to soothe them.

During the occurrence of these pathetic incidents the heroic Sandon had not remained inactive. All the grand soldierly qualities of his nature were called into play, and he still fought the foe with unflagging courage· With a mighty effort that taxed all his strength, strong as he was, he had piled up some of the cases until they nearly reached the rafters, then with the revolvers stuck in his belt, his sword girded about him, a rifle in his hand, and telling Hester to hand up the guns as he wanted them, he clambered to the top of his platform, which enabled him to look through the hole in the roof, and blazing away with a revolver in each hand, he bowled over the ruffians who were preparing to hurl another mass of blazing material into the godown.

It was a further surprise for the foe, who, baffled once more, howled again and again with hellish rage. But suddenly there arose from some of their number a great shout of alarm, and they began to scatter as a herd of sheep will do when a dog gets amongst them ; and as they fled there came to the ears of the beleaguered little party in the godown the welcome sounds of a true British cheer. This was succeeded by a volley, and a body of cavalry dashed into the compound, some sweeping through the gateway, others leaping their horses over the walls and sabring and cutting down the dusky ruffians without pity.

Succour had come at last. The gallant Felbey, fighting his way through all those who tried to oppose him, reached the cantonments, and making known Captain Sandon's position, a company of troopers were immediately ordered to gallop to the rescue. As they tore along the road, which was brilliantly illuminated by the burning bungalows, and riding over and cutting down crowds of rascals as they swept onwards like a tornado, it was a neck and neck race who should be first at the Pritchard compound. Thundering onward, and panting for vengeance on some at least of the

brutes who had that night deluged Meerut with so
much innocent blood, they hurled themselves into the
compound, and scattered the cowardly foe like sand
before a simoom.

As Sandon realized that help had come at last he
sprang down from his platform. He was grimed with
powder, smoke, and dust; it was difficult almost to
recognise in him the prim, faultlessly-dressed officer of
a few hours ago. Forgetting himself for a moment—
but his forgetfulness was pardonable—he put his arm
about Hester's neck, and kissing her with great warmth
said—

" My darling, you are safe."

Then he flung the boxes on one side that had formed
the barricade for the door, flung the door open as Felbey
was hammering on it with the pommel of his sword,
and the two comrades grasped hands again. The compound was soon cleared, and while Felbey and half-a-
dozen gallant fellows remained, the rest of the troop
pursued the flying rascals for some distance, until the
commanding officer ordered a halt and then led them
back to the compound.

In the meantime, Mrs. Pritchard had recovered consciousness, but she was delirious, and, seeming to forget
her children, she called frantically for her husband, and
struggled and raved to such an extent that it was as
much as two strong men could do to hold her. With
some difficulty she was placed on the saddle in front of
a stalwart trooper. The children and the ayah were
taken by other soldiers, and as Hester refused to ride
with any one, she and Sandon walked, escorted by half-
a-dozen men, including young Felbey. Two or three
times she reeled and seemed about to faint, and Sandon

had to support her. Her head had been bound up as well as could be done under the circumstances, and the bleeding stopped, but she had lost so much blood that she was very weak, and it was only by a supreme effort of will she succeeded in reaching the cantonments, then her effort failed and she sank into unconsciousness.

When the surgeons came they began to probe for a bullet, but they soon determined that the wound in her forehead was not a gunshot wound at all, but had probably been inflicted by a jagged stone, or an iron bar hurled onward with great force, causing a very ugly gash, and slightly fracturing the frontal bone. She was at once conveyed to the hospital, and every attention bestowed upon her; while Mrs. Pritchard, the children, and the ayah were placed in the care of some ladies who had been fortunate in escaping from the fury of the mutineers.

When Captain Sandon reached the cantonments, in spite of the mental strain he had endured for hours, and the tremendous exertions he had been compelled to make, he begged of his commanding officer to let him sally forth with a little troop of horse and pursue the rebels, but he was told to his amazement that the orders were that no pursuit was to be made, and troops would only be allowed to go out for purposes of rescue. No wonder that he and many other brave fellows chafed and fretted at this senseless restraint.

Slowly that dreadful night waned, and seldom before had British troops been compelled through the irresolution of their commander to remain inactive while their countrymen and women were being hacked to pieces; and seldom had civilians been called upon to endure a night of such mental strain and horror as was endured by the white residents in Meerut. The British soldiers —and they were some of the finest in India—numbered not far short of two thousand, and had only half that number been let loose against the mutineers, very few of the rebels would have escaped. When the whole station seemed to be in a blaze, and the yelling and frantic shouts of the infuriated mob was suggestive of hell broke loose, General Hewett moved a body of troops out, and they fired a few random volleys in the dark, nearly killing some European officers in doing so. But after this little fizzle the soldiers were ordered to withdraw to the European lines again. It was a terrible blunder—a fatal error. Many a valuable life that might have been saved was sacrificed ; and even those who survived endured suspense and agony which would have been spared if the troops had been sent out. As it was, the mutineers, having completed their demoniacal work, galloped off to Delhi without let or hindrance.

During the next few days the garrison was still kept inactive. No steps were taken to punish the inhuman rascals who had poured forth from the bazaars in their thousands to burn and slay, with the exception of the hanging of a few straggling maurauders who were caught red-handed and promptly strung up.

The women and children found shelter in a walled enclosure known as the Dumdama, and most of the officers—including the Generals and their staff—took up their quarters in a barrack.

During these days of enforced idleness, Captain Sandon was restless and angry, and his anxiety about Hester displayed itself in an unmistakable manner. She had been compelled to undergo a slight operation for the removal of some piece of fractured bone. The operation itself was comparatively trifling, but owing probably to the intense nervous strain she had endured on that terrible night in the godown, surgical fever set in, and some doubts were expressed as to whether she would recover. Mrs. Pritchard, fortunately, had so far regained her normal condition that she was able to undertake to nurse her, but her distress of mind was excessive, for no news had reached her from her husband, therefore she was in complete ignorance of his fate, and her fears for his safety were very great. She was aware how terribly cut up Sandon was, and knowing that she and her children and sister owed their lives to him, she necessarily displayed great tenderness and regard towards him. And on the third day after the operation, when he went to the hospital to make inquiries about Hester, she told him, by way of comforting him, that the doctors spoke more hopefully of her sister, and she added—

"There is no doubt that Hetty loves you. Last night, during the delirium of the fever, she did nothing but rave about you, and referred to you in all sorts of endearing terms."

So far this was consoling, and his hopes rose ; but while he was thus playing the lover, and yearning to clasp in his arms the woman who had won his heart, he was not forgetful that he was a soldier, and he did not hesitate to give expression to indignation and anger that he should be compelled to remain idle and keep his sword in its scabbard when there was brave work to be done. That very day, as it so chanced, a letter was brought by a faithful native bearer from a party of fugitive men, women, and children who had escaped from Delhi, and were secreted in a jungle. The writer implored that troops might be sent to rescue them. He said that the mutineers swarmed all over the roads, and had vowed to murder every white person they could get hold of. Therefore the fugitives dare not move from their hiding-place. They were in a dreadful state, for they had no food and no water, and unless they were rescued in the course of the next few hours they must all perish.

Captain Sandon happened to be in the General's quarters when this letter, which was in French, was brought in and read. He immediately asked that he might be allowed to go out with a little body of troops and rescue the people. At first the request was refused, for it was pointed out that a handful of men would be certain to meet with disaster, as the rebels and budmashes were swarming about the roads in thousands, and a large number of troops could not be spared, as it would not do to weaken the garrison. But Sandon was not to be turned from his purpose. He pressed his point. He said it was the first time women and children in peril had appealed in vain to British soldiers. He asked that a dozen men might be allotted to him, and he would do all that man could do to attempt the rescue. Somewhat reluctantly, permission was at last given, and he was told to select a party of twenty-four men. He had no difficulty in doing this. Every man in the garrison was ready to volunteer to go. Amongst his little company was Lieutenant Felbey, so that the two comrades were destined to once more share danger together.

While the men were saddling their horses and preparing for the venture, Sandon went to Mrs. Pritchard to tell her that he was going out on an expedition. He did not enlighten her on the smallness of his company and the desperate nature of the work before him. She was sufficiently well aware of the state of matters to suppose that he would run no risk, and as she bade him God-speed she said—

" Before you go you might see Hetty. She is much better, and has inquired about you."

He was delighted at this, and gladly followed Mrs. Pritchard to the little room where Hester, looking wan and weak, was lying in bed, her head enveloped in surgical bandages. She smiled faintly, and put out her hand to welcome him, and seemed very glad to see him.

They had a few minutes' chat together, and then he said in an offhand sort of a way that he was going out to bring in some women and children. She turned her languid eyes upon him with the remark—

" The women and children may be thankful that so heroic a man, and so good a soldier as you, is to undertake their rescue. If you cannot succeed, no one else could."

" Tut, tut, my dear, you mustn't speak of me like that," he answered, as the colour came into his face. " It is my good fortune to be told off for this duty, but there is not a man in the garrison who would not have gone if he had got the chance. I am simply in luck's way."

" You underrate yourself," she said. " How many are going with you ? "

" Oh, quite a little regiment," he answered laughingly.

" But how many ? " she urged.

" Well, a couple of dozen."

" Is that all ? "

"All! Why, my dear girl, it's plenty. Amongst them is young Felbey, and he is equal to a dozen himself."

"Ah, you speak lightly, though you cannot deceive me. But go; you are a soldier. God be with you, and bring you back safely again."

He construed this remark into something like a confession of love, and pressing her hand to his lips with the grace of a courtier he bade her adieu. Half-an-hour later the boot and saddle had sounded, and he and his little band of gallant troopers were riding forth on their perilous mission.

CHAPTER XXVIII.

THE TREACHERY OF THE RANEE.

THE news of the success of the mutineers in Meerut soon spread far and wide throughout North-West India. It had been anxiously waited for. Traitors who knew what was to happen had been keenly on the alert for the first signs of success. It was so well understood in native quarters that if the rising planned to take place in the strong military station of Meerut, where the number of British troops was greater than in any other station in the Punjaub, was not nipped in the bud, the revolt would roll forth like an impetuous stream that, bursting its banks, gathers volume as it goes, and sweeps all before it. But, perhaps, in no place had events been watched so anxiously as they were in Jhansi. The treacherous Ranee was thirsting for the blood of the whites. She had nursed her wrongs, or supposed wrongs, until they had crushed out every feeling of pity, and one great unconquerable desire for vengeance kept her in a state of feverish excitement. She was an ambitious woman, no less than a cruel and crafty one; and what she aimed at in her own particular case was freeing herself from the British yoke, consolidating her power, and extending that power until the ruler of Jhansi should be recognised as one of the most powerful rulers in India.

It was a dream, a wild, fantastic dream, perhaps, but she regarded it as one that was likely to be fulfilled if only Meerut should succeed. And so she kept her eyes, so to speak, fixed on Meerut, and listened for any sound that would convey the glad tidings to her that the hour of freedom had struck.

It has frequently been said that the Rajah of Bithoor, familiarly known to all the world now as Nana Sahib, and dubbed by the *Times* "the Tiger of Cawnpore," was one of the cruelest and most treacherous men who ever walked the earth. But the Ranee of Jhansi was not far behind him, either in treachery or cruelty. Like the Nana, she could murder and smile while she murdered. She could play the false friend with a consummate art that was little short of marvellous. She begot confidence by her plausibility, and no one knew better than she did how to conceal the blackness of her designs and the cruelty of her heart by a fawning manner and a smiling face. At first she had chafed and fretted and talked of her injuries, but she discovered that was a mistake. It was due to this that she succeeded so completely in throwing the little handful of British officers in Jhansi off their guard and disarming suspicion. She schooled herself to play a part. She entertained the officers of the garrison, she lent them her hunting elephants, she sent them presents, and she placed her servants at their orders. But all this time, like the crafty panther seeking its prey, she was watching her victims and crouching for the spring.

Life in Jhansi among the British was at the best monotonous. It was a hot and dusty station, and each day passed wonderfully like another. The European

THE TREACHERY OF THE RANEE.

officers only numbered nine, and some of them had their wives and families. The nine included young Hallett, who since his arrival had managed to make himself popular with his countrymen at least, but he soon fell into the Ranee's bad books. A few days after his arrival he was invited with a few of his comrades to the Ranee's palace, where they were entertained with the lavish display and prodigality for which she had become notorious. But though she might have succeeded in impressing him with the magnificence of her surroundings, she failed to make a favourable impression upon him as regarded her own personality, for that evening at the mess one of his brother-officers said to him—

" Well, what do you think of the Ranee, Hallett?"

" Very little."

" Why, how is that? Everybody likes her."

" Do they? Well, I don't. I should say that she is about as insincere a woman as you would be able to find in a long day's march. She has got the heart of a devil, I'm convinced of that, and I should be sorry to trust her farther than I could see her."

" Oh nonsense," exclaimed his companion somewhat patronisingly. " You mustn't take silly prejudices like that, or you'll never make your way in India. The fact is the Ranee is a capital woman. I don't know what we fellows should do without her. She keeps us going in elephants, and the feeds she gives us are things to be remembered. It's a deadly dull hole this, but the Ranee does her level best to relieve the monotony for us. And now take my advice, my friend. You, as a subaltern, have got to study your own interests; but those interests will suffer, believe me, if you display unfounded prejudices of that kind. The Ranee is an influential woman, and a staunch friend to the British."

"I quite understand that your advice is kindly meant," returned Hallett somewhat ironically, "but I have opinions of my own, and also a habit of sticking to them until I am convinced I am wrong. Of course, I am only a youngster, as you remind me, and perhaps when I have cut my wisdom teeth, and am something more than a subaltern, I shall acquire the art of dissembling. At present I am ignorant of it, and I repeat I don't like the Ranee, and am not going to say that I do. One has only to look into her fierce, restless eyes to understand her deceit. My impression is, that if this she-devil got half a chance she would cut all our throats and gloat over her deed."

"Oh, come, come," observed his brother-officer, "she is not so bad as that."

"Very well, we'll agree to differ," said Hallett.

The subject was now allowed to drop, but that conversation had not escaped the sharp ears of listening servants, and in due course it was repeated to the Ranee, with all the exaggerations incidental to gossip that is passed from lip to lip amongst Eastern races, and when she heard it she muttered—

"This insolent white puppy must be taught a lesson."

Then turning to her trusty factotum, Mata Singh, she told him what she had heard, and she added significantly, "Singh, you will see to it when the moment comes that this young fool is seized and brought before me. There are dungeons beneath my palace here, where my ancestors have found quarters for their enemies. In one of these dungeons this lad

shall rot in chains. I will torture him for his insolence."

Singh expressed his readiness to carry out her
commands to the very letter. He, like his mistress,
was burning to spoil the English, and he looked
forward eagerly to the hoped-for day when they would
be swept from the face of India. Another staunch
retainer upon whom she knew she could rely was
Chuna, the escaped prisoner from Meerut.

This man was a zealot in her cause, and he had
exerted himself to the utmost to corrupt the native
garrison of Jhansi. His efforts had been so far successful that the soldiers only waited a signal to rise and
massacre every white man, woman, and child in the
place. Had it not been for the Ranee's restraining
influence this rising would have taken place without
any reference to Meerut at all, but she knew perfectly
well that though she and her people might score a
temporary triumph, it would be very temporary indeed
unless the British regiments in Meerut were prevented
leaving there by strife within their own gates. If
the attempt in Meerut failed, then all would be lost,
but the reports that reached her almost daily spoke
most encouragingly of the prospects. One of the reports
which came from a moonshee or writer employed in
the commissariat department, ran thus—

" *These Feringhees are fools. They suspect nothing.
They have such unbounded confidence in themselves, and
such a supreme belief in their own infallibility, that
they refuse to believe it even within the bounds of possibility that a day of reckoning is coming. But this day
will of a certainty dawn, unless our people are content
to remain for ever in bondage, and to forget and forgive*

the stripes and persecution they have suffered at the hands of these barbarous taskmasters. That cannot be, however. We are not so effeminate as that. The blood boils in our veins as we think of our wrongs, and slowly but surely we are maturing our plans for a decisive blow. Knowing as we do how much depends upon us, we are anxious that there should be no miscarriage. If Meerut is successful, the reign of the British in India is over, and once again our race will rise to that position of power and greatness which they occupied before these accursed people crossed the seas to invade our territory. Therefore take heart, great lady. The greatness and power which erstwhile were the prerogatives of your house will return, and Jhansi shall once again be one of the mighty states of India."

This letter, which was typical of many she received, flattered the Ranee's vanity. In her hurry to reach the goal towards which she was pressing she never paused to consider whether or not the fawners and lickspittles who surrounded her were actuated by true patriotism, or were mere place-seekers, anxious to serve themselves and bring grist to their own mills. The history of her own house—that is, of the rulers of Jhansi—was a history of bloodshed and cruelty. They had kept their power by the sword, and their enemies had been smitten with a relentlessness of purpose which aimed at making the rulers of Jhansi greater even than the Moguls of Delhi. But the Ranee did not take this into consideration. She had been robbed of her birth-right, so she believed, by the English, consequently she bore them no love. She did not believe in being a puppet. She would be a ruler or nothing.

At last the supreme moment came. One night a

hot and dusty traveller entered Jhansi without let or hindrance. He had come from Meerut, and had all the appearance of one who had sped without sparing himself. He was one of the Ranee's spies, and he at once sought her presence, for he was the bearer of great tidings.

Prostrating himself before her, and bowing his forehead to the dust, he said—

" Rejoice, lady, for I bring you good news. All has gone well in Meerut. The Sepoys rose mighty in their wrath, and with fire and sword they swept the town clear of the hated Feringhees, whose bodies lie like unowned curs in the gutters, which have been washed with blood."

" And the white troopers, what of them?" the Ranee almost shrieked in the intensity of her excitement.

" Such of them as remain are paralysed with fear, lady, and are no more capable of offering resistance than an army of sucking babes would be."

" Aha! this is news indeed," she cried. " And what of our brave people, who have done this great thing?"

" Flushed with victory they have gone forth to Delhi, where the same thing has been repeated, and the power of the Mogul has been restored. The King of Delhi sits on his throne again, powerful as in the dead and gone days. But a new era dawns. The white Raj is destroyed for ever."

" Thou art sure of that?" she demanded fiercely.

" Aye, as sure as that death will come to all things that live."

For a moment a dark frown swept over her cruel face, and she muttered as if to herself—" The King of

Delhi is old, very old. His sands are all but run out. He is a mere puppet." These words showed the drift of her thoughts. Her house and the house of the Mogul rulers had ever been at variance, for the Moguls had sought to make Jhansi a subservient State—so that she had cause to fear a restoration to power of the fallen king. But her gloomy thoughts quickly passed away, and she sent an attendant to bid Mata Singh come to her.

"Mata," she said, when the man appeared, "the hour has struck at last; triumph will now be ours. Speed you to-night, silent as death itself, and proclaim the news to all friends; and, hark you, Singh, when to-morrow's sun sets there must not be a white man, woman, or child alive in Jhansi. Stay, one must be spared; Hallett, I think, is his name. He shall be spared for a bitterer death. Mark what I say. He is to be seized and brought here. Then he is to be chained in one of the dungeons and slowly starved to death. Revenge is great, and thus my enemies shall perish."

Mata bowed and retired. He was no less eager than his mistress to destroy the British rule, and a little later he left the royal residence to carry out his mission, muttering as he went—

"To-morrow; aye, to-morrow shall witness great things. The yoke shall be broken, the Ranee shall rule again, and I, her faithful henchman, shall receive my due reward."

The morrow came, and soon after reveille had sounded a native bearer placed a chit (note) in the hands of Lieutenant Hallett. It was written in English, and dated from the Ranee's palace. Of course it was not in her own handwriting, but that of one of her moonshees, or clerks. The note was worded as follows :—

" The Ranee of Jhansi presents her compliments to Lieutenant Hallett, and requests with much respect that he will do her the honour of calling at the palace as early as possible. The Ranee understands that Lieutenant Hallett has recently come from Persia, and she is anxious to obtain some information of a particular character about that country, which probably he can give her. She therefore begs that he will favour her with a visit."

This artfully-worded note was quite calculated to throw the young man off his guard. Although his opinion of the Ranee was by no means a flattering one, and he had with singular accuracy gauged her character to a large extent, he did not suspect treachery. Indeed, if the truth must be told, he was rather pleased by the notice she bestowed upon him, for it seemed in no way remarkable that she should make such a request. And as he had a couple of hours on his hands before the general morning parade, he went off to the palace, where he was received by several obsequious flunkies, and at once conducted to the Rance's presence.

Two hours later, to the summons of the bugles, the native troops began to assemble on the parade-ground, and the officers rode up and down, utterly unconscious of the danger that menaced them. The troops consisted of a wing of the 12th Native Infantry, and the 14th Irregular Cavalry. Hallett, to the astonishment of all his brother-officers, did not put in an appearance when the muster sounded, and as he was nowhere to be found, his absence was reported to the Colonel, who was exceedingly angry, and ordered that the young fellow was to be charged with breach of privilege and neglect of duty. Then the business of the parade was proceeded with ; but when the troops were called upon to form up in columns, they remained silent and sullen. The British officers saw at once that something was wrong, and the Colonel repeated the order with a stern peremp· toriness that produced no effect, however. Then he rode nearer to the mutineers, and shouted—

"Do you intend to obey the order or not?"

Instantly there stepped from the ranks a havildar-major, who answered saucily—

"No, we don't."

The parade was at once dismissed, and the men went back to their quarters very sullenly ; but an hour or two later they seized their arms, and rushed out, crying, "Death to the Feringhees."

Duly warned, however, of the inevitable outbreak, some of the officers, all the ladies and children, in all about seventy-five, had betaken themselves to the fort, which was defended for two days. Then some treacherous servant in the fort shot two of the officers, by name Gordon and Burgess, and this so reduced the defensive power of the garrison that the unhappy people abandoned all hope. Then came a messenger from the Ranee, saying that their lives should all be spared, and they should be afforded safe-conduct to Meerut. Believing this, they allowed themselves to be led forth, and were taken to a garden, where a body of the mutineers were concealed. These wretches sprang up as soon as the people appeared, and then ensued a scene of butchery no less terrible than that which, later on, was for ever to render the name of Cawnpore infamous. By the Ranee's order, not a man, not a woman, not a child was spared. Over seventy people were hacked to pieces in that fair garden, until the ground ran red with blood, and the very birds, that had erstwhile made sweet music in. the trees, fled in horror away. With insane ferociousness, even the bodies of the silent dead were subjected to the most fiendish outrages.

Jhansi had thus followed Meerut, and the mutineers were triumphant.

CHAPTER XXIX.

FOR LOVE AND LIFE.

WHEN young Hallett found himself in the presence of the Ranee, he noted that the apartment was crowded with armed men, and as he was about to approach her in order to pay her the compliment of kissing her hand, she waved him off with an imperious gesture, saying—

"Defile me not with your foul lips."

Then for the first time his suspicions were aroused, and he began to think something was wrong; but drawing himself up proudly, he replied—

"What means this? How have I offended you, my lady?"

He spoke in English, for the Ranee, although she did not write it, spoke and understood that language well.

"It means that you are an unclean animal," she snarled fiercely. "Therefore should I be defiled if you touch me. It means that you have spoken lyingly and disrespectfully of me, and for that you will pay the penalty with your life. It means that all your accursed countrymen will have bitten the dust to-day long ere the sun reaches its meridian. You would have died with them had I not been told that your foul tongue has maligned me; and for that I have allured you here in order that you may be chained up and slowly starved to death. Thus perish my enemies."

She looked like the savage she was as she spoke. Her face was the face of a merciless, pitiless barbarian, who was thirsting for blood. Hallett glanced hurriedly round. He realised that escape was impossible, but he resolved to sell his life dearly; and suddenly drawing his sword, which up to that moment he had been allowed to retain, he made a sudden spring forward in the direction of the Ranee, and there is little doubt he would have run her through the body had not one of the body-guards, with singular adroitness, precipitated himself on the young fellow, and the impact was so great that the two fell to the ground. Before the Englishman could even attempt to rise he was seized by half a dozen stalwart fellows, disarmed, dragged to his feet, and held so firmly that he was utterly powerless. A bitter cruel smile wreathed itself about the hard, cruel mouth of the Ranee, who said with a contemptuous sneer—

" Treacherous knave! It is in keeping with the *rôle* of your countrymen that you would play the assassin. But for this attempt upon my life you shall pay a double penalty. Hark ye, my people, and Mata Singh, see you that this, my will, is carried out. Every morning, so long as he shall live, let him be tied naked to the tail of a bullock-cart, and scourged through the streets, so that my faithful subjects may see that I know how to treat the enemies of my country. And two days from now have his foul and lying tongue cut from his mouth, and let it be brought to me, so that I may know that my orders have been carried out. Remove him."

Hallett was dragged from the room amidst the yells and groans of those around him. His heart turned to lead as he realised how small indeed were his chances of escaping the terrible doom which the fiendish Ranee had pronounced. It was hard to die young, to die in the first flush of his early manhood, and when a career seemed opening out before him, but it was doubly hard that his life should be sacrificed now that—after enduring so much and sacrificing so much—he was within a hundred miles of the woman he loved dearer than life. Blank despair seized him, and he resolved that if any chance offered he would destroy himself, and so cheat the treacherous Ranee of one part of her revenge at least.

The palace occupied by the Ranee was situated on the summit of a rocky eminence, that rose up by a gentle incline from the plain on the one side, and broke away in terraced precipices on the other. The palace was an old building, and, in common with places of that kind in India, it was provided with a number of dungeon-like chambers. In one of these chambers Hallett was placed. The only means of ventilation and light was that afforded by a sort of narrow embrasure in the rock. Glancing through that opening, the eye was enabled to range over a wide panorama. Hallett's first feeling was one of terrible, blank despair. It was only too painfully apparent that he had been treacherously entrapped, nor could he doubt for a moment that his comrades must have been killed, and that the native troops had mutinied. Otherwise the Ranee would never have dared to imprison him. No wonder, as he thought of these things, that his heart turned to lead. The Ranee had more than justified the opinion he had formed of her; and since she had made it evident that she had come by some means to know what he had said about her, it was not likely that she would show him the slightest mercy.

For some little time he remained in such a fever of suppressed excitement that he was dazed to a certain extent, and felt almost as if he must go mad. But after a while he grew calmer, and, as was but natural, he began to think of Hester. He was in ignorance, of course, of all that had taken place in Meerut, but he recalled every word of her letter to him, and it proved a sort of mental tonic, until, in spite of the desperate nature of his position, something like a glimmering of hope began to dawn. He was too energetic, too brave, to submit quite calmly to the carrying out of the Ranee's sentence upon him, and when once the reaction had set in, his spirits revived very considerably. If a weapon had been placed in his hands, and he had been told to cut his way to the woman he loved, he would have faced fearful odds, and have risked every possible danger. But though a man be as strong as Samson and as bold as a lion, what can he do if he is chained and caged? He may fling himself against his bars, and batter himself against his prison walls, but only to his own hurt. Some such thought as this came to the wretched young man as he paced up and down the narrow limits of the chamber. In such a case all that one can hope for is, that some unlooked-for, some inconceivable chance may favour one. This indeed is the only hope that can possibly be cherished. Slender it may be, and forlorn it is ; but even a forlorn hope sometimes succeeds. And so Hallett thought to himself—

" If fickle Fortune hasn't altogether deserted me, she may unexpectedly and in an unlooked-for quarter open up a way by which I can escape."

There was not much consolation perhaps in this reflection, but such as there was he comforted himself with it.

Slowly the dreadful day waned, and the night came. It so far brought him relief that he was enabled to obtain some sleep, which he did by making a pillow of his jacket, and stretching himself on the bare ground. He awoke with the dawn, feeling somewhat cramped and stiff, yet mentally refreshed. A cool, refreshing breeze was blowing in through the barred aperture, and placing himself in the direct line of the current of air, he drew it into his lungs and felt grateful, although the pangs of hunger were very keen, for he had had nothing to eat since the preceding morning. Everything was very still, and the growing light of the strengthening dawn was reddening the landscape. He leaned his head against the iron bars, of which there were three, and gazed dreamily out to where the river flowed far below.

Suddenly it occurred to him to test the strength of those bars, which he found were old and rusty. They had probably been there for generations, and the cement in which they had originally been set was cracked and honeycombed. It seemed to him that the middle bar as he shook it showed signs of weakness. He shook it harder, and he felt sure then that it was weak. Then did he put forth the lusty strength of his youth, and the lower part of the bar came away. It had broken from the part embedded in the cement. Having now got a leverage, it was relatively easy to force the upper part loose, and in a few moments he stood with the bar of iron in his hand. He would have been a strange man if he had not become somewhat excited, for firstly he held a weapon in that bar of iron, and secondly a way of escape seemed to have suddenly presented itself to him.

He managed to squeeze himself partly through the

increased opening he had made, and he noted that from the aperture there was a drop of something like twenty feet on to a ledge of rock ; and then as far as he could gather it was almost perpendicular down to the plain where the river flowed. No one perhaps save he who was in desperate need would have drawn much hope of life and liberty from that precipitous rock-face. But Hallett was in desperate need, and with an energy begotten by his condition, he used the broken bar as a lever wherewith to prize out one of the others, which yielded at last to the pressure thus put upon it, and it broke away from the top ; and by alternately pushing and tugging with might and main he wrenched it from the bottom holding.

He could now get through the aperture with ease. His first care was to tie the bar of iron to his waist with his handkerchief, for it would have to serve him as a weapon. Then lowering himself outside until he hung by the tips of his fingers, he paused for a few moments and dropped on to the ledge. Before he could steady himself the impetus carried him forward, and he found himself taking a series of flying leaps, as it were. Down, down he went ; it was impossible to stop. At last he pitched on to a turf-covered slope, down which he flew as if he had been shot from a catapult ; until breathless, dazed, half-stunned, he reached the level ground. He was bruised and bleeding, and so violent had been the shaking he had received in his breakneck descent, that he lay where he had fallen for some minutes, and felt as if and believed that the was dying. Then, as he began to recover his scattered senses, he heard a confused roar and shouting. His escape had been noticed, and the alarm was being spread.

Bullets whizzed near him by scores, but did not strike him.

At last the longing for life, and thoughts of the woman he loved, nerved him to another effort. So up he sprang, and running forward, he found himself at the entrance to a wooden bridge spanning the river. There were three or four excited natives standing there, and they showed a disposition to dispute his passage. The iron bar was still bound to his waist; he loosened it, and told the fellows to stand on one side; but instead of doing so, they made a rush for him. One fell stunned by a blow from the bar, and the others were scattered. He sped across the bridge, and gained the plain. There he paused, and considered whether it was not his duty as a soldier to go back and ascertain what was really the fate of his comrades, for he could only surmise that the troops had mutinied. He had no proof as yet. The proof came, however, even as he stood there, in the shape of a round shot, which was fired from a small gun placed on the terrace of the Ranee's palace. That shot would not and dare not have been fired had the English not been rendered powerless. It seemed to him conclusive evidence. Fortunately the shot went wide of its mark, and raised a huge column of dust which actually aided him by screening him for a while from his enemies.

He had always been noted for his powers of running, and they were to serve him in good stead now. On he sped, until half dead with fatigue, his breath spent, his limbs trembling, he reached a small native village. Nothing seemed to be stirring; the people were all or nearly all away, working in the fields. He saw before him an open doorway leading into a buffalo-stable; he dashed in, and in a little side-building leading out of it was a great heap of dried grass, used as fodder for the animals. Into that heap of fodder he threw himself, feeling as if he were really going mad with thirst and excitement.

In a little while, however, he fell into a sleep from which he did not awaken until the evening. Then he was disturbed by the peasants bringing in their bullocks after working in the fields. He lay very still and was not discovered, and when the animals had been put up for the night, and the men had retired, Hallett stole from his place of concealment. A leather bucket that had been used for watering the cattle stood in one corner. It was still half full of water, and of this water, impure as it was, the young man drank greedily. Feeling refreshed by the rest and the drink, he went cautiously forth. It was the supper hour of the natives, and that was in his favour. Sometimes creeping, and moving with the greatest care, he gained the outskirts of the village, which consisted of not more than a couple of dozen mud hovels. Suddenly he heard the neigh of a horse close to him. The animal, which was roped to a stake, was feeding in a compound. He entered the compound, and by the aid of the light of the stars he untethered the horse, made a bit and bridle of the rope, put it over the animal's head, and then springing on to the animal's back he rode forth. The horse was a poor, half-famished brute, but still it carried him well enough for the time, and presently he gained a road, which, from its direction, he guessed must lead towards Meerut, which he now wished to reach.

All night long he held on his way until it was broad daylight. Then he met a native woman carrying a basket of eggs and a can of goat's milk. He stopped her and demanded some of her goods; and drawing a couple of rupees from his pocket, he placed them in her skinny hand.

For this she permitted him to drink as much of the milk and suck as many of the eggs as he liked. When he had thus made a hearty meal, he inquired of her as well as he could—for his knowledge of Hindoostanee was very limited—which was the way to Meerut. She pointed to a road, which he took, and continued his journey until he gained a jungle, where there was a pond of water; here he decided to rest himself and weary horse. He lay concealed for hours, and when the darkness was falling pursued his way, riding all night, and lying concealed the following day, satisfying the craving of thirst and hunger with some dirty nullah water and herbs. That night he went forth again, and the following morning, weary, worn, and famished, he came in sight of a town from which columns of dense smoke and lurid flames were rising, and he heard the sounds of musketry. These signs were too significant to be ignored. It was clear there had been a rising there. Sick and weary of heart he turned aside and sought the shelter of a jungle, where he passed a terrible day, and he began to think that it was hardly worth while making any further struggle for his life; but this fit of despondency gradually passed away, and when the moon rose he decided on making another effort to save himself, although he was now weak and ill from the want of food. Thoughts of Hester, however, nerved him, so mounting his weary and half-famished horse, he rode forth northward again.

CHAPTER XXX.

WHEN Captain Sandon volunteered for the expedition to rescue the fugitives from Delhi, who were reported to be hiding in a jungle not far from that city, he little knew how desperate the service was. Owing to the supineness of the authorities in Meerut and other places, the mutineers swarmed over all the roads. It might be said with a strict regard for truth that the great revolt of the Sepoys had so far been allowed to go unchecked, and the unfortunate Europeans were abandoned to fire and slaughter. But Sandon was not the man to shrink from the duty he had undertaken ; while Felbey and his little band of heroes were equal to a small army, for now that they were freed from the restraint of the station, they showed that they burned with a desire for a terrible revenge. Sandon himself shared the spirit and enthusiasm of his men. He remembered his murdered brother ; he thought of the awful massacre during the last few days of helpless women and children in Meerut, and as he rode on beneath the great calm canopy of heaven, there was within him the turmoil and the bitterness of an avenging thirst for blood.

Within five miles of Meerut the little band came upon their first obstacle. A stream was before them,

and on the opposite bank of that stream was an encampment of rebels, who at once opened fire with two
small mountain-guns, which carried death to two of
the English soldiers. Sandon did not hesitate for a
moment as to the course to be pursued. He formed his
men up in open line. In his clear, ringing voice he
gave the words of command : " Walk—Trot—Gallop—
Charge ! " Then like a cyclone suddenly let loose from
the caves of the wind, that little body of horsemen
swept over the stream and into the native camp. The
rebels made a vain effort to stand firm, but they went
down like nine-pins, until the ground was strewn with
their dying and dead. Then the rest fled in confusion,
and some of the English troopers dismounting, and
loading up the two mountain-guns, turned them upon
the flying enemy with disastrous effect. In this en-
counter four of Sandon's followers had been slain, so
that his little party were much weakened. But the
survivors spiked the guns, piled up all the baggage,
accoutrements, and tents which the surprised rebels had
left behind, and set the heap on fire ; while the ammunition that was found was tossed into the water.

Flushed with victory the column swept on, and ere
the day closed they had to fight another pitched battle
with an overwhelming number of rebels, who for a
time surrounded them, and the English were compelled to fight back to back. But at last they dispersed
their foes with terrible loss, though they themselves
had suffered cruelly and were reduced to twelve only ;
while amongst the slain was brave young Felbey, who
had done great execution before he fell. He had fought
like a lion at bay, and had met a soldiers's death.

Sandon's grief was very great and very sincere when

he saw that his noble companion had fallen. But it was the fortune of war, and he knew that on the morrow it might be his turn. As well as they were able the survivors buried their fallen comrades, and then weary and worn they threw themselves on the ground, their arms in their hands, their horses close to them.

With the dawning day the men rose, and munching their breakfast rations, which was of necessity small, they led their horses to a stream to drink; then mounting rode forward again, and before noon encountered and defeated without loss to themselves a band of armed rascals who were evidently bent on plunder. Continuing their journey towards the Mogul city, whose gorgeous domes and minarets could be seen afar off glittering in the brilliant sunlight, they suddenly heard a shout of welcome, and beheld about a hundred yards off three men, evidently Europeans. These men rushed forward to meet them, and informed Sandon that they were members of the band of fugitives who had managed to entrench themselves in the jungle near a stream, but they were in a terrible plight, and unless succoured at once must inevitably perish.

When Sandon and his men reached the encampment, the first man to come forward and greet him was his friend Colonel Pritchard, who had been wounded in the head, and looked ghastly ill. He could scarcely find voice to speak as he feebly grasped his comrade's hand; but when at last words came to him, he gasped out—

" Tell me, how fares it with them ? "

By " them " he meant his wife, his children, and his sister-in-law. Sandon understood, and with something of his wonted cheeriness he answered—

" Well—they are well, all of them."

" Thank God, thank God," murmured Pritchard, as he covered his sunken eyes with his hands, and when his emotion had passed he led Sandon aside and said brokenly—" If I could only have seen with your eyes things might have been different with me. But now I am striken with a mortal disease, and can hardly hope to live long enough to see my dear ones again. On the first outbreak at Delhi, where I had been suffering from an attack of dysentery, I managed with the assistance of half-a-dozen brave comrades and a few civilians to protect a number of women and children. We got them out of the city, hoping to reach Meerut, but almost immediately were attacked by a body of rebels, and we suffered great loss. With the remnant of our party we managed to make our way to this spot, where we have waited and hoped, as it seemed in vain, for succour to come to us. Without protection it is impossible that the party can move forward, for our fighting force only consists of six men, including myself, and I am all but helpless. We have fourteen women and nine children all more or less sick with us, and three civilians who are also very ill, and can render no assistance. We have no medicine, no comforts, and our little stock of provisions is exhausted."

It was a pitiable story, and as Sandon once again gripped the emaciated hand of his friend, he said firmly, and with a certain sternness begotten of determination—

" We will save you. Courage. Things are not as bad as they might be."

As Sandon's men moved about, weak and suffering women and pale-faced children came forth from the

wretched shelter that had been made for them by inter-
lacing boughs of trees, and kissing the soldiers' hands
or grasping their knees, pleaded to them to save them.
As the food supply was all but absolutely exhausted,
Sandon selected six of his men, and ordered them to
ride out on a foraging expedition, he leading them.
When they had ridden a few miles, they came to a
village. At first some opposition was shown to them
by the villagers, especially by one determined man,
who, armed with an Enfield rifle which he had evidently stolen, called upon his fellows to slaughter the
Englishmen, and with his rifle he aimed and fired at
Sandon. The bullet missed its mark, however, and
Sandon at once drew his revolver and shot the fellow
dead. This cowed the others, and Sandon forming his
men up in line declared to the assembled crowd that he
would shoot every man in the place and burn the village
down, unless all the arms were brought forward,
together with a waggon-load of provisions. As there
could be no mistaking that he meant what he said,
some of the people sullenly retired to comply with his
demand; while in order to guard against treachery,
Sandon formed a cordon with his little band round a
number of men and youths, and the stern English
soldiers sat like grim statues on their horses, a sword in
one hand, a revolver in the other.

When an hour had passed, two heavily-laden drays
drawn by bullocks were observed coming along the
village street. Among the things thus brought were a
number of old Brown Bess guns and a quantity of
ammunition. The provisions principally consisted of
rice, native cheese, and flour, together with some fruit
and sweetmeats. Sandon made the drivers of the

bullocks proceed ahead, and having given the head man of the village an order for payment of the things supplied, he and his followers brought up the rear, and in this manner they proceeded to the place where the fugitives were encamped, and the relief thus brought proved invaluable. Sandon and Pritchard resolved to retain the bullocks and the waggons as a means of transport for the women and children, but the drivers were allowed to return to their village. That, as it turned out, was a fatal mistake. During the night the fellows must have carried word to the rebels in Delhi. The sentries who had been placed on duty by Sandon reported that a body of the enemy was advancing. Instantly all was bustle in the little camp. Very hastily an extemporised fort was formed by the bullock-waggons, the bags of rice, and such other things as were likely to form shelter to the defenders and present obstacles to a rush on the part of the attackers. The women and children were placed in safety as far as it was possible to do so. Then Sandon and Pritchard disposed of their men to the best possible advantage. The enemy was about one hundred strong, and was composed entirely of Pandies—that is, rebel soldiers. They approached within a hundred yards and opened fire, but not a single shot took effect, and instantly a volley was poured into them which stretched several of their number on the ground never to rise again. This loss caused the others to withdraw to a safer distance, and to take advantage of the shelter the trees afforded. From their position they kept up a desultory fire for some time, with the result that two of the bullocks were shot. For hours the fight was carried on, and the enemy was still further reduced but the defenders suffered no loss. Then the enemy ceased firing, but did not retire. The two English officers took advantage of the lull to strengthen their position as much as possible. The command virtually devolved on Captain Sandon, for Pritchard was so ill that he could hardly move, and his voice had become so weak that he had difficulty in making himself heard.

With what might almost be described as superhuman efforts the men worked; and in spite of the want of proper appliances, they succeeded in throwing up a rough sort of parapet, and some of the most active of the ladies were instructed in the loading of the muskets.

The night fell and was passed in suspense and dread. Twice did some of the enemy try to steal into the camp, but the vigilance of the brave little band of defenders defeated the attempt, and each time inflicted loss upon the foe. In the morning a fresh body of rebels came up with two eight-pounder guns which they had brought from Delhi. It was evident that if these guns were got into position and fire was opened upon the camp all would be lost; but Sandon was not the man to remain inactive in the face of this terrible danger. So ordering every man who could do so to mount, two volleys were poured into the insurgents, and before they could recover from the confusion this threw them into, the defenders swept out of their shelter and hurled themselves against the foe, and in less than a quarter of an hour were actually in possession of the guns, which, with ringing cheers, they turned upon the Sepoys and scattered them. Then the guns were dragged to the camp; and this heroic feat evoked cheers even from the sick women and the children. As the ammunition for the guns had been captured as well, Sandon felt that he could now hold out for some time and keep the cowardly foe—for cowardly he was—at a respectful distance. But it was very certain that unless the defenders were relieved they must ultimately succumb. Sandon therefore decided that by some means or other word must be sent into Meerut. But he could not spare an effective man for this duty; and while he was debating with himself as to what was best to be done, a half-caste youth, who had been born in Delhi and brought up as a Christian, volunteered for the service, notwithstanding that he was very ill. His offer was accepted; and as soon as it was dark he stole away on his perilous errand. A little later Sandon and four men made a sortie, and catching the enemy napping, punished him severely, and returned to the camp with a quantity of rice and some arms.

For many days the noble little band of English soldiers kept overwhelming numbers at bay. The two guns proved of immense service; but they were only fired when absolutely necessary, in order to spin out the ammunition. The eagerly-looked-for and expected aid from Meerut came not; and the inference was, the youth had failed to reach the city.

The state of the besieged was now becoming more and more pitiable. Women and children died, and their poor bodies could not be buried, while those who lived envied those who were dead. Colonel Pritchard had grown so weak and was so emaciated that he could no longer stand, and he was placed in the rear, where a bed was made up for him, and the ladies afforded him such comfort as they could. Sandon's fighting force had been reduced by one trooper, who was shot dead while out in the open collecting fuel.

Things were desperate indeed now, and even Sandon began to take a gloomy view, for unless the enemy drew off there seemed to be nothing for it but capitulation, though, as far as he was personally concerned, he resolved to die sword in hand. His magnificent courage, his splendid fighting qualities, his abilities as a soldier had been the means so far of keeping the rebels at bay; but there was a limit even to his powers, and already he was beginning to feel the strain. Want of proper rest and food, coupled with anxiety, had told upon even his cast-iron constitution.

One morning just as the sun was rising the camp received a reinforcement in the shape of one man—a young man, haggard, gaunt, and famished-looking. He had come from Jhansi, and his name was Hallett.

CHAPTER XXXI

THE DYING MESSAGE.

For days and days Hallett had been wandering about the country, dodging predatory bands of rebels; travelling by night and sleeping by day. Quite unable to get any information, except what he gathered inferentially, he was in ignorance of the exact state of affairs, though it was very obvious to him that the mutiny had been very general. He managed to get to a place called Bhiwani, a little to the north-west of Delhi, where he learnt that Delhi was absolutely in the hands of the rebels, and that all the Europeans had been massacred. He then set off to try and reach Meerut, when passing near the encampment of the fugitives he was attracted by the firing, and creeping cautiously up to ascertain from whence it proceeded, he recognised the British uniform of the defenders, and by making a detour he succeeded in reaching them. As an English officer he at once reported himself to Sandon, stating his name and rank. The name did not strike Sandon at first, and therefore in this ragged, dust- and travel-stained, half-starved man he did not recognise the lover of the woman whom he also loved.

Although Colonel Pritchard was not in effective command, owing to his illness, he was still by courtesy recognised as being in nominal command, and so

Hallett was taken to him; and as the sick man put out his withered hand for the other to take, he said feebly—

" You are surely the Jack Hallett of whom there has been so much talk, and with whom my sister-in-law seems to have been infatuated."

Hallett soon made it clear that he was the identical person; and Pritchard could not refrain from telling him that it appeared as if Fate had for some special purpose directed his footsteps there. Naturally Jack inquired tenderly and anxiously about Hester; but all that Pritchard could say was, that when he left Meerut she was well. He did not mention to Hallett that he had a rival in that very camp, for the painful circumstances and peril in which they were all placed rendered silence on such a subject the kindlier course. But Hallett soon heard that Sandon had come from Meerut since the mutiny broke out, and so he did not hesitate to inquire of him how Hester fared. Then, and not till then, did Sandon recognise him; but he too held his peace for the same reason that had actuated Colonel Pritchard.

When Hallett had partaken of food, and had removed some of the encrusted dust by means of a bucket of water, he felt and looked a new man. And it was not long before he gave proof to his commanding officer of his powers and courage as a soldier. He was a valuable addition indeed to the tiny garrison, and Sandon was too brave and too honourable a man to show any ill-feeling towards him because they were rivals. As there was now no longer any room to doubt that the first messenger must have fallen into the hands of the enemy, Sandon decided to send some one else to Meerut for succour. And in order that there should be no insidious distinction made, he arranged that every man in the camp, with the exception of himself and Pritchard, should write his name on a slip of paper, which should then be screwed up and put into a bag with a number of blanks. A lady was next deputed to draw out a slip, and the first name she drew was to be the man for the perilous ride. Of course Hallett took his chance with the rest; his name, however, did not come out first, but the name of a trooper called William Andrews. Hallett was disappointed, though he said nothing; but he tried to console himself with the thought that having survived so many risks, and got within a dozen miles of the woman who was his hope and stay in life, he would surely be spared to once more hold her in his arms, and hear again from her lips that she was his. That thought nerved him, inspirited him, and he even began to dream dreams of the future.

When darkness descended, Trooper Andrews, mounted on one of the best horses left in the camp, started on his short but dangerous journey, and in order to divert the attention of the rebels, the defenders opened fire upon them, which was returned with interest, and for a quarter of an hour a terrible fusillade was kept up. When it ceased the muster-roll of the garrison was called, and there was one who did not answer to his name. That one was Lieutenant Hallett, and search being made for him he was found lying outside of the defences seriously wounded, and beside him was a dead Sepoy. Hallett reported that he saw the man creeping like a stealthy wild beast round to the back of the camp, and rushing up to seize him, the native stabbed him in the breast with a long knife, but instantly Hallett shot him with his revolver. What the man's exact object was could only be guessed at, but no doubt he was reconnoitring, and wished to carry information to his friends.

It was soon seen that Hallett's wound was of a very dangerous character, and in the absence of medical attendance and surgical appliances, little could be done for him; but the women, or such of them as were able, did all they could for him under the circumstances. The poor creatures, in spite of their misery and suffering, were like ministering angels, and imparted consolation and hope to the sick and the dying.

It soon became evident that poor Jack was doomed. He knew and felt that to be the case himself. It was precious hard, after all he had gone through for Hester's dear sake, to die as it were on the threshold of her door. But no man can avoid his destiny, and when Jack saw that death had set its seal upon him, he requested Captain Sandon to come to him.

"Captain," he said, with difficulty, for when he attempted to speak the blood gurgled into his throat, "Captain, we are strangers, but soldiers, and one soldier when he is stricken with death in his country's cause may entrust another with a sacred message. It is very probable you will live to get back to Meerut, and if you do so, I, as a dying man, pray you seek out Hester Dellaby, the sister-in-law of Colonel Pritchard, if she be living, and tell her my last words were of her. She was to have been my wife, but it is willed otherwise. Give her this small case—it is her portrait. When I left England I told her I would wear it next my heart for her sake, and it should keep me straight. I have done so; it has never gone from me; and now into your keeping I give it, and charge you in the name of God deliver it up to her with my last message."

He ceased speaking, for his voice had entirely failed, and Sandon, kneeling on the ground beside him, held his hand and pressed it with the true grip of a noble soldier, and he whispered in the dying man's ear—

"I will do all that you wish."

Hallett lay upon an extemporised charpoy, placed under some palm-boughs, and the only light on the pathetic scene was that which came from the subdued glow of a smouldering wood fire a little way off. Sandon still knelt there and held his comrade's and rival's hand. Hallett made another effort to speak, but failed, his voice being suffocated with the upward rush of blood. And presently a tremor passed over him, then he was still, and the pressure of his hand relaxed. Sandon rose, and beckoning to a lady who was sitting on the ground weeping, he muttered—

"He is dead."

And as the brave man turned away he passed his hand over his eyes, for tears had actually gathered there. Into the jungle at the back of the defences went four soldiers carrying a fifth, who was dead, with them. The fifth was ill-starred Jack Hallett, who, wrapped in a military cloak, was silently laid in a soldier's grave. The usual honours which are observed at a military funeral had to be omitted in this case for fear of arousing the enemy. Two pieces of stick tied at right angles to each other to form a rough cross were placed over the grave to mark the spot where the young lieutenant was sleeping the last sleep, which neither the blast of bugle nor the tuck of drum should ever more disturb.

For two days the wretched and half-famished fugitives waited in eager and anxious suspense for signs of the expected relief, but none were forthcoming. Then did black despair seize again upon every one, for it seemed as if they were all doomed. Trooper Andrews could not have succeeded in his mission. And to make matters worse, as the day was closing the enemy opened fire again, and they were only kept from making a rush by the cannon which the defenders handled so well. While the fight was at its hottest a ringing cheer was heard—an unmistakably English cheer—and the enemy were suddenly attacked in the rear. The relief had come at last; women wept and children screamed with joy, and Sandon and his half-dozen heroes threw themselves upon the foe, who were thus hemmed in and were utterly annihilated. Andrews had got through safely, and in compliance with his urgent messages a party of fifty troopers went out to the relief. •

With dawn of day the fugitives were gathered together and escorted to Meerut. Colonel Pritchard was borne upon a litter, and it was only too plain to see that death had marked him for its own. He lived long enough to see and recognise his wife and children and Hester, and as he bade the latter adieu he murmured faintly—

" Be kind to Sandon. He is a noble fellow."

That night the Colonel passed to his rest and was buried in the English cemetery where so many of the victims of the great Mutiny were laid.

As may be imagined, the death of her husband was a

terrible blow to poor Mrs. Pritchard, and the only measure of consolation she could find was in the fact that her two dear children had been spared to her. Hester, too, was much cut up. She had quite recovered from the effects of her wound, but she had suffered great anxiety on Hallett's behalf, for news had reached Meerut of the revolt at Jhansi and the massacre of all the Europeans. Therefore she had mourned for Hallett as for one dead.

For two or three days after his return, Captain Sandon saw nothing of Hester, though she heard his praises being sounded by men and women, who spoke of him enthusiastically. At last he sought an interview with her. Then did he tell her of the message of which he was the bearer, and he delivered to her the likeness entrusted to him by her dying lover. She received them in silence. She had no words, no tears. It seemed as if her cup of bitterness was full to overflowing, and that Fate had been unduly cruel to her and him in bringing him through so many perils only to separate them for ever at last, when they were almost within embracing distance.

Sandon, like the brave and noble man he was, respected her sorrow and held his peace, merely wishing her a quiet adieu, and telling her that he was about to start with his regiment to take part in the siege of Delhi. Then with a passionate outburst of hysterical grief she shook his hand and prayed God to guard him.

So they parted, and he went forth to that scene of hellish strife which was raging around the Mogul city.

CHAPTER XXXII.

PEACE !

In a quiet home in peaceful England, in one of the most beautiful parts of beautiful Devonshire, dwells a widow lady with her son and daughter and her sister. The widow is Mrs. Pritchard, her sister is Hester Dellaby. It is getting on for three years since the great Mutiny declared itself in the station of Meerut, and struck sorrow into the hearts of so many families. Quiet and subdued now is poor Mrs. Pritchard, for deep and abiding shadows have fallen across her way in life, and for her the world can never be the same world it was before that awful Indian experience. Her dear children have been preserved to her, and for that blessing she is unspeakably thankful; indeed, had it not been for that, her life might have ended for aught she would have cared, for both her father and her mother had paid the debt of nature.

Hester had grown much more of a woman, and her beautiful face had taken on an habitual expression of thoughtfulness which seemed a little out of place. Often when alone she would sit for a long time gazing on vacancy, as if her thoughts were far, far away. Perhaps that was not to be wondered at, for no impressionable and sensitive woman could have gone through the experiences that had been hers without growing more thoughtful, and developing a tendency to view life through a somewhat sombre medium. It was very, very rarely indeed that either she or her sister referred to India. It was a tabooed subject, for it could not be discussed without reviving many bitter memories.

Would-be suitors had sighed for some favourable look or word from Hester, but to all she was as a statue. Men said she was cold; and women whispered that her heart was buried in India. She herself neither confirmed nor contradicted what people chose to say. She wanted to live her life as it suited her; and though she was staid and meditative beyond her years she could hardly help that. She could not change her nature, could not entirely remove the blight that had fallen upon her youth.

One glorious spring morning, when the great heart of Nature seemed to be pulsing with a new-born joy, Mrs. Pritchard sat at an open window from whence a glorious panorama of sea and shore was obtained. She had been perusing the *Times*, and looking up, she addressed her sister, who was engaged in making a water-colour sketch of a vase of spring flowers that stood on the table.

"Hetty," dear," she said, "here is an item of news that will interest you. I see that the *Gloriana* troopship has arrived with the headquarters of the 12th Royal Lancers on board. Amongst the officers occurs the name of Brevet-Lieutenant-Colonel Sandon, V.C."

"Indeed," exclaimed Hetty, with more animation than she was in the habit of showing, while some accession of colour seemed to redden her fair cheeks. "But it can't be the Captain Sandon we used to know, for we heard, you remember, that he was killed during the siege of Delhi."

"It must be the same, dear," answered her sister. "Listen," and she proceeded to read. "Amongst the officers whom the *Gloriana* has brought home is Brevet-Lieutenant-Colonel Sandon, who has so greatly distinguished himself during the great Mutiny, and has been awarded the Victoria Cross for his gallant services during the siege of Delhi. When the rebel city was stormed by our troops on September 14, 1857, Lieutenant-Colonel (then Captain) Sandon was attached to one of the assaulting columns which stormed the breach at the Cashmere Gate. Captain Sandon was one of the first officers to enter the breach, where some desperate fighting took place. In spite of a severe wound he received, he refused to retire, and by his heroic example he so encouraged his men, who showed a disposition to waver, that they rallied, and made such a tremendous onslaught on the rebels opposed to them that the position was won. Later on in the day, although suffering greatly himself, Captain Sandon rescued at the imminent peril of his life a private of the 53rd regiment, who was surrounded by Sepoys. The man had received a terrible wound in the left arm which partially disabled him. The gallant officer killed two of the enemy and drove the others off, and when the private fainted from loss of blood, Captain Sandon lifted him up and carried him to a place of safety. We understand that Lieutenant-Colonel Sandon intends to resign his commission, and settle down on his splendid estate of Beechholm in Surrey, which he recently inherited from his uncle."

"Yes," remarked Hester quietly, as tears gathered

in her eyes, " it is our Captain Sandon." Then she went on with her painting for a few minutes, but suddenly rising she put away her materials and said—" I am going for a stroll, Madge. I've got a headache."

Mrs. Pritchard made no answer, but that evening when the lamps had been lighted, and the children had gone to bed, she and Hester sat alone, and looking up from some needlework she was engaged upon, she fixed her eyes on her sister's face and said—

" Hetty, dear, I have written to Colonel Sandon with our joint congratulations on his arrival home. Have I done right ? "

" Yes, of course you have," answered Hetty, with a bright, glad look in her face such as it had not worn for many a long day. " We owe our lives to Sandon, and we should surely have been wanting in common gratitude not to have sent him some welcome."

In less than a week from that evening an answer came from the Colonel, and in it was this passage—

" Glad indeed I am to hear that Hester is with you and is well. I wonder if she still thinks kindly of me. When may I come to see you ? "

By return of post went back the widow's answer—

" We shall be delighted to see you at any time you like to come. We can only offer you humble accommodation in our humble home, but the welcome will be hearty and sincere."

A few weeks later, on a golden evening in early June, a handsome, bronzed man wandered listlessly with a lady by his side along a fern-fringed path bordering a Devonshire stream. And presently the two came to a stile, where they lingered, and while she stood with modest, down-cast mien, he took her gloved hand, saying—

" Hetty, for over three years I have nursed my love for you. Your face has been ever present before me. I have seen it through the cannon's smoke ; and it has been like a vision of sweetness to me amidst the horrors of the battle-field. Have I earned the right now to ask you to share the future with me ? "

A moment's pause, then she raised her eyes to his and murmured the one word—

" Yes."

Their lips met in ratification of the compact ; and arm in arm they wandered home, as the young moon rose and shed a lustre of silver sheen over the landscape, which was so peaceful, so beautiful, so truly English. That evening, when the dinner-table had been cleared, and Colonel Sandon had lit a cigar, little Amy stood beside him, and stroking her fair golden ringlets, he asked—

" Amy, how would you like to have me for your uncle, eh ? "

" Oh, so much. You dear, dear old man ! " cried the child, with the excitement of delight. " But how can you be my uncle ? "

" Well, you see it's this way. Hetty is your aunt. Now, if I become Aunt Hetty's husband, I shall be your uncle. Don't you see ? "

" Oh, I say, isn't that jolly ? " exclaimed Master Fred, who, seated at one end of the table, was busy carving some orange-peel into grotesque shapes. " I always knew you liked Aunt Hetty, because I remember once in Meerut you kissed her hand in the garden. And I know she likes you, because when we came here and we heard you were dead she used to cry."

Then Mrs. Pritchard spoke, and these were her words—

"Colonel Sandon, a brave man deserves a good woman, and in my dear sister I am sure you will find a perfect wife. You wooed her in stormy times, you have won her in peace, and I pray earnestly to God that he will grant you both a future of usefulness and restful happiness."

"Amen to that," murmured Sandon, with impressive fervour. And a little later, when Mrs. Pritchard had gone off with the children to see them to their beds, Sandon folded his arms about Hester's neck, and said— "What a dear, dear woman you are!"

"Ah!" she sighed, with a sigh of exceeding great joy, as she pillowed her head upon his breast.

THE END.

www.ingramcontent.com/pod-product-compliance
Lightning Source LLC
Chambersburg PA
CBHW060519030726
47498CB00004B/1004